BLEED LIKE ME

Cath Staincliffe

CORGI BOOKS

TRANSWORLD PUBLISHERS
61–63 Uxbridge Road, London W5 5SA
A Random House Group Company
www.transworldbooks.co.uk

BLEED LIKE ME
A CORGI BOOK: 9780552168724

First published in Great Britain
in 2013 by Bantam Press
an imprint of Transworld Publishers
Corgi edition published 2013

Addresses for Random House Group Ltd companies outside the UK
can be found at: www.randomhouse.co.uk
The Random House Group Ltd Reg. No. 954009

The Random House Group Limited supports The Forest Stewardship
Council® (FSC®), the leading international forest-certification organisation.
Our books carrying the FSC label are printed on FSC®-certified paper.
FSC is the only forest-certification scheme supported by the leading
environmental organisations, including Greenpeace. Our
paper-procurement policy can be found at
www.randomhouse.co.uk/environment

Typeset in 11.25/14.5pt Sabon by Falcon Oast Graphic Art Ltd.
Printed and bound by CPI Group (UK) Ltd, Croydon, CR0 4YY.

2 4 6 8 10 9 7 5 3 1

For my agent, Sara – thank you for everything

Day One

1

Rachel was running. Running for her life. Air burning like acid in her chest, feet pounding the tarmac. Everything around her, the shops and passers-by, lampposts and railings, smudged, a blur of shape and colour.

She risked a glance behind, hair whipping in her eyes, almost losing her balance as one ankle buckled, and she saw the car was gaining. He was at the wheel, his face set with intent, eyes gleaming, mouth curved in a half-smile.

Running her down, running her to ground. For a moment, her legs stalled, numb, weak as string, before she took flight again. Arms slicing the air, throat parched, sweat cold across her skin and the thud of her heart ever louder in her ears. Then the roar as he gunned the engine, the screech as the car leapt towards her, close enough for her to smell burning oil and petrol fumes high in her throat. Dizzying.

The thump of impact. Hurling her forward, a

bone-cracking crunch and Rachel fell, sprawling along the gutter and into the pavement's edge, legs twisting the wrong way beneath her, skinning her chin and shoulder and the length of her forearms. Smacking her head against the kerbstone. A jolt that turned the world black and brought vomit scalding her gullet.

The engine cut out and then she heard his footsteps, the smack-smack of best Italian leather on the gritty stone.

She tried to draw away but was pinned, paralysed, and her attempt to shuffle brought scarlet pain licking through her hip. She tried to cry for help but her voice was frozen too and all the people had gone. She was alone with him.

'Rachel,' he said sadly, 'Rachel, Rachel, what will I do with you?'

Tears burnt the backs of her eyes. Then his hands were on her, yanking her over, ignoring the howls she gave.

Nick, shaking his head, disappointed in her. 'I warned you,' he said.

And he had.

'I can't trust you, Rachel.'

That was fucking rich, that was. She'd have laughed if the pain hadn't been so brutal.

He lifted his foot, pressed the sole of his shoe on her neck. His eyes drilled into her.

There was something she must do, must remember to do, something . . . The knife! She still had the knife. Her fingers tightened round the handle. She kept her gaze locked on his. Just stab his leg and then . . .

'We could have been so good. But you wouldn't listen, would you? Threatening me. You silly bitch.' He pushed down, his mouth tightening with the effort, crushing her windpipe.

She raised the knife, so heavy, her arms spasming with cramp, and plunged the blade into his calf and heard the sudden high scream, half pain half rage, that he gave as he stumbled back.

Rachel couldn't move. Her legs wouldn't work. Nick bent over her, grabbed her hand, peeling back her fingers to get the knife. 'You bitch, you mad bitch.' He spat the words, spittle landing on her face.

'Bastard,' Rachel whispered.

He had the knife.

She would not beg.

He moved closer, the knife ready, smeared with his blood. His eyes brilliant with hatred. He touched the tip of the knife to her cheek. 'I've got to kill you,' he said softly, 'you know that.'

Panic skittered in her chest, making her shudder uncontrollably. The pain from her hip rolled over her in waves.

Fuck you, she thought. Fuck you, Nick Savage. Fuck you to hell and back. She lunged for his arm, determined to fight, grabbing at his wrist, but he dodged, lifting the knife away.

Swiftly he moved back, stooped with the knife and swept it under her throat.

Rachel felt the spill of warm blood across her neck and down her chest, heard the gurgling noise she made, saw his smile, wide, gleeful. She tried to scream but her throat was full of blood. No air. Help me!

She reared awake, choking, sucking in breath, the knife in her hand.

The room full of snow, white, floating, spiralling down. Touching her neck, sticky, itchy. And something sharp in her mouth, making her retch. She felt for it with her fingers, drew out feathers, curled and slick with saliva. Feathers, not snow. Her pillow slashed. She spat more feathers from her mouth, wiped them from her neck.

Alive.

Awake.

Rachel Bailey wept. Huge noisy sobs while the feathers swung and floated in the silvery beams of first light that stole into her bedroom.

2

Gill Murray had barely got her coat off when the call came through. Suspicious death. Serious Crime Division wanted her as SIO, senior investigating officer. The syndicate were next in line for any new case, so the shout had come to her. She got the location, Journeys Inn on the far side of Oldham, and left word with her sergeant, Andy Roper.

Probably a bar brawl, or some payback exacted after last orders, she speculated as she drove, heading out of town past the slow-moving traffic coming in the other direction into work. Some scrote getting mouthy with some other, blood on the floor. But why hadn't they heard about it till now? Why hadn't the landlord called them out last night?

Don't get ahead of yourself, she thought, looks suspicious, might not be. There are plenty of sudden deaths that turn out to be natural: hearts stopping, brains stroking out. Or suicides. Or accidents.

The road climbed out of the valley past old

warehouses and sheds edging the canal and a scattering of new industrial units, and switched back on itself as the incline became steeper. Terraced houses sprouted in little hamlets, more or less merged these days, some looking abandoned, threadbare, with boarded windows, others maintained well enough.

She travelled up through the Larks estate, social housing built in the sixties, three-bed homes with pebbledash and open-plan front gardens. The estate was laid out like a maze, Gill knew; the main road bisected it but either side there were endless semi-circular drives that sprouted more crescents and cul-de-sacs and all looked interchangeable. Up on the brow of the hill was Journeys Inn. As Gill's car crested the rise, she could see a row of vehicles parked on the roadside in front of the pub, among them CSI vans and two squad cars.

Journeys was an old coaching inn. Three storeys high with six windows on each floor at the front and probably the same at the back, thought Gill, though she could not see from where she was. She pulled in behind the other vehicles. The scene had been secured with tape which ran along the perimeter wall of the pub by the road and across the drive at the side which led behind the building. A sign pointing that way read *Car Park*.

Stepping out of the car, Gill felt the breeze coming over the hills. Beyond the inn lay open country, the mix of heather and bracken that covered the slopes interrupted here and there by dun-coloured grass. The bracken a blaze of vermilion in full autumn glory. It was not dissimilar to the view from her own house a few miles further to the east. Gill estimated the nearest houses, on the Larks, were perhaps three hundred yards from the pub. So no immediate neighbours, no one overlooking the place.

Gill got out and opened the car boot, fighting against the wind as she unfolded a disposable paper suit and pulled it on. She did the same with a pair of gloves, covered her shoes with protectors and opened a face mask, leaving it round her neck until she got into the scene. Immediately, she was hot, and with the mask on she knew her glasses would soon steam up.

Gill showed her warrant card to the man staffing the crime scene perimeter at the entrance to the drive. He signed her in and she ducked under the tape and followed the designated path that had been marked out along the lane. To her right, parallel to the side of the pub, was a long single-storey building, roof long gone and the internal walls reduced to piles of stone. Probably stables for the inn, during its heyday. The car park at the back was almost deserted. Just a small grey hatchback parked at the far side.

The ground was hard-packed earth, rutted where heavy vehicles had churned up mud. Much of the lot was overrun with weeds, cow parsley and dandelions and nettles, suggesting it wasn't prone to heavy use.

Either side of the main double doors were picnic

tables, the wood grey and splintered, and to the right in the corner a play area with a rusting swing set and a climbing frame. There was a second single door almost at the corner of the building. CSIs had protected both entrances with tents.

The main doors were ajar and Gill read the brass plate above them: *Owen Cottam, licensed for the sale of alcoholic beverages for consumption on the premises.*

'Gill Murray.' The man, suited and booted like Gill, came out of the building.

'Gerry. You CSM?' Responsible for managing the crime scene.

'Coordinator,' Gerry said. 'They tell you we've got three victims?'

'Three! Oh, God.' Gill felt the kick of adrenalin speed up her pulse though she was professional enough to appear calm and collected.

'Three separate scenes. Gonna be a long day,' he added.

Week, month, Gill thought. Each scene would have its own crime scene manager and Gerry would oversee them all.

'Take you up?'

Up. She heard the word and revised her expectations. Upstairs. Not a bar fight, then. Unless they'd a function room upstairs and someone got killed without any of the other guests noticing. And again, how come the landlord hadn't summoned help till now?

16

The interior of the inn was gloomy. No one had turned any lights on. A cardinal rule of crime scene management. Touch nothing, preserve the scene. The CSIs would bring in any lighting required, to enable photographs and video to be taken of the scene, to allow the techs to document and recover any evidence. After all, who knew if a fingerprint might be on the light switch. Might tell a crucial part of the story. There was always a story.

Gill followed Gerry through the pub to the right with its smell of damp carpet and beer and old cooking oil and cigar smoke. Years since the smoking ban but nicotine still tainted the air.

The place was cavernous, though some attempts had been made to section off the space with booths and some raised sections. As her eyesight adjusted she could see that the banquette seats looked greasy with use, and the fussy wallpaper, Regency stripes, had come away in some places. Design circa 1980s, Gill guessed, thirty years out of date.

A door marked *Private* led off the bar into a narrow hallway, with an external door to the right (the one she'd noticed from the outside) and stairs leading up to the left. The tenants' entrance. So they could come and go without traipsing through the pub itself.

The fire door at the top of the stairs had been propped open and they went through it, took a quarter turn to the left on to a short landing. 'Bathroom on the right,' Gerry said, 'kitchen and living room on the right.' Both doors were shut. The landing led to a hallway that ran down the centre of the building with doors off either side. Stepping plates had been placed on the carpet along the hall to protect the scene and small markers sat here and there, indicating potential evidence.

Gerry turned left. 'First scene – master bedroom,' he said. The room would look out on to the road at the front. Viewed from the road it would be in the extreme right corner of the building.

Gill could hear the murmur of voices, the sound of the CSM and CSI techs already busy at work. She pulled her mask on. They stepped inside. Gill greeted the people there, who were filming in the light from a stand of specially rigged lamps, then focused on the scene.

The victim lay in the double bed. Face up, eyes closed, covered by the duvet from the waist down. Her hands were out of sight. The woman, dark-haired, looked to be in her late thirties, Gill thought. She wore a nightdress. From the short sleeves you could see it had once been blue with sprigs of dark blue flowers printed on it, but now the bulk of it across the whole of the woman's torso was dark red, the colour of drying blood. The smell, sickly sweet, hung in the air.

The room was otherwise undisturbed. Make-up and jewellery on the dressing table. A round stool in front of it. A fitted wardrobe along the outer wall, easy chair by the window, blue velvet curtains closed. Wicker laundry basket by the door. Gill noticed the bedside tables, his and hers, water glasses and lamps on both, alarm clock on his side, a mobile phone, indigestion mixture and book on hers.

'No sign of a struggle,' Gill said.

'No defence wounds, or nothing visible anyway,' Gerry agreed.

'She's not been posed,' Gill said.

'Don't think so,' he said. 'Be hard to move her without getting blood everywhere.'

Gill peered closer. Could see two puncture slits on the chest where a sharp implement had pierced the nightdress and the woman's body. The puckered fabric, knitted to the congealing blood around the edges of wounds.

A sudden volley of barking made Gill start. *What the fuck?*

'Pet dog in the kitchen,' Gerry said, nodding back towards the stairs. 'The next one's this way.'

In the hall, crime scene tape demarcated the next crime scene, in the adjoining room. In order not to contaminate either by tracking evidence with them, both Gill and Gerry changed into fresh paper suits, boots, gloves and mask. Sealing the ones they had already used in bags and labelling them.

For the same reason a separate team of CSIs were at work in this room under the guidance of their own crime scene manager. And a further log was being kept of who entered and left each scene.

A plaque on the door read *Penny*, the letters made out of pink and red hearts. A girl, perhaps eleven or twelve, lay prone on her bed, face partly hidden by her dark hair turned to one side. The back of her pyjama jacket was thick with blood. The duvet was hanging off the foot of the bed, smeared with blood. Gill noticed the girl had painted toenails, glittery pink. She was slightly built, bony ankles and slender wrists. Just a child. Gill felt her guts tighten in response, the pity of it, always that extra sense of tragedy with a child involved, but it would not affect her ability to do her job. If anything, she would strive even harder.

Gill surveyed the room. One wall had fitted wardrobes, white with folding shuttered doors, the others were a mix of posters, One Direction and Justin Bieber, and drawings: cartoon figures, anime style, *Penny* signed at the bottom of them. The girl had liked to draw. There was a photograph too, which Gill looked closely at. A family group on a sofa. The woman from the room next door with a baby in her arms; a man, well built, with a moustache and close dark hair, had a toddler on his lap. In between the adults was Penny. They were smiling for the camera. The toddler had one hand up, touching the man's cheek; the child was turned slightly towards the man and his mouth was open as though he was telling him something.

A row of stuffed toys – a dragon, a panda, a meerkat – occupied a long shelf next to a desk cum dressing table. Homework and make-up littered the table and mounted above it was a flat screen television.

Though the bedding was less neat here, still there was very little disruption. In both cases it looked to Gill as if the victims had been attacked where they lay.

'They could have been sleeping,' she said to Gerry.

'Looks that way,' he said.

The dog barked again, fast and furious. Gill turned to Gerry and gave a nod to say she was ready for the next. They moved further along the hallway to the end of that crime scene cordon and repeated the business of changing their protective clothing and logging in.

The next scene was the bedroom at the far end, at the back of the building.

The man was on a single bed, partially on his side, head bent backwards, hands closed on his breastbone, the gaping wound on his neck curving open, giving a glimpse of the tube of his oesophagus and a gleam of white bone. Blood had sprayed on to the headboard and the wall behind the bed. His fingers and T-shirt were stained with it. The man had very short hair and his eyes were open, filmy. Part of a tattoo showed beneath the sleeve of his top.

'Owen Cottam?' Gill asked. The name on the licensee plate. Had someone broken in and slaughtered the three of them? But he didn't bear any resemblance to the man in the family snapshot.

'No IDs yet,' said Gerry.

'Not the man from the photo next door. Too old to be a son,' Gill thought aloud, 'only looks a few years younger than the woman. Sleeping in a single room.' She looked again at the savage cut. Sensed the enormity of the crime. Three dead. And the killer? 'Looks like they used a knife.'

'We found it in here,' Gerry said, 'under the bed.' He asked one of the men in the room for the knife which was in a rigid, clear-plastic knife tube. Gill took hold of the tube. The weapon, a sizeable kitchen knife, non-serrated, was smeared with blood.

'Fast-track this for swabbing and prints,' Gill said. 'The whisky bottle from the bathroom as well.'

She scoured the room, the curtains still closed but some light coming in through the gaps where the hooks had gone missing. A Man City scarf the only decoration. Chest of drawers with clothes spilling out, more clothes littered on the floor. A small telly and a gaming console. Xbox. Same as Sammy's.

'Who called us?'

'Brewery. Delivery arrived at eight to find the place deserted, no one answering the door and the dog howling the place down. Wagon driver rang his boss who assumed Cottam had done a runner, abandoning the dog.'

'Bit of a leap,' Gill said. 'Might just have nipped out for milk and a paper.'

'Except no one else was responding,' said Gerry.

'Maybe there was some existing trouble with the

business, then,' Gill said, 'if their first thought is he's done a moonlight flit.' All questions that would be asked and hopefully answered once the investigation got under way.

'Local bobby came out, found it all locked up and forced entry.'

'Found a bloodbath,' Gill said. 'Which door?'

'The single one. The family entrance,' Gerry said. 'Look at this.' He took her back along the hallway, to the room opposite the daughter's. A child's bed and a cot. Everything, the blue décor, the duvet covers, the toys scattered on the carpet, the train frieze running around the walls, screamed little boys.

'No sign?' Gill asked. *The baby and the toddler. The toddler with his hand up to his father's face.*

Gerry shook his head.

'Upstairs?' Gill said: the third storey.

'Padlocked. Been up – full of junk, nothing else. And the cellars are clear.'

No more bodies. Small bodies. So where were the other children?

The dog was yelping and whining, scratching at the kitchen door.

'Can we get shot of Fido?' Gill said.

'In hand,' he said.

'Right,' she said, 'I'll call the coroner.'

Ten minutes later Gill had secured the coroner's authorization to order forensic post-mortems on the three victims. Next she contacted the Home

23

Office pathologist and asked him to attend the scene.

Gerry called her name from the ground floor. Gill peered down.

'Someone here with intel on the household,' Gerry said.

Gill descended, went through the pub and outside. The sun was warm and Gill was steaming inside the protective suit.

'Jack Biddle, CID,' the man waiting for her introduced himself, then began to read off the facts. 'Owen Cottam, publican, aged forty-five . . .'

Not the man in the single bed then, she was right about that.

'. . . wife Pamela, forty, daughter Penny, eleven – just moved up to high school.'

Gill nodded. 'You know the family?'

'My lass is at school with Penny.' He swallowed but retained his composure.

Hearing the names, learning them, names that would become second nature, part of her waking life as the investigation progressed. People she'd come to know inside out. 'Looks like Pamela and Penny,' Gill said. 'We've a man as well, ten years younger than Pamela perhaps, very short hair, tattoos.'

She saw a flicker of recognition in Biddle's eyes. 'Pamela's brother Michael Milne. The two little ones, Theo and Harry?'

'Not here. How old?'

'Toddlers.' He dipped his hand, palm down by his

knee, indicating their stature. 'I can check the ages.'

'Thanks,' Gill said. 'No sign of them or Cottam. Any ructions you heard about? Domestic violence, family feud?'

Biddle shook his head. 'Nope.'

'Any criminal associates, prior offences?'

'Nothing,' Biddle said. 'Magistrates approved his licence every time.'

'Car reg?'

He read it off. No match to the Vauxhall at the edge of the car park. 'Blue Ford Mondeo.'

'Whose is that?' she asked, pointing at the car.

'The brother's – Michael's.'

Gill had a sudden chilling thought: had the boot been checked? 'Give me a minute,' she said and went to ask Gerry.

Minutes later a CSI came down from Michael Milne's room with a set of car keys, accompanied by a woman with a camera. She ran off a series of shots of the Vauxhall before the boot was opened. Gill was holding her breath but when they found only a pair of wellies, a carrier bag of old drinks cans and a leaking can of motor oil she could breathe again. Drew in a strong draught of air perfumed with the smell of moorland. The CSI went to look in the old stables too, though as they were pretty much open to view anyway, Gill didn't think the children would be there.

'You think Owen . . .' Biddle broke off, trying to digest the news.

'Yes,' Gill said, 'I think he's our suspect. Killed his daughter, his wife, his brother-in-law, then took off for the hills with his sons. I'm sorry. We have to find the bastard.' She gazed out over the sweep of the hills. Sheep dotted here and there. Heard the burbling of a grouse on the wind. *Before it's too late.* She didn't say it out loud. And hard on the heels of that thought came another. *It probably already is.*

3

'Family annihilation.' Janet caught the urgency in Andy's voice as she walked into the incident room. The buzz was palpable, people talking across each other. 'That's what they call it in the US,' Andy said, his lean face brightening as he set eyes on Janet.

'Multiple homicide,' Rachel said. Rachel looked rough, Janet thought. Her friend burning the candle at both ends again, no doubt.

'Whereabouts?' asked Kevin.

'In the UK,' Rachel said slowly, tapping her own head.

'No, where's the murders?' Kevin said.

The term woodentop could have been invented for Kevin but this time it was Rachel who'd got the wrong end of the stick.

'The Larks,' said Andy. 'Journeys Inn.'

'You're joking!' Janet stopped by her desk, jacket over her arm.

'You know it?' said Andy.

27

Suddenly there was another agenda, a subtext beneath the interchange. Forcing her to censor her words slightly. 'Used to go there when the kids were little, walk and a pub lunch.' Leaving out Ade's name. Because Ade, his name, the very fact of his existence, was there like a pit, a snare, a trapdoor, something to stumble over. The small matter of him being her husband something that she and Andy were trying very hard to ignore, to forget about, to glide over.

'Three dead,' said Andy, all businesslike. 'Believed to be the wife, daughter and wife's brother, still awaiting formal identification. Gill's on her way back. Suspect Owen Cottam, landlord there, missing along with two younger children.'

There was a pause as they each absorbed the information. Janet felt dizzy, the floor swirling under her feet. She could feel Andy's eyes on her. She pulled out her chair and sat down. Felt sick and bloated. Her hand moved protectively across her abdomen over the scar where they'd sewn her up after surgery. Injuries sustained in the line of duty. She shouldn't be feeling like this. She'd recovered well over the last six months. Been back at work after three.

'You okay?' Rachel, standing opposite, leant forward, hands on her own desk.

'Fine.' Janet smiled. Rachel stared, head tilted, waiting for something closer to the truth.

'Okay,' Janet said sotto voce, 'I'm knackered. Up till the early hours on homework duty with Elise, the

28

Long March and the Cultural Revolution. Then Taisie has a nightmare at half three and the alarm's set for six. What's new?'

'Why's she having nightmares?' Rachel asked.

'Because she can?' Janet shook her head. It was one thing after another with Taisie. No sooner through one crisis or drama than she swanned in with another. 'And because she's stupid enough to watch some 18 certificate Japanese horror movie at the sleepover she went on, even though she knows she'll freak out after.'

Gill arrived then, issuing instructions as she walked. 'Briefing in ten. Get me sandwiches – no onions – and coffee. Andy, bring the press office in, we'll be holding hands on this. All other actions suspended for the foreseeable. Kevin – exhibits.'

'Yes, boss, course boss.'

Gill, DCI Gill Murray, was Janet's age, late forties, but the similarities stopped there. Friends for years, Janet had finally joined Gill's team seven years ago. Gill was a human dynamo with an ability to think strategically; she relished the role of leading her syndicate. Janet knew her own skills were as a communicator, an interviewer. And she'd rather sit opposite some witness or suspect and persuade them to tell her the truth than command a team, oversee development, play the public relations game and manage resources.

Gill could inspire, she had inspired many a young detective, but cross her and she was a formidable foe.

Even when she was working all hours, like now, Gill crackled with an energy and zeal, a lucidity and clarity that Janet envied. But also found exhausting at times. Of course Gill only had one teenager at home, but she'd managed the last four years as a single parent since Dave had left. Recently Sammy had moved in with his dad, to Gill's dismay. But even when Gill had been looking after him on her own she had still managed eighteen-hour days and turned up for work looking impeccable. Hair neat and shiny, a practical cut that skimmed her chin, trademark red lacquered nails, clothes clean and pressed. Gill was one of those people who could get by on four hours' sleep a night.

And I, thought Janet, getting up with her notebook and pen, am most definitely not. *Gill's driven. I'm just driven up the wall.*

Godzilla, as Rachel most frequently thought of her boss, was briefing them on the Journeys Inn crime scene and the unfolding manhunt for suspect Owen Cottam. The whole team were there. After two years, Rachel felt like she belonged, as much as she belonged anywhere. They were a mixed bunch. Pete, the doughnut man, solid, steady, paunchy, balding. And next to him, big man Mitch, ex-army. Turn his hand to any job, Mitch could. Loads of experience, well travelled, he was the oldest detective constable in the syndicate. He'd a quiet confidence, perhaps from knowing he was good at what he did, and he could handle himself in a fight, of course. Andy, at the head of the table beside Gill, was their sergeant, which set him apart in his roles and responsibilities. A sharp dresser, bit of a mod about him: Rachel could just see him on a scooter, a Lambretta. Andy was single and now and again she wondered what that was about. Not bad looking, probably the best of the bunch, but Rachel had never actually clicked with him; he was a bit cool, a bit distant – and he was her supervisor. Lee, on Rachel's right, he was more of a thinker, letters after his name and widely read. Sort that made Rachel feel uneducated. She learned from Lee, soaked it up like a sponge, stuff she could regurgitate to impress Nick. Back in the days when she was still trying. Before the assassination attempt. Lee was the only black member of the syndicate. Lee was the one who got sent on courses for offender profiling, criminal psychology and behaviour analysis.

Then Janet, of course. Rachel couldn't imagine the syndicate without Janet and usually the two of them were paired up, which Rachel liked. And Kevin Lumb. They got that wrong by one letter. Kevin Dumb it should have been, the div, like an eight-year-old. Kevin and Rachel the youngest on the team, but she was light years ahead of him most of the time.

'Question one,' the boss said, 'why is Owen Cottam our prime suspect? We have three members of the family dead in their beds, father and two youngest children missing. As is Owen Cottam's car. No sign of

31

burglary or forced entry, no evidence of a struggle. Cottam is not a known associate of the criminal fraternity and there have been no problems, no forfeiture of his personal pub licence. Of course he was CRB checked prior to being granted that by the local authority in Birkenhead. To date no talk of any enemies, any feuds or threats made to the family, though we'll need to see what we get from house-to-house and talking to friends and family.'

She stopped for breath and then continued, 'Nothing is ever sure in this game, you all know that, but to date there is nothing to suggest a third party was involved. Knife recovered from the third crime scene is being fast-tracked for evidence, as is a whisky bottle and items belonging to Owen Cottam. As far as the public is aware we urgently wish to speak to Owen Cottam in connection with our inquiries. And we want to find two children missing from home. We are setting up for a child rescue operation running concurrently alongside our murder investigations. Priority of course is to prevent further loss of life. That means we have the authorizations in place as of now for telecoms, warrants and so on so we can work in real time.'

That appealed to Rachel. Their work on the Major Incident Team was investigating murders and the information was usually gathered slowly and painstakingly with often frustrating waits for data from telecom providers and financial institutions and the like. Those protocols went out of the window when a life was at risk. Already data on Owen Cottam would be flowing in to be logged and analysed by readers and actioned by receivers for the various strands of the investigation.

'Border control, ports and airports, alerted,' the boss said.

'Found his passport at the pub,' Kevin said.

'Kevin's exhibits officer on this one,' Godzilla said.

Sooner you than me, Rachel thought. Keeping track of all the potential evidence from a scene meant you were stuck in the office for the duration. Drowning in evidence bags and chain of custody forms.

'His computer has been removed for examination,' the boss said. 'As yet nothing obvious leaping out at us, no Google maps or ferry sailings. His phone is missing.'

'Do we know if he has access to firearms?' Mitch asked. Rachel knew he'd be trying to assess how dangerous the man was.

'No guns licensed to him,' the DCI said. 'Now, we've ANPR, of course,' referring to the automatic number plate recognition system that had fast become a major tool in police work, routinely recording vehicle registrations on major routes nationwide. 'So if Cottam's in the Mondeo we'll find him before too long. Soon as we're done here I want Rachel heading house-to-house, looking for witnesses. Good revision for your sergeant's exam.'

Rachel nodded, a glow of satisfaction at being

allocated the task. She glanced across at Janet, who winked at her.

'Next of kin have been notified. Pamela Cottam's mother, Margaret Milne, is on her way over from Cork. Post-mortems expected to start later this afternoon. A complex scene means the CSIs will be there for several days. Cottam has a father, Dennis, in Liverpool and a brother, Barry, Preston way. We are talking to the brewery and his family as well as his neighbours on the Larks. So far the picture emerging is that of a regular guy, a family man. Lee.' The boss raised a finger to him. 'We'll be liaising with a forensic psychologist on this and a hostage negotiator obviously,' she said, 'but in the meanwhile Lee can tell us something about this particular type of homicide.'

Lee nodded; he'd got a psychology degree and was studying for a master's in his spare time. Rachel knew he was fascinated by what made people tick, what pushed them over the edge to kill, why one individual would take a life when another similar person would not. Frankly, Rachel didn't give a toss. They'd done it: her only interest was in catching the toerags and seeing them banged up for it. Whether their parents had been a walking disaster zone or they'd been bullied at school or there was something buggered in their brain chemistry was neither here nor there to Rachel. You broke the law – you paid the price. End of.

Lee put his pen down and tugged at his tie, loosening it as he began to speak. 'We average a handful a year, single figures, though that's on the rise: in periods of recession we tend to get an increase. Economic hardship is often a trigger point. The man loses his job, or gets into debt, and views that as catastrophic failure. He reasons he's better off dead and the family too.'

'Why the family?' Janet asked.

'The profile of this sort of man is a dominant, often controlling personality. He sees himself as the provider, the head of his family, and he regards the family as extensions of himself. Part of him. He won't leave them behind to face the disgrace, the collapse of lifestyle and so on.' Rachel thought briefly of her ex Nick Savage and his downfall. From shit-hot criminal barrister to criminal. One minute he's defending clients, the next he's on a charge himself. Attempted murder. The city centre flat and the bespoke suits exchanged for a cell in Strangeways and prison sweats.

'All for one and one for all,' Pete said.

'Except nobody else gets a say,' Janet pointed out.

Lee continued. 'In many cases, the wife's been having an affair or wants to end the marriage.'

'Is that not just revenge?' Godzilla said.

'May well be,' Lee agreed. 'In that situation the wife is killed to punish her but the children are killed because the father doesn't want to leave them behind. It's almost like a duty. I'm better off dead and so are they. Of course research is limited because few of the men survive to explain their motives or thinking.'

'But Cottam has,' Rachel said.

'So far,' Andy added.

'Why didn't he just finish the job?' Rachel said. 'He's done three of them, why suddenly stop and leg it with the youngest two? And the dog,' she said. 'Usually they kill the pets too, don't they?'

'That's right,' said Lee.

'Usually planned?' Godzilla said.

'Yes,' Lee said. 'Media coverage tends to emphasize the good father runs amok angle but in most cases the men have prepared to some degree, acquired the means, decided when to act, and so on.'

'Not exactly in the heat of the moment, then,' Janet said.

'Could the flight be part of the plan?' Rachel asked.

Lee shrugged. 'Unusual.'

'Or maybe there's trouble in the marriage, they're splitting up, all he wants is to abduct the kids and run?'

'Doesn't explain our three victims, especially the girl,' the boss said.

Rachel shrugged. Early days; they were still working out what the hell was going on.

Her Maj picked up and waved one of the reports through from the CSIs. 'Initial observations suggest our victims were asleep when attacked. Bodies on the beds. No sign of struggle. Nothing to suggest they were moved or posed.'

'What order?' Pete said.

'Still waiting for more on that from the scene.'

'The wife is usually first,' Lee said.

'And the knife was in the brother's room, Michael, so he'd be last,' said Rachel. Made sense.

'He intended to kill everyone,' Lee said, 'himself included.'

'What stopped him?' Rachel said.

'And why didn't he take the weapon with him?'

'Plenty of questions we need answers to,' the boss said, 'though top of the list,' she held up an index finger, 'is, where is Cottam now? If we're to find Cottam before he completes his grisly little mission we need to know everything about him: boxers or Y-fronts, where does he go on holiday, who are his mates, childhood haunts, health, money, favourite colour? We're appealing to the public for sightings.' Gill held up a photograph of Owen Cottam. Rachel looked at it: tall, thickset bloke, not overweight but solid looking, thinning hairline, moustache. Nothing in the man's expression to suggest he was a monster, a nutter who'd stick a knife into his eleven-year-old daughter as she slept.

His wife, okay, Rachel could understand that. She had fantasized taking a knife to Nick Savage on many an occasion during their relationship over the past two years. First when she found out he was married and had kids and that she, Rachel, had been his bit on the side. Disposable, irrelevant. Then when he'd learnt she was pregnant and told her to get rid of it. No discussion. After that he'd come squirming back to her, talked her into thinking he really did care, but he was just watching his back. Because by then Rachel knew Nick was dirty, had broken all the rules by sleeping with a juror during a trial. She had that over him and to protect his own skin he'd tried to have her killed. Some dick in a car tried to mow her down. She'd dreamed of taking a knife to him, cutting his balls off, countless times since then. So, if there was jealousy going on in Cottam's head the wife was halfway understandable. But not the daughter, nor the brother-in-law.

'I'm now going to show you the video of our scene, taken by our crime-scene coordinator,' Godzilla said, starting the recording. The video began. The boss making odd comments now and then. The camera taking them up the stairs and into the family's flat. Surveying each crime. First the wife, then the girl. The man, Michael, his neck agape, slathered with blood. Rachel felt her stomach churn and her wrists prickle. Her own dream still too close, a cloying aftertaste.

'Now, from her phone we can see that Pamela Cottam texted a contact, Lynn, at eleven fifty-two last night. Janet, you talk to her, then join Rachel,' the boss said. She continued, allocating further tasks, sounding off a rapid-fire list of actions, each accompanied by a sharp nod of her head. A bit like one of those office toys, the bird drinking the water. And those mad hand gestures she did, hand-jive crossed with karate.

Rachel shivered, waiting for the briefing to conclude, eager to get out and on with the job.

When Janet went to see her, Lynn Garstang was at work. She was the friend who had exchanged texts with Pamela Cottam the previous night. The last person known to have communicated with Pamela before her death. In this age of social networking and camera phones, someone would soon be tweeting about the police activity at Journeys Inn, so the police press office were on the brink of releasing a statement rather than let rumours flourish over the ether. Local officers had informed immediate next of kin of the deaths – messengers bearing the worst possible news. It was terrible when the family heard about a loved one's violent death on a news broadcast. The shock compounded by a sense of betrayal at the failure of the authorities, their appalling insensitivity and disregard. Even if names weren't made public, with a place so specific as a pub it didn't take a rocket scientist to work out who were the victims behind the headlines. But getting the news out into the public domain, alerting people and enlisting their help in an effort to save further lives, was paramount. If there was any comeback, Janet knew it was Gill who would face the music and explain to the relatives the very sound reasoning for the publicity.

The call centre was in a double industrial unit off the ring road. Janet showed her warrant card to the woman at the front office and asked for Lynn and whether there was anywhere private they could talk. The girl's face went still with curiosity but she bit her tongue and showed Janet into a tiny meeting room the size of a lift, a bare round table, two chairs and a slim filing cabinet the only furniture. Presumably where staff were hired and fired.

Lynn was rake thin, her face hollowed at the cheeks, her dark skin dry-looking. Janet wondered if she had been ill or lost weight or normally looked like that.

'Hello,' Lynn said, looking a little puzzled but waiting for enlightenment.

'Please sit down,' Janet said. 'I'm DC Janet Scott from Manchester Metropolitan Police. You're a friend of Pamela Cottam?'

'Yes.' Her smile faded. Her eyes, dark eyes, locked on to Janet's.

'I'm afraid I have some very bad news,' Janet said. 'We were called to Journeys Inn earlier today and found the bodies of three people. We believe them to be Pamela, her daughter Penny and Pamela's brother Michael.'

Lynn's eyelids flickered and her mouth moved for a couple of seconds before she said, 'Bodies?'

'I'm very, very sorry,' Janet said, talking slowly, for Lynn would need time to comprehend what was being said. 'An investigation into the deaths is now under way.' Important to use the word death. To make sure that there could be no misinterpretation.

'I . . . I'm sorry.' Lynn put her hand to her forehead. Her voice shook. 'Pamela? And Penny and Michael?'

'We think so. We have yet to complete the formal identification but we believe those are the victims.'

'But how? Was there a fire?'

Lynn had finally found some explanation that half made sense but before she could elaborate on it, let it take wing and find some comfort – *a fluke, an accident, a tragedy* – Janet said, 'No, we're treating these deaths as suspicious. I'm afraid all the indications are that the victims died as a result of knife wounds.' She couldn't say for definite until the post-mortem results were in, and even then they'd have to be very careful in the wording of such information. That was something that was drilled into them throughout training. It got so it became second nature, qualifying statements with phrases that, if held up in court, made it clear that the police had not made assumptions but had been punctilious about facts, only making categorical statements where they had the hard evidence to prove them.

'A knife?' Lynn said.

'We believe so,' Janet said quietly.

Lynn sat for a full minute, her mouth slightly ajar. Then she spoke again. 'The boys, Theo and Harry, they're all right?'

'They're missing,' Janet said. 'So is Owen.'

There was another pause. Lynn covered her eyes with her hands. Janet could hear her breathing. Then

41

Lynn moved, her face wet with tears. 'I don't understand,' she said. 'Why would anyone do that? And then take Owen and the boys?'

'We are still trying to establish what happened,' Janet said, 'but at this point there is nothing to suggest that an outside party was involved.'

A fraction of a second, then the shock fell through Lynn's face and she recoiled. 'You think . . . Oh, God,' she said. 'Oh my God,' hands pressed to her cheeks.

'I am sorry,' Janet said again. 'If you feel able I'd like to ask you some questions. We're trying to find Owen and the little ones.'

'Right,' Lynn said huskily.

'Pamela texted you last night?'

'Yes, about Tuesday.'

'You were going shopping?'

She halted, momentarily surprised that Janet knew this, but then said, 'Yes.'

'Was there anything unusual about the message, the time, or the content, anything at all?' Nothing had been obvious to the police.

'No.' Lynn shuddered, losing control of her muscles. 'I'm sorry,' she said.

'It's the shock,' Janet told her. 'Let's get you some tea.' She went out and asked the receptionist if she could bring some sweet tea for Lynn as she had been the bearer of bad news. The girl paled and said of course. Once that was accomplished, Janet began again, not knowing how much longer Lynn would be capable of talking. 'You're close friends, you and Pamela?'

'Yes,' she said.

'How long have you known each other?'

'For ever. We met when she first came over from Ireland. Chambermaids. I was her chief bridesmaid. She was mine. I'm their godmother, all three of them.' Her face contorted and she began to sob. Janet had some tissues in her bag. Always. Tissues, warrant card, alert alarm, pepper spray, radio, antiseptic spray (for scratches or bites – less exposure to that in serious crime than in uniform), phone, money and keys.

Lynn thanked her for the tissue and wiped her nose.

'Did you see much of them?'

She cleared her throat. 'More recently, with us being nearer. I moved to Manchester while they were still in the Lakes and then they went to Birkenhead then here, Oldham, and so we saw more of each other then.'

'How was the marriage?'

Fresh tears ran to her chin; she wiped them away with the back of her hand. Sniffed hard. But didn't reply straight away. Janet felt she was trying to frame her reply. 'Fine. I think.'

'Did Pamela talk about it, about Owen?'

'Not often. But sometimes he could be a bit, well, I'd call it controlling.' She made it sound like a question, as though seeing if Janet agreed. Janet made a neutral sound, encouraging her to say more.

'Like he always wanted to know where she was,

what her plans were. She didn't have much privacy. Much life of her own. Maybe some marriages work like that.'

Janet thought of her own. She and Ade shared pretty much everything; the logistics of work and home made it crucial. Only now she had secrets, now she told lies and misled Ade if she wanted to catch half an hour with Andy.

'Wouldn't have suited me,' Lynn said, 'but then my bloke left as soon as a better offer showed up.'

'You have any family?'

'Twin boys, two years older than Penny. How am I going to—' Emotion flickered over her face again.

'Did either Owen or Pamela ever get involved with anyone else?' Janet said.

'No,' Lynn said, 'no, she loved him. And he thought the world of her.'

'Would she have told you if she had been seeing anyone? Or if they'd had problems?'

'I think so,' Lynn said.

'Is there anyone else she might confide in?'

'No, she didn't really see anyone else. When we first met up there were a few of us became mates, but over the years . . .' She pulled a face.

'What about the pub, the business?'

'She said things were getting tough. Everyone's having a hard time. We see it here,' Lynn said.

'Did she mention any debts, owing money?'

'No – nothing like that.'

'When did you last see her?'

'Three weeks ago. We went for a drink in Manchester. She seemed fine. She never said he was depressed or anything. He must have been, he must have had a breakdown, mustn't he, to do that?' Her voice was thick now and she shuddered again.

Not necessarily, thought Janet. The debate about mad or bad was an endless one, practised by shrinks and criminologists, kicked about by police officers, the public and lawyers. But according to what Lee had said so far, and supported by the relative normality in the scene surrounding the victims at the inn, Cottam had not gone barmy and raged about in an orgy of destruction, he'd waited and acted when he had been sure of least resistance. While his loved ones slept. The wounds were efficient, not excessive. Janet had seen countless murders, plenty of stabbings, all sorts of obscenities. This was measured, if such a thing can be said to be so.

'We're nearly done for now,' she tried to reassure Lynn. 'Can you think of anywhere Owen might go to escape notice?'

'My mind's gone blank,' Lynn said. 'Erm, he went through a fishing phase. When Michael first came over. It didn't last long. I think Michael probably got on his nerves a bit.'

'How come?'

'Well, he was a bit shy in company, but if he knew you well he could talk the hind leg off a donkey, just drivel really, stream of consciousness. Maybe not what you want all day long on the river bank. That poor boy,' she said suddenly. 'He was harmless. And Penny . . . Oh, God.' Her composure, such as it was, collapsed and she began to sob, gulping air and in between asking, 'Why? How could he do that? Oh, God, why?'

4

Janet joined Rachel at the church hall on the Larks estate which they were using as a meeting point for the house-to-house. She handed out plans of the estate to the team of uniformed officers who were working door to door, while Rachel briefed them. Janet could hear an aggressive edge in Rachel's tone and knew that her friend was finding it difficult. Bark first, before they do, was Rachel's approach to most encounters. Probably worrying that she'd mess up. She needn't have bothered. None of these PCs would dare undermine her. They were all too keen to get stuck in, hoping to find something useful for the investigation.

As they peeled off and left the hall, Janet said, 'That was fine.'

'Yeah?' Rachel said guardedly.

'Well, you could have relaxed a little bit more, perhaps made eye contact now and then.'

'I did make eye contact,' Rachel objected.

'With the distant horizon, maybe.'

'So what're you saying? I was crap?' Rachel set off for the door, clutching the file.

'No, Rachel. I'm saying you are good at your job and you need to believe that so you have confidence, and that confidence shows. You were just a bit ... prickly.'

'Prickly?'

Oh, she should never have said anything. 'We're all on the same side,' Janet said, 'but sometimes it feels like you're not sure about that. Rachel Bailey against the world.'

'Don't you start,' Rachel said. 'I get enough shit from Godzilla about being a team player.'

'It matters,' Janet said, 'especially if you get your sergeant's exam – you'll be managing people. It's not just bossing them about.'

'Shall we get on with this?' Frowning in irritation, Rachel shook the plans in her hand.

'Wait.'

'Now what?' Rachel's scowl deepened. But even scowling she was attractive, large brown eyes, high cheekbones.

'Feather.' Janet reached out and pulled a curled white feather from the back of Rachel's hair. 'Two.' She picked out the other one. 'You been pillow fighting? No wonder you look knackered. Anyone I know?'

'Shut up,' Rachel said, pushing through the double doors.

'Seeing him again, whoever he is?' Janet said.

'Nah,' Rachel said.

They turned left on the crescent which led up to the top of the estate. Their remit the twenty-five properties closest to Journeys Inn.

Janet wasn't sure what was going on in Rachel's personal life. Since the whole sordid, sickening business with Nick Savage, Rachel had barely mentioned men. Barely mentioned anything outside work. Couldn't blame her really. Betrayal didn't come any bigger. Celibacy probably an attractive option, sensible. But Janet knew Rachel didn't do sensible. Never for very long, anyway. There was a chaotic, self-destructive side that seemed to be her default position when under stress. And she seemed drawn to danger. Janet worried about her. It was like watching a toddler trot towards an open fire, or teeter on a window ledge.

Janet thought about the Cottam kids. Two and a half and eighteen months. Talking, walking but powerless, dependent. Still alive? Anybody's guess. But the way it worked in a hostage situation was you assumed the best as you planned for the worst.

They reached the edge of the estate and Janet was panting, the pain in her side a dull throb. She turned away, pretending to survey the view, the roof of the inn visible above the back of the houses.

They split up, Janet taking the even numbers and Rachel doing the other side of the road. The estate was quiet, that time of day when anyone who had anywhere to go, school, work, shopping, had gone.

Janet got no answer at the first two houses but at the third, where a car was parked on the pavement outside, a woman wearing a dressing gown answered. Eyes soft with sleep, hair messy, face marked with creases on one cheek.

'Sorry to disturb you,' Janet said, holding up her warrant card. 'DC Janet Scott, Manchester Metropolitan Police. We're investigating a serious incident at Journeys Inn.' She paused, expecting the woman to show some recognition: the scant details had been broadcast, stating that the police were investigating suspected murder after three bodies had been found at a public house on the Larks estate. TV and press crews were arriving to film the pub and the hive of activity there as the CSIs went about their work.

But the woman just looked puzzled.

'Could I have your name?' Janet said.

'Tessa Bowen.'

'Date of birth?' Janet noted her answer. 'Does anyone else live here?'

'No, just me. What sort of incident?'

'Suspected murder,' Janet said, and saw the colour drain from the woman's face.

'Good God. But who?' she said, pulling her dressing gown tighter as though it might offer protection.

'We've yet to formally identify the victims,' Janet said. 'But they are believed to be members of the Cottam family, a man, a woman and a child.'

Tessa's hands flew to her mouth and she swayed.

Janet asked if she needed to sit down, if Janet could come in.

The lounge was dominated by a bright red leather sofa. They sat either end of it. 'A child?' Tessa said. She looked dazed. 'And a man and a woman. Pamela? But Owen was fine this morning.'

Janet's stomach fell. 'You saw Mr Cottam?' She jotted notes in her book.

'Yes – about half past six. I took the dog back.'

'The dog?'

'Yes. She's not their dog but they're looking after her. Billy, the owner, he's in hospital, operation for bowel cancer. He's my neighbour, number four.' She tipped her head to the right. 'He needed someone to take the dog.'

'Yes.' Janet nodded, waiting for the rest of the story.

'So, erm, Pamela and Owen said they'd have her, till we knew what was what with Billy.' She stopped and looked at Janet, bewildered.

'So this morning?' Janet prompted.

'I was coming back from work, night shift, Oldham Royal, I'm a nurse. And, erm, Pepper, the dog, she was on the road.'

'Whereabouts?'

'The other side of the hill, about quarter of a mile beyond the pub. I stopped and fetched her – took her up round the back. Owen answered the door.'

Janet gave a small nod, not betraying the flush of

51

adrenalin that increased her heartbeat. They would have to establish the time and all the other hard details but now she just needed Tessa to finish the story, to let it flow as much as possible, while it was still clear in her mind, unmuddied by the fallout of shock and speculation.

'He said she must have got out,' Tessa said.

'They kept her in the house?' Janet checked.

'Yes, they have to. The gate on the drive's never shut. And I said, she'd better not have got in with Grainger's sheep or he'd be up there with a shotgun. Or get the police round.' A look of alarm bloomed across her face. 'They weren't . . . ?'

Shot. 'No,' said Janet.

Tessa swallowed, her hands clenched tight in her lap. 'The boys, they came downstairs while we were talking.'

'Theo and Harry?'

'They're all right?' Tessa said.

'We believe Mr Cottam has taken them with him.'

'Oh.' She gave a little gasp.

'You saw the boys, and then?'

'That was it. I came home.'

'Tell me more about Grainger?'

'He owns a lot of the land beyond the pub. The farmhouse is further down the valley, going away from town. There've been a few problems: kids from the estate on those mini motorbikes, and dogs worrying the sheep. That's why I said that to Owen about

52

Pepper. She's been in there before and Billy managed to get her back before she did any damage, but Grainger, he always calls the police.'

'That's very helpful,' Janet said. 'We're going to need a full witness statement from you and it would be very useful to do that at the police station. I realize this is a lot to take in. Can I make you a cup of tea?'

'No, I'm fine, thanks. I'll just get dressed,' Tessa said.

'Of course. I'll come back in half an hour and we'll get you down to the station then,' Janet said.

Tessa stood up but paused at the door. 'How could he do that?' she asked.

'We don't know,' Janet said. 'We only have a limited amount of information at the moment.'

'He wouldn't do that,' she said, 'he just wouldn't.' She bit her lips together and shook her head, looking up at the ceiling. 'The boys – do you think they're going to be all right?'

Janet didn't reply. What answer could she possibly give?

Rachel could see that what Janet had found out from Tessa Bowen was crucial to the inquiry, giving them a possible last sighting of Owen Cottam, and she radioed through the information immediately. She was keen to get her to the station and take a written statement.

'I've left her getting ready,' Janet told Rachel, 'said

we'd call back for her. Do you think we'd better check out this Grainger fella, just in case he went ballistic, saw the dog worrying his sheep and decided to teach Cottam a lesson he'd never forget?'

'Thought farmers did it with shotguns?' Rachel said. Not that they came across many on their patch as a rule; not a lot of call for farmers in North Manchester, not unless it was a cannabis farm. Fair few shotguns though. Sawn off, usually.

'Oh, yes, invariably,' Janet said.

'Besides, what's he done with his nibs and the nippers? Fed 'em to his pigs?'

Janet closed her eyes, a pose of martyrdom.

'What?' Rachel said.

'Your turn of phrase leaves a lot to be desired.'

'Tell your mum was a schoolteacher,' Rachel said. 'What was yours?'

A failure. 'Housewife,' Rachel invented. 'Wait!'

'What?'

Rachel scrabbled through her pockets. 'Okay. Thought I'd lost the keys for a minute.' She hadn't but it served to derail the conversation well enough; now she could shift it to safer ground.

The track to Grainger's farm was halfway down the hillside, a turning to the right, tarmac part of the way then given over to dirt and stones. The gate into the farmyard was shut and various warning signs plastered about made it plain that no one was welcome. An impression reinforced by the broken stile just at the side of the gate and the rotting public foot-path sign half hidden by brambles.

In the farmyard there were some geese, big brutes, and Rachel was glad they were the other side of the barrier. A dog, out of sight, was barking its balls off, which brought a man from one of the outbuildings.

Rat-faced, Rachel thought, no chin, spike of a nose, daft-looking moustache, like something you'd buy on a sheet of cardboard from the toy stall on the market.

'Mr Grainger?' Janet said.

'Who's asking?'

Always a good start. Rachel and Janet flashed their warrant cards. 'We're investigating a serious incident at Journeys Inn,' Janet said. 'Have you been aware of any disturbances, anyone entering your property, any unusual traffic in the area?'

Rachel briefly imagined catamarans, penny-farthings, air balloons. Should have eaten, her mind jittery because she'd not.

'No,' he said and turned to spit.

Fuck's sake, Rachel thought. Wild west. Just need the chaps and spurs. 'What can you tell us about Mr Cottam?' she said.

Grainger pursed his lips, gave a shrug. Bored, in-different. Rachel wondered if he'd change his tune once he heard the story. Would that get his tongue wagging.

'You know him?' Janet said.

'By sight.'

'Neighbours though,' Janet pointed out. Grainger said nothing.

'You seen him recently?' Rachel said.

A cat stalked across between the barn and the farmhouse, tail held high, ignoring the geese, though the birds moved and grouped as if they'd attack.

Grainger shook his head. 'Saw his car, this morning,' he said, 'early.'

Rachel felt a prick of interest. 'What time?' she said.

'Quarter to seven, ten to.' *Minutes after Tessa had returned the dog at six thirty.*

'Was he driving?' Rachel said.

'Wasn't near enough to see.'

They didn't get much more from Grainger. He'd not seen the dog, Pepper, and claimed to know little about his closest neighbours. But curiosity finally overcame his mealy-mouthed act and he said, 'What's this incident then?'

'Suspected murder,' Janet said. And Rachel saw the blink signalling his surprise. Quick recovery though.

'The wife?' he said.

'Why d'you say that?' Rachel asked him.

'Usually is. Wife or husband, and if you thought he was in the car . . .'

Columbo.

Janet did the formal spiel. 'We have three victims, identities are not as yet confirmed.'

He didn't speak. Just gave a nod.

'We'd like you to call into the station as soon as

possible, make a witness statement.' Janet handed him a card. His hand shook as he took it. *His age? Or does he actually give a fuck?* He tipped his head again.

Janet phoned through to the incident room, then and there, told them they'd a key witness sighting of Cottam's car from the farmer and that he'd be in to make a formal statement.

'Central casting,' Rachel muttered as they retraced their steps to the car.

'They're not all like that,' Janet said. 'I met a very nice farmer once, literate, witty, sociable – friend of Gill's.'

'I believe you,' Rachel said sceptically.

'Just like "all coppers are bastards", eh?' Janet said, a nod to the graffiti initials *ACAB* that were still regularly daubed on walls and shop shutters and hoardings and reflected the attitude of many of the people they had to deal with day in and day out.

'Right,' Rachel said, ''cept me and you.'

Gill had attended the post-mortems. Watching in turn as the pathologist did external then internal examinations, combed the hair, taped the body and scraped the fingernails, swabbed the orifices. Photographed and measured the wounds, inspected, weighed and measured the organs.

Back in the office she received excellent news: they'd an ANPR report of Cottam's Mondeo heading north on the M6 near Penrith.

'Andy.' She put her head round her door, into the outer office. Told him about the breakthrough.

'Good,' he said. 'So we know he's still moving.'

Alive. 'Yes. Heading up to the Lakes, perhaps? Old stamping ground. I'm going to contact both Lancashire and Cumbria police,' she said. 'Bring them up to speed.'

She made those calls, alerting her colleagues in the neighbouring forces to Cottam's movements so they could brief their own officers. Then her phone rang – the front desk. Margaret Milne, Pamela and Michael's mother, had arrived. The family liaison officer who'd met Mrs Milne at Manchester Airport would remain her point of contact with the police. Normally one or two of Gill's DCs along with the FLO would accompany the next of kin to identify the victims, but on this occasion, Gill intended to go herself.

Gill knew Janet and Rachel were heading back in with an eyewitness who could place Owen and the two boys alive at six thirty that morning. Had he killed them after that, then taken the bodies with him? As yet there were no additional crime scenes other than those of the first three victims, no ominous pools of blood in the hall, or the living area. If he had killed the boys, why remove them? The fact of their absence seemed to suggest they were still alive when Cottam fled the scene.

Gill would use Janet to talk to Margaret Milne. Janet was her best interviewer. After the stabbing, in

58

March, when Geoff Hastings had almost killed Janet, in that long week that followed when it was touch and go, Gill didn't dare to think Janet would ever come back to work. The best she could hope for was that her friend would survive and be able to have some quality of life in the aftermath.

An attack like that, life threatening, was no easy thing to come back from. Gill knew coppers who would never work again, at any job; others, physically maimed or psychologically troubled, were shadows of their former selves, their previous talents and abilities ruined by the trauma. Janet's strength, her solidity, her resilience, amazed Gill. Not only had she resumed her duties after convalescing but she retained her ability to empathize with the people she interviewed, to make them comfortable enough, safe enough, to open up. To woo them into her confidence so that talking, telling her what she needed to know, was easier than not.

Rachel could take the eyewitness and Janet the bereaved mother.

On her way downstairs her phone rang again. *Chris* on the display. A little burn of pleasure inside her. She answered the call. 'You heard?'

'Can't think why. Triple murder, two missing kids.'

'So tomorrow . . .' she said regretfully.

'You putting me off?' he said.

'God knows when I'll get home. You know the score.' And he did. Working in the National Policing Improvement Agency, consulting on hard to solve murders, going wherever in the country he was needed. The same job that Gill had done, had loved, until her hubby Dave shag-bandit Murray had finally been caught doing the dirty and left her for the whore of Pendlebury. Leaving Gill holding the baby; well, the fourteen-year-old. Sammy needed at least one parent in the family home on a regular basis. Gill's high-flying career went out of the window and she took on the syndicate instead. Still working senseless hours but near enough to drive home afterwards and have breakfast in the mornings with her son. And now even that had gone . . . She tore herself away from thoughts of Sammy's recent flight into the toxic bosom of Dave's new family and back to Chris.

'I miss you,' Chris said and she felt her stomach drop.

'Me too,' she said. It was impossible. If she wasn't up to her eyes he was in Cornwall or Northumberland or wherever. Then when they did schedule something together, like now with him taking leave to come up for a week, she was landed with a trio of dead bodies and the prospect of more to come.

'Could still come up,' he said.

'And do what? Twiddle your thumbs while I'm here night and day?' Nice thumbs he had, like the rest of him. 'Book a flight somewhere,' she said. 'Treat yourself.' She imagined him at the beach: tall, really tall, but he carried it so well. She loved his height, his youth, her toyboy. 'Send me a postcard.' And the fact he really liked her, her mind as much as her body. They spent hours talking about work and he got it, got the same buzz she did from solving the puzzles they were set, from strategy and insight. With Dave she'd shared anecdotes but there'd been an undercurrent of resentment on his part. Although he'd lumbered up his own career ladder, more or less winched up by a crane, she thought sourly, he had never had the smarts that Gill knew she had. Of course back then she'd done that whole modest act, so he wouldn't look dim. No need with Chris. Equals.

'Think of it as research,' she said. 'Find somewhere perfect we can go together next time I take leave.'

'Do you ever take leave?'

'Yes,' she protested, though probably not always her full quota.

'Okay,' he said. 'Talk to you later.'

'Sardinia,' she said. 'Sardinia sounds nice. Or New York?' and ended the call.

Margaret Milne's complexion was so grey Gill wondered if the woman was having heart failure. She asked her if she'd like anything to eat or drink or whether she would like to see a doctor if she wasn't feeling well.

'No, thank you,' she said, her voice wavering.

'Perhaps just a cup of tea,' the FLO, Julia, suggested. No one wanted her keeling over when they got to the mortuary.

'Okay. Thank you.' She nodded.

While tea was fetched, Gill gave the woman her condolences. 'I'm so very sorry for your losses,' she said, 'for what has happened to Pamela and Michael and Penny. And I promise you we will do everything in our power to find and punish the person or people responsible.'

'Owen,' Margaret Milne said, her lips puckered as though the name itself was bitter.

'If he's responsible,' Gill said. Important to acknowledge that they were working on assumptions, bloody likely ones, but assumptions all the same. Until the evidence was in place and firm enough everything was modified with 'alleged', 'probable', 'believed to be', not 'known to be'. Not least because giving a grieving relative information that sounded cast-iron and was later disproved caused extra anguish.

'And the babbies?' she said, her Irish accent sounding stronger.

'No news. We believe Owen took them with him when he left the area this morning. Our sole aim now is to prevent any further loss of life. We have specialist staff, hostage negotiators and so on, ready to act as soon as we find them.'

The tea arrived and Margaret Milne picked up her cup then stared at it, at a loss. And she hadn't even seen the victims yet. Her son and daughter, her granddaughter.

'After we've been to the mortuary, if you are able to

confirm that it is Pamela and Michael and Penny, we'd very much like your help.'

'How?' She looked astonished, as though Gill had suggested something improper.

'You can tell us about the family, about Owen and Pamela. It may help us know where to look.'

'Yes, of course,' she said. She put her cup down, her hand shaking, spilling some tea over the edge. 'Can we go?' she said, her mouth twisting and twitching. 'Please can we go now?'

Gill smiled and got to her feet, shared a swift glance with Julia, knowing how bloody heartbreaking the next half-hour would be.

With a dignity that was painful and humbling to witness, Margaret Milne solemnly identified her forty-year-old daughter Pamela, her eleven-year-old granddaughter Penny, and her twenty-nine-year-old son Michael. She stood in the viewing room facing the window, tears coursing silently down her face. Then she turned to Julia and asked when she would be allowed to touch them.

'We have to wait for the coroner to release the bodies,' Julia said quietly. 'It may take some time. The defence have the right to request an independent post-mortem, you see.'

The woman nodded her understanding but held her arms out, fingers opening and closing around empty air. Gill knew that powerful urge, had seen it before, the desire to clasp the person, to hold them close. She had witnessed it at murder scenes where a relative or sometimes even the culprit clung to the victim, raining kisses on them, rocking them, willing them back to life. At road traffic accidents where parents cradled shattered children or drivers held hands with their lifeless passenger. And when she had accompanied the bereaved to funeral parlours and seen them stroke their loved one's hair or cheek. A tactile way of understanding that the person was dead and gone. That the essence of them wasn't there any more. Their heat and vitality and spirit had departed.

'Do you need a moment?' Gill asked, eager to get Margaret back to the station, to move things forward, aware of time passing from the metronome ticking in her pulse. For somewhere out there were Cottam and his children, at grave risk of death.

Margaret Milne turned to face her, slowly wiped her cheeks with her fingers and shook her head. 'No,' she said numbly.

Gill dipped her head and turned and led them out of the mortuary into the bright of the day.

5

'But won't it be weird for you?' Rachel said, cramming half a sausage roll into her mouth and swallowing before she continued, 'me being a sergeant and you still a DC?' Snatching a break at the station before their respective interviews. A snack at their desks. She hadn't had breakfast earlier, couldn't face it, so had spent all morning with her stomach feeling as if her throat had been cut. An image of Michael Milne flashed into her mind. The napkin of blood across his chest. And the sickening powerlessness as Nick stooped over her in the dream, slid the knife under her throat.

'Why should I?' Janet said, 'Gill's my boss, our boss, several rungs up, and I can handle that.'

'Yes, but—'

'What?' said Janet.

'She's your age.'

'Ancient, you mean?'

Rachel rolled her eyes. 'And she's years of experience. But me—'

'Elbowing us oldies out, queue jumping,' Janet tutted, 'all mouth and attitude, still wet behind the ears.'

Rachel grinned. 'Something like that.' She ate the rest of her snack.

Janet took a drink. 'You'll be a good sergeant, I'm a great DC. No problem.'

Then Rachel thought of the trial, and Mr dickhead barrister Nick Savage, and everything went cold and hard again.

'What?' Janet said.

Rachel sighed, about to speak, but Kevin came through then, his arms full of exhibits from the crime scene. Everything to be logged and kept safe. 'Skiving again?' Kevin said as he drew close. Rachel considered sticking out her foot, tripping him arse over elbow, serve the snidey little tosser right, but that might damage the exhibits and it'd be her in trouble, never mind the risk to the case.

'Pencil first, Kevin,' she said, 'then you can rub out all your mistakes.'

'Comedian,' he sneered.

Once he was out of earshot, Rachel glanced up at Janet, who was still patently waiting for an explanation. Rachel pressed her fingertips on to the crumbs of pastry on the paper bag. 'It's just . . . when we go to trial, Nick – he could take me down with him, Janet. I'd lose my job. My warrant card.' The prospect of that, like a bloody great pit, waiting to swallow her.

She had always known it would come to this, some-thing like this, no matter how far she'd come, run, from her shitty life and her scrappy family, no matter how much she studied and trained, no matter the hours or the commitment or the fact that this was all she had ever, ever wanted; sooner or later she knew she'd be found out, failed, chucked out. End up on a bench in the precinct with a can of cheap cider, spout-ing crap like her miserable excuse for a father. Or missing presumed couldn't-give-a-fuck like her mother, who swanned off when three kids and a feckless feller got too much for her.

'It's an offence, perjury,' Rachel said. 'I could get sent down.' Join her sad-sack little brother who was behind bars for armed robbery. Some irony there, given she'd not exchanged a word with him since he was caught. Janet didn't know about that, about Dom or her mum and dad, but she knew about the perjury.

Janet said, 'Look, I grant you, he's a nasty piece of work, and I told you—'

'You told me,' Rachel echoed bitterly.

'But he is charged with attempted murder, with try-ing to kill you, and if he even mentions that it'll backfire because it'll show Nick was colouring outside the lines. Using you to get confidential information that he'd then manipulate to try and get his slimy client off.'

One professional to another, that's how Rachel had seen it. What's said in the bedroom stays in the bedroom. She'd told him of her elation at nicking notorious crime lord Carl Norris and the jibe she'd made as she put Norris in the custody suite: 'Who's laughing now, pretty boy?' But Nick broke the rules. Months later, the relationship in tatters, Rachel had been summoned to give evidence as arresting officer at Norris's trial. And was horrified to discover Nick acting as Norris's barrister. Cross-examining her, Nick sought to undermine the basis for the arrest and flung the phrase back at her in court. Which she then denied. Lying under oath. A stick to beat her with. And Norris walked.

But when Rachel found out, just by chance, that Nick had been shagging one of the jurors during that trial, she'd some leverage of her own. By then, though, Nick had turned over a new leaf, she'd given him a second chance (maybe third – she wasn't counting). All seemed hunky-dory until she was nearly mown down.

'The evidence against him is overwhelming.' Janet's blue eyes beaming intelligence, reassurance, at her.

The tape recording. Rachel's stomach turned over at the thought of it again. Nick Savage in a car with big-shot career criminal Carl Norris. Nick oh so carefully explaining how Rachel might be a 'problem' seeing as she'd found out Nick was screwing a juror during the trial where Nick was defending Carl Norris. And clever-dick Norris oh so carefully taping the whole conversation. For the police.

'Chop chop!' Gill swept in, clapped her hands together.

'Any more on the ANPR?' Janet asked.

'Not as yet.'

'His phone?' said Rachel.

'Not using it. Not switched on, our telecoms reckon. Update at the briefing.'

Sod Nick Savage. Maybe Janet was right and he wouldn't derail her career. He'd go to trial and get found guilty and spend the next ten to fifteen years banged up with a load of low-lifers, bored out of his skull or too anxious to sleep. Posh boy like Nick wouldn't exactly be one of the lads inside, and without Carl Norris watching his back he'd be fair game.

Rachel sank the last of her coffee and grabbed her bag. If she was quick she'd have time for a fag before sitting down with the witness from the Larks.

Rachel had gone through Tessa's account with her once and was now reworking it, seeing if there was any more useful detail to be gained. Taking the bare bones and adding flesh to them. Some witnesses felt frustrated by the process, sure they'd told you everything, and were then surprised that a carefully phrased question suddenly illuminated fresh information.

'You said it was still dark when you saw the dog,' Rachel said. 'Were there any lights on at the pub?'

Tessa considered the question. 'I don't remember seeing any, but the light in the hall came on just before Owen answered the door.'

So it sounded as if Owen Cottam had been upstairs

when Tessa called and he'd put the light on to answer the door.

Rachel had seen the plans of the property. The separate entrance to the family's first-floor accommodation led into a short hallway with a flight of stairs. A second doorway off the hall gave access into the pub itself. That had been locked when police arrived.

'The dog went past Owen and up the stairs,' Rachel said. 'How long would you estimate you were at the door for?'

'Not long, maybe ten seconds.'

'How long had you waited for him to answer the door?'

'A couple of minutes. I'd knocked twice. No one answered at first so I tried again. I thought they might be asleep.' Tessa blanched.

'How did he appear, Owen?'

Tessa swallowed. 'A bit breathless,' she said. 'I thought it was the stairs.'

'Anything else? Try and picture him.'

'Not drowsy but tense,' she said, then pulled a face, 'but maybe I'm saying that because I know now—'

Rachel interrupted, not wanting her playing mind games with herself. 'See him at the door. What's he wearing?'

'Erm, sweatshirt . . . green . . . yes, bottle green, and, er . . . jeans, I think.'

'Shoes?'

'Yes.' She sounded surprised.

'Fully dressed?'

Because he hadn't been to bed, Rachel wondered? Or had he got dressed ready to leave the house? The first seemed most likely, especially if his original intention had been to wipe out the whole family including himself.

'How does he seem tense?' Rachel said, deliberately using the present tense to help Tessa recapture the memory.

Tessa tilted her head back in concentration. 'His eyes,' she said, straightening up. 'They were sort of darting around. That, and the way he was breathing, and I felt like he was itching to get shot of me. But then—'

'Yes?'

'Well, we weren't that pally. He was a bit like that anyway.'

'Like what?' Rachel said.

'Impatient, practical,' she said, 'I don't quite know how else to describe it.'

'That's fine,' Rachel said. 'Could you hear any other noises from the house?'

'No, not till the children—' She choked on the word, coughed and recovered. 'Till they came and called out.'

'Before that,' Rachel drew her back a step, 'tell me anything else you can remember about Owen. Any marks on his hands or his clothes?'

'No.'

Two minutes would give him time to wash his hands, Rachel thought.

'Any smell?' *Blood say, or sweat? Sweaty work, murder.* He might have avoided any major blood spatter but there would almost certainly be microscopic traces on his clothes.

'I think . . . there was a smell of alcohol but I couldn't say if that was from him or just with it being the pub.' You'd want a drink, wouldn't you, Rachel thought. Or several. Before embarking on the grisly task. Dutch courage.

'Okay, the children . . . ?'

'The little one, Harry, he called out "Daddy" before I saw him at the top of the stairs. Owen, he . . . I don't know how to describe it, like he, like he flinched, like he was really irritated.'

'Show me,' Rachel said.

'Sort of . . .' Tessa drew back her lips exposing her teeth, a snarling movement, blinking her eyes. More of a grimace than a flinch. She coughed and laughed and then blushed deeply. 'I feel ridiculous.'

'Don't, this is really helpful,' Rachel said. 'What was Harry wearing?'

'A sleep suit. Blue and white, some pattern.'

Details which would be fed through to the team. A check would be made to establish if the item was still at the scene, and meanwhile someone would scour children's clothes designs to find a match. If the garment was missing then an image of that item would be used in the search and could assist when investigating alleged sightings.

'Then Theo came after him,' Tessa said. 'He was sort of whining a bit.'

'But you'd not heard that before you saw him?'

'No. He was rubbing his eyes, just tired, cranky. You know how they get?'

Not really, Rachel thought. Whinging kids she'd rather avoid like the plague. Even if she had decided to go ahead and keep Nick's baby when he wanted her to get rid of it. Lost it anyway. All for the best. Sure was now. *Yes, babe, Daddy tried to get Mummy killed. That's why we never see him.*

'He had pyjamas on, Theo. Tiger stripes. It's his nickname.' Her voice shook now, almost breaking. 'Tiger, they call him.'

'You all right to carry on?' Rachel said, not wanting particularly to give her the option. Learning from Janet and Andy that recognizing distress was important to acknowledge but needn't be an exit sign. 'Have some water if you like?'

'I'm fine. The kids got halfway downstairs before I left. Owen said, "Thanks, I best . . ." and nodded his head to the kids.'

'So most of the conversation took place before the children came down?'

'Yes.'

'You went straight home from there?'

73

'That's right,' Tessa said.

'Is there anything else you can think of?'

'No.'

Rachel thought about the fact that she knew the little kid's nickname. 'How well did you know the family?'

'To say hello to and through Billy, really. He drinks in the pub and takes the dog with him. That's why I suggested asking if they'd have Pepper while he went into the Royal. Pamela and Owen and me, I wouldn't say we were friends or anything. I used to go along when they had quiz nights, a few years back now, if I wasn't on shift. But that's dropped off.'

'How did you find them, Owen and Pamela?'

She shook her head, shrugged. 'Normal, ordinary. Pamela was the chatty one. I'd say I knew her best. Just normal,' she said again. 'Busy with running the place and the kids.'

'And Penny?'

'Nice girl. They all were.'

'What about Michael?'

'He was very shy, blushed if you spoke to him—' Then her face was crumpling again. 'Sorry,' she said.

'You're fine,' Rachel answered. 'Take your time.' Normal, Rachel thought, normal family man. Neighbour on the doorstep and upstairs three corpses still warm. How the fuck did he hold it together? Dog barrelling past him, kids mithering. The plot unravelling. Yet he appeared normal enough to send her on her way with no clue as to what had happened in the rooms above.

The soft interview room was designed to be comfortable and homely: sofas and low coffee tables, boxes of toys for times when youngsters accompanied a parent or carer. Proper lamps instead of fluorescents.

Not that any of this would register with Margaret Milne, mother of Pamela Cottam and Michael Milne. Janet knew she would be knocked sideways with shock, with bursts of grief, still trying to absorb the nightmare her world had become.

Janet brought in tea, biscuits, tissues, water. She had her notebook and pen.

Margaret Milne sat at one end of the three-seat sofa but from her eyes Janet could see she was a million miles away. It was Janet's job to drag her back to the here and now and hoover up all the information she had about her family.

'My name is DC Janet Scott,' she said. 'I'd like you to call me Janet. Can I call you Margaret? Is that okay?'

Margaret Milne gave a nod, blinking as if the light was too bright. First names, the first part of the contract, the bond that Janet would build. The more Margaret trusted Janet, the more fruitful the conversation would be.

'I'm so sorry for your loss.' Janet fixed her eyes on Margaret, who turned away momentarily, looking into the corner of the room, away from the sharp sting of reality. Janet kept talking, softly and slowly. 'I can only imagine how devastated you must be and I wish none of it had happened and we didn't have to do this, but I need your help. We need your help to try and find Owen and Theo and Harry.'

Margaret nodded. Janet needed her to start vocalizing, to speak, for the longer she stayed mute the harder it would be to draw answers from her. But she wouldn't exert any pressure. Outside the room, teams were racing against the clock, scurrying around furiously as the manhunt unfolded, but in here time stood still for Janet while she got Margaret Milne to share her stories, to unravel the tangle of her family's life and perhaps reveal clues as to why Owen Cottam had acted as he did and where he might be.

'Tell me about Pamela,' she said.

Margaret took a breath. 'She's a lovely girl.' She tripped over the tense. 'Never any trouble.' A pause. Janet waited, gave half a smile.

'Always in work.'

Janet thought momentarily of her own mother. If Geoff Hastings had succeeded, how her mum would have framed it. *Couldn't wish for a better daughter but I never wanted her to join the police. She could have done anything: teaching or law or been a professor. Very bright – but she wouldn't listen. Went her own sweet way. And now. And her two girls . . .* Janet squashed the voice in her head and concentrated on

Margaret, who was now finding her stride, her words a little less jerky. Forty years of a life to convey, forty birthdays, three children, all those milestones and setbacks and the level times in between.

'They met in the Lake District,' Margaret was saying. Then she hesitated. 'He was managing the bar at the hotel—'

'Owen,' Janet murmured, seeing the name was becoming poisonous to Margaret. But censorship would not help the flow.

She nodded. 'Owen.' Her chin trembled. 'Pamela was maître d' – in the restaurant. They got married up there, in the Lakes, and Penny was born. They had a little house in the grounds. It was lovely,' she said, then again as if puzzled by the senseless reversal of circumstances, 'it was lovely.' No doubt thinking, how did we get from there to here, from that to this?

'Penny was born in 2000,' Janet nudged her gently.

'After that they took over a pub in Birkenhead. And when that closed they moved here. To the Journeys.'

Janet knew that they were tenant landlords, and that the tenant leased the premises and the equipment and stood any profit or loss. She also knew that pubs were closing in epidemic proportions.

'Theo was born in 2009 and then Harry the year after,' Margaret said.

'Any reason for the gap – nine years after Penny?' Janet asked.

Margaret shook her head. 'It just didn't happen. I

think they wanted to get on their feet at first, so they waited a while, and then when they did try again . . .'

Janet smiled.

'Michael moved in then, just before Harry came along. He wasn't getting anywhere at home. He's got learning difficulties; mild, but . . . he couldn't really manage on his own.' She shook her head. 'And we're out in the sticks. Nothing for him there—' Again Margaret broke off, the brutal truth knocking her sideways again. If Michael hadn't come to live with his sister, he'd still be alive. Margaret would still have one child left.

'So Michael moved in,' Janet said.

'He started helping out over Christmas and stayed. I'd say it was great for Pamela, especially with the little ones; she didn't need to do as much in the bar. Though it's always the same if you live and work in the same place, never really off duty.'

Janet nodded. 'What did you make of Owen?'

'I thought he was grand.' Tears swam in her eyes. 'Put in the hours, hard worker, always liked them looking nice, the children and Pamela.'

When she didn't elaborate Janet said, 'And how were things between Pamela and Owen?'

'Good,' but Janet caught an echo of doubt and waited so that Margaret carried on. 'He liked things doing the right way. Bit of a perfectionist. They'd the odd row about that sort of thing.'

'Recently?' There was something there: Janet

could practically smell it in the air, in the hesitation.

'Things were hard, the business side.' Margaret frowned, ripples across her brow. 'He worried,' she said.

'Was he ever violent?'

'No, she never said. Just, you know, a bit of a shout now and again. What man doesn't?'

Janet could hear the undercurrent running beneath the flow of words. The sickening dawning prospect that *the odd row* and *a bit of a shout* had mounted up to mayhem, slaughter, murder.

'I have to ask you this, I'm sorry,' Janet said. 'Were either Owen or Pamela involved with anyone else?'

'No,' Margaret said emphatically.

'They were married for eighteen years,' Janet said. 'That's a good while. Were there ever problems?'

Margaret shook her head. 'No, not between them.'

'Thank you. And what about alcohol? Drugs? Any problems for either of them?'

'No, not a problem, but Owen liked a drink.'

Janet tried to unpick the phrase. Liked a drink as in an odd tipple or glued to the bottle?

'How was he when he was drinking?'

'How do you mean?'

'Did it alter his mood, his behaviour?' Not wanting to put words in Margaret's mouth, or ideas in her head.

'He was quieter; the same, really. Perhaps a bit . . . short-tempered.'

'Like what?'

'If the children were being bold, or noisy, he might tell them off. That's all.'

Janet recognized the Irish turn of phrase. Bold meaning naughty. The Irish, the biggest immigrant population in Manchester, something like a third of the citizens having some Irish blood. Janet had, through her father's side. Still heard Irish accents often and particular words that differed from English. Running messages meant going on errands. Janet had once been told drugs were hidden in the hot press – Irish for the airing cupboard.

A depressed drunk then. Someone whose troubles magnified with each tot. 'Would he drink at work?' Janet asked.

'Yes,' Margaret said. 'To be sociable. Not too much.'

'Did Pamela ever say anything about his health?'

'No. I don't think he went to the doctor's in all the time I've known him.'

'You mentioned things being hard with the business. What can you tell me about that?' Janet asked.

'Just with the recession and that. People have less money in their pockets and there's a lot out of work round there,' Margaret said.

'On the Larks?'

Margaret nodded.

'They were settled there?'

'Oh, yes. They'd no plans to leave. Penny had just

gone up to secondary school. They'd not want to uproot her.'

'Did you ever hear of Owen being involved in anything illegal?' Janet said.

'No, no – he'd have no truck with that sort of thing.'

'Did either of them owe anybody money? Borrow money?'

'I don't know.' Margaret shrugged. 'It wasn't my business. That would be between the two of them.'

Janet nodded. 'How often did you see them?'

'Two or three times a year I'd come over, but Pamela rang me every Sunday. Regular as clockwork.' Her lip trembled.

'When did you last see them?'

'August – the bank holiday week.'

'And yesterday, did Pamela ring?' Janet asked gently.

Margaret gave a nod and pressed her hand to her mouth, her eyes flooding with tears. Perhaps she was realizing that yesterday was the last time she would ever speak to her daughter.

'I'm sorry,' she blurted out.

'It's fine,' Janet said, 'I understand.' She passed over the tissues. 'Are you all right to continue?' Margaret Milne nodded. Her face was watery, wobbly, as Janet resumed. 'How was Pamela when you spoke yesterday?'

'Grand. Same as ever. She'd told me that Penny had played—' She stopped abruptly, took several painful breaths, then said, 'Penny had played netball on Saturday and they'd won. She'd got a goal.'

'What else?' Janet said.

'The weather getting colder, and Theo not being so good the week before. He gets awful earache, but he was better.'

'Tell me about the boys. Harry – the little one.'

'He's a bright spark,' his grandmother said. 'Runs rings round you, that age, into everything? But he sleeps like a lamb.'

'And Theo?' Janet said.

'He's the sensitive type. Harry – you can put him down and he's spark out, but Theo has to have the light on and you have to sit with him. He has bad dreams.' Again she stopped. Bad dreams. But this isn't a dream, Janet thought, this is real. But at this stage too enormous to comprehend.

'What does he like, Theo?' she said.

'Oh, trains. He's train mad.' Margaret almost smiled. 'Michael was the same. Penny's very good with him. With both of them. If they're busy she'll put them to bed or get their tea.' She started to cry again. Janet allowed her time to recover from the deluge of emotion. Watched her breathing settle, the hitching of her shoulders ebb away. Margaret reached for another tissue.

'Does Owen do much with the children?' Janet said.

Margaret didn't answer immediately. 'A fair amount,' she said, 'but Pamela is the main one. He 'wouldn't take them to the clinic, say, or buy clothes.'

'Feeding, changing: he'd be able to do that?' Janet said. *If he hasn't already harmed them.*

'Oh, yes.'

'Harry's eighteen months now. Is he walking, talking?'

'Both. Only a couple of words, though; he's not making his sentences yet,' Margaret said.

'And Theo, he'd be able to talk.' Janet didn't want to say 'ask for help' – the boy would trust his father and not approach anyone unless Owen abandoned them. She was trying to find out in general about the children's abilities and assess how dependent they would be on Cottam.

'He's shy with strangers,' Margaret said.

'Is he in playgroup or nursery yet?' Janet asked.

'No – still in nappies. Clingy, too. Pamela wasn't all that sure about taking him for a while yet.'

'Can you tell me how Owen and Michael got on?'

'They were great,' Margaret said. 'I'd say Owen was like a role model, you know? Michael would have followed him around all day. His dad died when he was very young, but Owen knew how to manage him. They both did.'

'So there was no tension?' Janet said.

'No. Owen would soon have put his foot down if there was.'

Janet wondered if Pamela would have reported it to her mother even if there had been.

'How did he discipline the children?' she asked. 'If they were being naughty?'

'They might get sent to bed.'

'Did he ever smack them?'

Margaret looked trapped. Her eyes flew from side to side. 'He might. Just a smack, same as anyone.'

Except not everyone believed that hitting children was any more acceptable than hitting adults.

'Did Pamela smack them?'

Margaret hesitated.

'Margaret?'

'The same,' she said, 'only if they were really naughty. A tap, that's all, and then a cuddle later.'

'Thank you,' Janet said. 'But you don't believe Owen ever hit Pamela?'

'I know he didn't,' she said.

How can you know? How can you be sure? Was she just insisting on what she wanted to think was true?

'I can't believe it,' Margaret burst out. 'He loved her, he loved them all. They were his life. How could this happen? How could he do this? Where are they? Where are the children?' She wept again, her questions ringing round the room, desperate, and impossible to answer.

6

The briefing room, packed with her MIT as well as specialists from forensics and crime scene management, fell quiet as Gill entered.

The mood was attentive, focused, while Gill made introductions, an edge of impatience in the air, pent-up frustration because as yet Owen Cottam had eluded them. Gill surveyed her team, working out that since she'd taken over the syndicate she hadn't lost anyone. No transfer requests, no retirements or redundancies. They had all worked hard to get on to the syndicate (barring Kevin who'd been rehomed when Gill's mate more or less gave up on him and Gill rose to the challenge) and once on board they liked the billet. Five men, two women and Gill. A good spread of skills and experience. A good balance.

'We have significant results back from forensics,' she said. 'Fingerprints recovered from the knife left at the third scene match those found on a bottle of whisky in the bathroom and items around the property belonging to Owen Cottam – bedside lamp and alarm clock. He'd not bothered to wipe the knife. Why?'

'If this is what we think it is,' Lee said, 'he wasn't trying to hide the crime. He wasn't expecting to be around to answer any questions or go to trial. He'd be dead along with everyone else.'

'Okay,' Gill said, 'we'll start with the live investigation,' Gill said. 'Owen Cottam at large, registered keeper of a Ford Mondeo, vehicle captured by ANPR at eleven fifty on the M6 near Penrith. We now have a second result from ANPR timed at three twenty-nine close to Ribbleton.' The screen on the wall showed the map, initially on a small scale so people could understand the context, see the major towns and road networks, then Gill zoomed in so they could see in greater detail. 'So he's heading back down the M6, retracing his route. Why? Calls from the public now being actioned. Last verified sighting of Cottam . . .' Gill looked to Rachel, who appeared to have just woken up.

'Six thirty this morning, neighbour returning the dog spoke to him briefly. She also saw the two youngsters. At six forty-five Mr Grainger who has the farm on the far side saw the car but got no visual on the driver.'

'No other activity logged,' Gill said, checking with Andy that that was still the case.

He agreed. 'His phone has not been switched on. He

hasn't made or received any calls, he hasn't accessed his emails or used an ATM.'

'He's gone off the radar,' Gill summarized.

'Why's he still using the car?' Mitch said. 'He must know we can ping him.' Ian Mitchell had a young family himself, second marriage. Gill suspected he'd be feeling this case particularly keenly, though it would never affect his judgement or his consummate professionalism.

She held out a hand, inviting contributions from the floor.

'Not found an alternative,' said Janet. 'If the kids are still with him, he can't just dump it and start walking.'

Gill nodded. 'They're a liability, limiting his options,' she said.

'Why did he take them?' Rachel said. 'Why didn't he wait for Tessa to go then finish what he started?' The way she put it was almost brutal but Gill could hear the puzzlement in her voice. Rachel wanted to make sense of the man's actions. Because then she could better second guess what he might do next and how they might catch him.

'Lost his nerve,' Mitch said.

'If I can?' The criminal psychologist, Leonard Petty, a small, round-faced man with a liking for hair oil and kipper ties, spoke up.

'Please,' Gill invited him to say his piece.

'A sense of control, of being in charge, is central to

the personality here. The likelihood is that the murders were planned. Cottam executed the first three killings effectively and while the victims were asleep. No fight, no words exchanged, nothing to interfere with the scenario he'd envisaged. I think it's probable that he intended to do the same to the two youngest children. When the dog was returned and they woke, his plans went out of the window. He hadn't anticipated having to attack anyone who was awake, anyone communicating with him. Rather than lose control, which is his default position, he will delay and construct a new plan to regain his sense of being in command of what happens.'

'Why didn't he kill the dog in the first place? Why let it out?' said Pete. An astute question. Pete might be a sloppy dresser – Gill looked at his shapeless fleece and tracksuit bottoms and thought that he'd reached an age where he was letting himself go to seed – but his work remained methodical, good on detail.

'It wasn't his dog,' the psychologist said. 'The family were looking after the pet for a neighbour. He only wants to kill those he sees as close family. To take them with him. Not to abandon them. Think of it as suicide by proxy. His ultimate goal is to end his life, but first he must make sure he includes his nearest and dearest.'

Janet sighed and shook her head.

'He couldn't risk it, either,' Rachel said suddenly, eyes flashing bright. 'He could maybe have gone back in and thought up a way to kill the kids, then hanged himself or whatever, but Tessa told him that if the dog had been worrying sheep Grainger would have the police round. For all Cottam knew they were already on their way. He hadn't time.'

'Another interruption.' Gill saw the sense of it. 'Running buys him time. Good. Yes?' Gill glanced at Leonard Petty: this was his territory. She'd plenty of experience with low-lifes and losers, but whilst there was some overlap this was not their usual run-of-the-mill inquiry.

'That's right. He's regrouping.' Petty smoothed his tie. 'He needs to take control again so he can play things out to his satisfaction.'

Another three lives, Gill thought. Which would be a disaster, a nightmare of huge magnitude. Performed with the whole country watching.

'Right, lads,' she said crisply, 'what do we know about Owen Cottam?'

Andy began rattling off the facts collated from the spider's web of intelligence gathering. 'Born 1966 in Preston, one brother, Barry. Father Dennis a garage mechanic, mother a bookkeeper, left to remarry and emigrated. Owen and Barry chose to remain in the UK. Owen was unremarkable at school, member of the rugby team. Finished school at sixteen, worked with his father for the next four years, then moved up to the Lakes and worked there. First as a handyman then bar and cellar man at the Greyhounds Hotel. Met Pamela

Milne and married in 1993. Moved to Birkenhead in 1999 and ran the Colliers Arms for the next six years. Took over tenancy of Journeys Inn in 2005. Penny born in 2000, Theo in 2009 and Harry in 2010.'

'Relations between the couple said to be generally amicable,' Gill said.

'So far,' Rachel said sceptically.

'Yes,' Andy agreed, 'there must be something there. She's playing away . . .'

Janet shook her head, gave a little snort.

'. . . or she's threatened to leave, taking the kids.'

'So now it's her fault?' Janet sounded ruffled.

'Considering motive, not fault,' Gill reminded her. Don't blame the victim, a holy grail. 'Leonard?'

'Infidelity, the end of a relationship, it's often a factor,' he said, 'but not always,' sounding a note of caution.

'We have the eyewitness, Tessa, and Margaret Milne's statements. Anything else from house-to-house?' Gill said.

Rachel found the page in her report. 'Well known in the area, liked by some people, described as a good bloke, that sort of thing. Others pegged him as a bit moody, left the socializing to Pamela. But no bad blood. Also described as a bit quiet as in keeps to himself.'

'Not quite mine host,' Gill remarked. 'Local bobbies?'

'As we know, never any problems with his licence,'

said Pete. 'Sorted out troublemakers when he needed to. Couple of parking fines, the odd speeding ticket. No known criminal activity or associates.'

'Family.' Gill moved them on to another element. 'Brother and father expressed shock when told of events. Not in a million years and so on. I've spoken in person to the father and advised him we may want to make an appeal.' *One father to another, father to son.* 'Radio and television broadcasts.'

'Cottam's hardly going to turn himself in,' Rachel sneered.

'Very unlikely, but we have to be seen to be exploring every avenue,' Gill said. Procedures that had to be followed, laid out in the rule book. 'The chances of Cottam's responding to the appeal might seem remote, but it gains us human interest, sympathy, adds to likely public efforts to assist.' Two sides to policing – protect and serve, fighting crime and maintaining the trust of the population. The great British public needed to believe that an appeal was in their interest. A high profile case like this would be scrutinized and found wanting if people weren't reassured as to how it was being handled. Gill could already see down the line to the case reviews to come. She needed to know that the team were doing everything humanly possible and then some.

'Finances?' She looked to Pete.

'Living beyond their means.'

Hardly the high life, Gill thought. The pub had a

shoddy, tired appearance which the family flat above shared. Furniture was mismatched and mostly cheap, the soft furnishings too. The kitchen/living area looked as though it had been fitted twenty years ago or more, the sandy brown worktop fraying along the edge with water damage. The room had smelled of dog and a faint whiff of gas. Tiling behind the counter top in cream and flecks of burnt orange, every so often a feature tile, a picture of a tree. The rustic feel circa 1980s.

Other things were newer, the flat-screen televisions and the computer. And the clothing that Gill had seen all looked in good condition.

'The pub wasn't doing much of a turnover,' Pete said.

Smoking ban, people drinking at home.

'Should have tried a sports bar,' Kevin said. 'Massive screen. Course, you've got the outlay—'

'Kevin.' Gill yanked his lead, stopped him wittering on. Kevin was Gill's crown of thorns. Struggling to make the grade and Gill had sworn she'd knock him into shape. It was just taking way longer than she'd anticipated.

'There were rumours on house-to-house it was losing money,' Rachel pointed out. 'There's no work on the Larks; his clientele's mainly benefit drinkers.'

Pete said, 'I spoke to the brewery. They were talking about pulling the plug after New Year. Tenancy is up for renewal then. Informed Cottam by registered letter,

92

which he received on the thirtieth of September.'

'Something like that could be a trigger?' Gill said.

Leonard nodded. 'Definitely.'

'He'd debts too,' Pete said. 'Credit cards – only paying off the interest. Payday loans.'

'Owen was owing.' Kevin grinned, looked round the room for a response. Got a scoff and rolling eyes from Rachel, a slow blink from Janet and a shake of the head from Lee. 'Rhymes, doesn't it?' Kevin, crap at reading the signs, dug his hole even deeper.

'Kevin,' Andy said wearily.

'What was he spending it on?' Gill asked Pete.

'Clothes, food, essentials, nothing flash. Utility bills. His car's six years old, pick one up for six grand.'

'Still – it's a Mondeo,' Mitch said. 'Lot of car for the price.'

'Tells us what?' Gill said, not wanting them to get into a *Top Gear* riff. Mitch was mad about cars.

'Not flash,' Andy said, 'but he's looking at reasonable quality.'

'Anything flash round the Larks and it'd soon disappear,' Rachel said.

'The family had a holiday to Minorca in May, not paid that off yet,' Pete added.

'He was already in debt by then?' Janet asked.

'Oh, yes,' Pete said.

'Keeping up appearances,' said Lee. 'He had to be seen to be providing for his family. He'll keep the illusion going as long as possible.'

That would tally with the clothes, Gill thought. People would see the kids well dressed and assume the household were managing well.

Janet raised her pen and addressed Leonard Petty. 'What's he feeling then, about things going down the drain?'

'Shame and anger. This is his responsibility. Any failure in that regard would be excruciating for him. He won't admit to anyone it's happening. He feels outraged, betrayed that his livelihood is on the line. It's common enough: the recession, businesses folding, layoffs, but as far as this man is concerned it's his problem and his alone. He's been singled out, his status about to be destroyed, his self-esteem undermined.'

'Even for us,' Gill said. Numbers in the police force were going to be cut in an effort to make savings. At what cost, she thought? As people became poorer, more desperate, as unemployment increased, crime would rise, with fewer officers to deal with it all. Crime stats had been falling. It was something she was proud to be associated with, but the future was far more uncertain.

'Did we find a will?'

'Yes,' Andy said. 'They both had one. Standard stuff – spouse inherits and then the children.'

'Okay. Moving on to our crime scenes,' Gill said, 'we're awaiting further forensics but already we can agree a likely sequence of events. Last customers left the pub at eleven twenty-three.'

Rachel picked up the thread. 'A group celebrating a thirtieth birthday with whisky chasers and rounds of pool.'

'CCTV from the pub tells us all was well then,' Gill said. 'Pamela, Owen and Michael clearing up.'

She played the film. There was little communication between the three adults as they went about the routine. But it was unnerving witnessing the footage, so mundane and unremarkable, knowing what was to come. 'No reports of anything out of the ordinary,' Gill went on. 'Pamela Milne texted her friend Lynn after going upstairs.' She gave Janet the nod.

'The women were due to be going shopping in Manchester,' Janet said. 'Pamela suggested Tuesday in her text. Nothing untoward in the exchange.'

'No CCTV in the flat itself,' Gill said. 'The cameras are inside downstairs and outside covering the entrance and the car park. We see nothing until three in the morning.' The film showed Owen Cottam entering the pub from the internal door and going behind the bar. He opened a bottle of whisky and then went into the small room behind the bar. The screen went black.

'He switched the system off then. Note he is fully dressed and wearing clothes the same as or similar to the ones described by Tessa when he spoke to her at six thirty in the morning. Until forensics give us more hard data all we can be sure of is that between eleven thirty last night and eight, when the wagon driver from the brewery arrived, Cottam used a knife recovered from the property to kill his wife and his daughter and his brother-in-law. The sighting of the car by Grainger, the neighbouring farmer, before seven makes me think we can probably shave an hour off that. Analysis of drops of blood on the landing between the three bedrooms should help us confirm which direction Cottam was walking in and therefore the order in which the attacks took place. We believe he was interrupted during or soon after the attack on Michael, leading him to abandon the weapon in Michael's room. The bottle of whisky, three-quarters empty, with a smear of blood visible on the label, was recovered from the bathroom. Owen Cottam's fingerprints are on the bottle, which is the same brand as the one he had on the film from the bar. Evidence suggests he washed his hands in the bathroom after the attacks: blood traces in the sink and on a towel. Cottam shut the dog in the kitchen and fled the property between six thirty and eight with the two younger children. Mitch, friends and associates?'

'Not finding many,' Mitch said. 'Seems to have kept himself to himself, family man.'

'Acting alone?' Gill said, and Leonard nodded. 'Not likely to have any allies.'

'He wouldn't trust anyone else to help, would he,' Lee said. 'He believes he's on his own. Any emotional investment he has is with his immediate family. Not beyond that.'

'That's right,' Leonard Petty said. 'So although we know he might be looking for places to regroup we're not expecting him to contact friends or wider family.'

'What places will be of interest?' Gill said.

'Possibly remote, isolated, where he won't be at risk of identification,' Leonard Petty said.

'What if he's clever, though? You've two kids, you want to go unnoticed, why not go where there's loads of kids. A theme park or summat,' Rachel said.

'In plain sight.' Gill considered it.

'More risky, I'd have thought,' said Janet.

'I agree,' the forensic psychologist said. 'He wants to be somewhere where he believes he can control the scenario. Somewhere to take stock and redesign his plan.'

'He didn't take the knife, so we don't know how he might be trying to kill them,' Pete said.

'He could buy another knife,' said Kevin.

'He's got a car,' Rachel pointed out. 'If he's got a bit of hosepipe he could have already done it. That's what I'd do, or jump off a cliff with them.' Rachel blunt as ever.

Gill tipped her head to Leonard Petty, inviting him to respond.

'Hard to second guess, but it's an eventuality we should prepare for if we do find the vehicle,' he said.

Gill imagined it. The Mondeo in some lay-by. Unremarkable until someone sees the line of tubing snaking in the top of the window. Catches a glimpse of the driver's face, or the kiddies' – red as toffee apples: the side effect of cyanotic poisoning. 'Let's hope the bastard didn't have time to take anything with him. That he's still trolling up and down the M6 trying to work out where to go, what to do. You'll all be entitled to overtime thanks to the powers that be.' A cheer went up. She knew most of them would have put the time in regardless. Not interested in their social lives or feet up in front of the box in the midst of a case like this.

'So, Rachel, take the father and the brother. As well as general background we specifically want a list of locations. We want to know where Cottam might be headed.'

Rachel had only just lit up, sucked a lungful of smoke in and closed her eyes when she heard someone approach, footsteps fast on the ground, setting her nerves jangling as she swung round prepared to bolt.

'Found you!' Her sister Alison, for fuck's sake.

'I wasn't lost.' Rachel took another drag, willed her hand to stop shaking.

'Well, I've been ringing you for the last fortnight,' Alison said, bossy big sister act, hands on her hips. 'Thought you'd given up.' She nodded her head at Rachel's fag. 'Those things'll kill you.'

Who cares, thought Rachel? Something's got to. 'What're you here for, Alison? Only I'm working. Busy. Very busy.'

Alison was about to hurl something back. Rachel could see it: *Busy? You have no idea. I've three kids and a job as well.* But then something clearly dawned on Alison, bringing light to her eyes and making her mouth drop open. 'God, it's not the Journeys Inn thing, is it?'

'Yes.' Rachel sucked more smoke, another couple of tokes, getting ready to head back inside.

'That's awful, that,' Alison said, 'awful.' Then quieter, more confidential, a greedy look on her face, 'Do they know where he is? Why he—'

'Can't discuss it.' Rachel dropped her fag, ground it out. 'So . . .'

Alison crossed her arms. 'Another couple of months and Dom'll be released.'

'Jesus Christ,' Rachel breathed, 'not that again.'

'What d'you mean, *that again*? He's family, Rachel. We're all he's got.'

'Count me out.' Rachel had been over this time and again. Dom had messed up, silly pillock, made his bed, he could lie in it. She didn't need a convicted criminal for a brother, convicted of armed robbery. Imagining how well Godzilla would take that little nugget of information.

'What's prison for?' Alison said.

'Low-lifes? Scumbags?'

'Rehabilitation,' Alison said.

'Spare me the philosophical debate.' Rachel began to move away.

99

'He needs us, Rachel. He's done his time, he's paid for his mistake. No support and he is way more likely to get into bother again. Is that what you want?'

What did she want? For it never to have happened. For Dom to have stayed on the straight and narrow. Got a job, found someone to spend his wages on. For Dom to have grown up and got his act together, instead of throwing it all away. 'What's done is done.'

'He'll listen to you,' Alison said. 'He always was closest to you. He always asks after you, you know. You washed your hands of him.' She was getting aerated now. 'Four years – not one visit, not even a birthday card. How do you think that's helped his self-esteem? Fresh start, Rachel, doesn't he deserve that?'

Rachel didn't want to think about it. About Dom who she'd tried to raise right after her mum had sodded off and left them to it. Her dad a waste of space, living his life in a triangle: bookies, pub, home, with occasional appearances at the dole office. Alison tried to keep everything going. Rachel had finally escaped, left it all behind. Now Alison was wanting to drag her back into it. 'He *didn't* listen to me, did he? Or he wouldn't be there. Look, now is not the time—'

'When the hell is, then?' Alison shouted. 'You're never in if I come round. You ignore my calls.' A couple of bobbies going round to the entrance halted, sussing out if help was required. Rachel raised a hand, showing them she was okay.

'You'd rather he went back inside?' Alison said. 'All I'm asking is you see him, buy him a meal now and then. Be his sister. Please, Rachel?'

Rachel ground her teeth. She didn't need this. Not on top of everything else.

'What is it?' Alison rattled on. 'He'd cramp your style, would he? Now you've got the brilliant job and the fancy luxury conversion and you're hanging round with big-shot barristers. Looking down on the rest of us.' Alison didn't know about Nick Savage. Rachel had told her he was off the scene but left out the bit about him trying to get her killed. 'Joined the Masons, have you? Funny handshakes?'

'Don't be daft.'

'You're just writing him off, me and all? Is that it? You're too good for us now?'

'It's not about you. You didn't commit armed robbery with a sawn-off shotgun.'

'He was a teenager, Rachel. He was young and daft.'

'He had a choice,' Rachel said. That's what made her so mad, that the stupid little scally could have taken another road. Turned down the offer of a rock solid way to make easy money and stayed honest.

'We all make mistakes,' Alison said. 'You could get a bloody medal for it.'

'You know fuck all about me.' Rachel suddenly hot with rage.

'I'm your sister, you daft mare, course I know about you. And he is your brother.'

'I've got to get back,' Rachel said.

Alison swung her head, chewing the side of her cheek. Obviously furious with her. Disappointed. She didn't move as Rachel walked back in, already craving another smoke and imagining the bottle of wine waiting for her at the end of the day.

7

Dennis Cottam had the weather-beaten, whittled look of someone whose life had been one of manual labour. Skin leathery and brown. Outdoors all hours, running his car repair workshop. Grease monkey, thought Rachel, something ape-like about him, not in his manner – not crude or uncivilized – but in his physicality: bald with a deeply wrinkled brow, bristles dark around his mouth, arms with muscles and tendons like ropes and hands larger than his frame warranted, out of proportion to the rest of him somehow. He'd got startling blue eyes, like Janet's, curly hairs thick on his forearms.

'Mr Cottam? DC Rachel Bailey. Someone said I'd be coming?'

'That's right.'

Local officers had already made the initial visit, broken the news to Cottam senior, established whether he'd had any contact with his eldest son (not for a couple of months) and advised him on what he should do if he did hear anything. Ferried through any facts they collected to the inquiry.

Dennis Cottam lived in an end terrace next door to his workshop and garage. The house looked clean and tidy from the outside, like its neighbours.

'Barry's not here yet,' he said, his knuckles pressing at his chest, the only sign that anything was wrong.

'That's fine,' Rachel said. 'We can make a start.'

He took her through. The rooms had been knocked through to create an open-plan living area. The furnishings were plain, modern: a small chocolate-coloured sofa and chair, pale grey paint on the walls. Rachel wondered if Dennis had picked it. Or if there was a woman involved.

She sat in an upright chair beside a small table, presumably where he ate his meals. He sat in the armchair, then started, 'Would you like a drink, tea or coffee?' Worried about forgetting his manners.

'No, thank you,' Rachel said. He was dazed, she could see that: the way his eyes wandered, drifting, the halting nature of his interaction with her. 'Can I just go over what you told the officers earlier? You've not heard from Owen since August when you all went for a pub lunch.'

'That's right. Busman's holiday for them but it saves them the cooking . . .' he cleared his throat, 'Pam and Bev, Barry's wife.' He pressed his fist against his chest again. You can cry, mate, Rachel thought, I'll not bother. But he fought against it and picked up his story. 'There's a place near the reservoir, Hollingworth way. Big playground. We got into the habit of going there, two or three times a year. Handy for everybody, the driving like.'

'How was Owen, then?'

'Same as ever,' he said, shaking his head steadily, 'same as ever.'

'Have you ever known Owen to be violent?'

'No,' he said, then shrugged. 'He could hold his own, if things got out of hand, any trouble at the pub. But no, no.'

Some people knew, Rachel thought, saw it coming, their sons or brothers or fathers always quick to anger or picking fights. Bullies or hard men. Heads full of jealousy and envy and *fuck you, mate*. Not necessarily psychos but a fist or a bottle the weapon of first resort. And when such men killed, the relatives would berate themselves for not having done something, not having said something. Unless they were cut from the same cloth, when it'd be more a case of *so-and-so had it coming. Only so much a bloke can take*.

Dennis Cottam though, Rachel could see, had never imagined this, not in his darkest dreams. And was still trying to absorb the new reality he had been plunged into.

'Did Owen say anything about the business?' she asked.

'No. Ticking over, that's the impression I had. Why? Was there a problem?'

'We've heard the brewery had plans to close the pub in January. And Owen was carrying a lot of debt.'

He stared at her, then frowned and rubbed his chin with one hand. 'He never said a word. Is this why?' His voice rose. He stood quickly. 'He needed money?' A look of disgust pulled his lips back; his teeth were yellow, uneven. 'I could have lent him money. If it was about money.' He was appalled. 'Why didn't he ask me? I could have sold the garage, for pity's sake.'

'Dad!' The man who interrupted looked more like Owen than his father, stocky rather than wiry, with a paunch and a florid complexion. 'Dad?'

'He was in debt,' Dennis Cottam, his voice still loud, still agitated, said to him. 'She said they were due to close the pub down.'

'Good God.' Barry sighed heavily. 'Just sit down,' he said to his father. 'Sit down now.'

Rachel nodded her thanks and introduced herself formally. 'You'd not heard about that either?'

'No,' Barry said.

'And you last saw Owen at the get-together in August?'

'Yeah. We were expecting to see them in a few weeks' time, as well,' he said. 'Christening.' Instead of which they had funerals to attend. Rachel knew from her briefing notes that Barry and Bev had two children, the younger a baby.

'He was a good bloke,' Barry said. 'It doesn't add up, you know.' He jiggled his car keys in one hand.

106

'I understand it's a terrible shock,' Rachel said. Important to acknowledge the impact of the crime, though for something this massive it was hard to find big enough words. Rachel could practically smell the grief. About to destroy them. All she could do was get them to focus on the practical.

'We'd like your help in trying to think of places where Owen might go. It might be somewhere he spent time as a child or more recently, it could be related to an interest or a hobby or work. I'd like to go through every place you can think of starting from when he was little. Was he born here?'

It took nearly an hour, with a pause for a cup of tea, to list a lifetime's locations. Everywhere from the hall where the Boys' Brigade band met, where Owen briefly played bass drum, through a campsite in Morecambe Bay where the Cottam lads went as teenagers and the further education college in Preston where he did a day release course to get his car mechanic's qualification, to the holiday apartment in Malaga that Barry had rented for both families just before Theo was born. In between there were diversions to the TT races in the Isle of Man and a trip to New York.

'Where was he happiest?' Rachel asked. Which sounded like a fluffy touchy-feely question but might help.

There was silence for a moment, then Dennis said, 'Meeting Pamela.'

'And recently, we thought, with the boys coming along,' said Barry. He always wanted boys.' He spoke softly, the unspoken questions suffocating in the room: *Where are the boys? What has he done to them?*

Rachel cleared her throat. 'What about your wife, his mother?'

'She's in Australia,' Dennis said. 'Melbourne.'

'Was Owen in touch with her?'

'No,' they said together.

'It wasn't easy, her going like that, not for any of us,' Barry said.

'Was he resentful?'

'We both were. What kid wouldn't be?'

With you on that, pal.

The list would need close examination and assessment as to which were the most likely places to carry out further investigation or surveillance. Any further identification of Cottam's vehicle on the ANPR system would help narrow it down but it was still a massive undertaking.

'We may wish to do a televised appeal,' Rachel said. 'I believe my boss, DCI Murray, spoke to you on the phone earlier about that?'

'Yes.' Mr Cottam nodded. 'Anything, of course, anything.'

'How would you describe your relationship?'

'He's my son,' grief lancing through his blue eyes, sharp and frank, 'my flesh and blood.'

'Would he trust you? I need to ask because that

could affect how he'll respond to the appeal. Or whether we ask Barry to do it, for example.'

'We weren't all that close, to be honest,' Barry said. 'We'd only meet up with the families – that sort of thing.'

Rachel nodded.

'I don't know any more,' Dennis Cottam said, his voice hollow with desolation. 'I don't know anything any more, with this . . .' His hands sought his chest again, first one hand, then the other, knotted, pressing hard. His face tight with effort. 'I don't know who he is any more,' he said. 'The man who did that . . . he is not my son.'

It was cold when Janet left the building, a hint of frost in the air. And a hint of chemicals too, petrol and something else, but preferable to the stale air in the office. Janet couldn't wait to get home. Still feeling queasy and too hot. Taisie had been ill with some bug a couple of weeks earlier and Ade had caught it but Janet thought she had been spared.

'Janet, wait,' Andy called after her.

Back in April it was Andy who'd picked her up, scooped her up, as she lay bleeding in the hallway after Geoff Hastings had stabbed her. Her vision had failed by then and the effect of sudden blood loss had plunged her into shock. The initial stunning pain had dissolved. She couldn't feel anything. Everything spinning, sliding away from her: words, language, meaning, identity. But Andy, his words, somehow reaching her through the veil, 'I love you,' passion and anguish in the declaration. Since then he had waited, discreet and on the sidelines, while she had healed. Calling at the hospital and then occasionally at her home over the three months of her recuperation. Her mum and Ade looking after her, managing the girls.

Janet had slept with Andy just the once, before all that, after the works' Christmas do. A moment's madness, she thought at the time. And crazed with guilt afterwards she swore not to do it again. The thought of cheating on Ade was hard enough but the prospect of what a separation or divorce might mean for her girls hit her as unbearable.

The attack had ripped away those certainties, making her acutely aware that life is a fleeting gift. Making her wonder. And leaving her with a hunger, a sense of aching frustration. Work was fine, she loved her job and she loved her kids, but the notion of them growing older and independent was increasingly attractive. And the thought of another twenty or thirty years with Ade made her stomach sink. Yet when she looked at Andy, when she heard his voice, when she walked into the office and caught sight of him, she felt the thrill like something magnetic between them.

'You okay?'

'Yeah,' she said, dragging the word out, the inflection making it sound more like so-so. Could he tell she was feeling under the weather? Could anyone else at work? What if it wasn't a passing bug but a result of the attack and the subsequent treatment, the repairs to her intestine and stomach? The surgeon had said they'd need to monitor for any complications, particularly adhesions, which were not uncommon and would require further surgery.

'Perhaps we—' He moved in closer as he spoke.

'Shh.' She shook her head.

'I want you,' he said. The declaration sent a wave of pleasure through her. She stepped towards him, although the still small sensible voice in her head was whispering caution. *Stop it, stop now.* Knowing that being caught having a knee-trembler with her sergeant would be disastrous, on oh so many levels.

A slam of a car door made Janet spring back and she held her breath and listened until she heard the engine start and the vehicle drive away.

'I'm going home,' she said quietly.

'Janet—'

'I really am going,' she said. 'I want you too but not now, not like this. And I need more time.' The words at odds with what her body was clamouring for. She turned to walk away, then swung back. Kissed him until her head began to spin and she was drunk with him. Then she walked unsteadily away.

Gill had texted her son Sammy three times in the past week, left messages on his voicemail too. 'All

111

right? Just wanted a quick catch up, kid. Get in touch.'

And heard nothing. She wasn't sure which was worse, the anger she felt, which built up and made her want to smash something – preferably Dave the dickhead's balls – or the sadness. Dave whom she blamed for the whole debacle. Sammy had only been able to jump ship and move in with Dave because his dad had lured him there, rolled out the red carpet, showered him with money, promised to get him a car whatever his results. And Dave had done that to punish Gill for having the brass-necked audacity to start seeing someone. No matter that Dave was the cheating shag-bandit who'd broken up the marriage in the first place, choosing his tart from Pendlebury over his family and leaving Gill and Sammy to their own devices.

'She doesn't interfere,' Sammy had said the day he announced his defection.

Maybe not with you, pal – she interfered big time in my marriage. It stuck in her craw.

Now Gill rang Dave's number, steeling herself, straightening her back, promising herself to stay calm and collected whatever Captain Thunderpants said.

'Gill,' he answered coldly.

'Is Sammy there?'

'He's about somewhere. Why?'

'Put him on, will you?'

'I'll see if he wants to talk to you. You've tried his mobile, have you?' Almost gloating.

112

Gill blazed. 'Just put him on the fucking phone!' She heard him sigh then a clatter and a rustling as he moved.

Gill had never been to the house in the four years since the split and imagined it to be a crowded little town house, no character and not enough space. Liking the picture of Dave having his style cramped while she and Sammy had remained in the beautiful family home.

'Hello?'

'Sammy, it's Mum. How's things?'

'Cool.'

'Have you been looking at open days?'

He was applying to uni, still uncertain as to which courses. She had spent hours looking at options with him and helping him redraft his personal statement and then suddenly he was gone.

'Yeah.' Monosyllables. It wasn't really what she wanted to know, what she really wanted to ask was *Are you happy? Do you miss me? Please come home, will you?* Now that the case had broken she couldn't even ask him out to eat because she'd be working sixteen-hour days for the duration.

'Have you booked them?' she said.

'Not yet.'

'Well, you need to get it sorted. How are you going to choose if you've not been to visit?'

'I know,' he said, suddenly irritable, and she felt herself losing the battle. Hearts and minds.

It's very quiet without you. I miss you so much, longing to say it but determined not to. Guilt-tripping not her style. Needy Mum neither. Her brain scrabbled around searching for something else, something to get him talking. It never used to be like this; time was she could barely shut him up. Her Sammy. 'What you been up to?'

'Dunno.'

For Pete's sake. 'Been out anywhere?'

'Alton Towers.'

'Right.' He loved the roller coasters. Last time the two of them had been he'd talked her into riding with him. Fantastic and utterly terrifying. 'Good stuff! You keep your breakfast down?'

'Course,' just the edge of a laugh bubbling there.

'Your dad go on with you?'

'Nah.'

'Pussycat,' Gill scoffed.

'Emma did. And we went straight back on,' he said gleefully. Gill grew cold. Hating the thought of that bitch having fun with her son. Knowing she had to swallow her jealousy.

'Wow,' she managed.

'Dad wants his phone,' Sammy said.

'Okay, look, keep in touch, will you? Just message me or whatever. Let me know you're still alive. That you're okay. I worry.'

'Course I'm okay.'

I don't know that. You could be pining or lonely or

114

bored senseless and I wouldn't know. A year's time and he'd likely be gone for good; she had expected to have him for these last few months, as he finished his schooling. It felt as if Dave had snatched it away to get back at her. 'You take care,' she said. 'Love you, kid.'

'Yeah,' he grunted, 'later.' The phone went dead. She resisted the temptation to hurl it across the room, instead slapped the wall with her hand. Which hurt like hell, stinging her palm and bringing a burning pain to her eyes.

Then she set about updating the policy book on the various actions of the inquiry and outlining her reasons for each decision she had made.

The house was in darkness though the security lighting in the car park came on as Rachel drove in. Once inside her flat, she headed straight for the kitchen, poured a large glass of red wine and drank half of it before shaking off her coat. She felt hollow, cold even though the room was warm enough. And hungry. It took her three minutes to sort out a chicken noodle meal in the microwave and another three to demolish it.

She refilled her glass and sat down to check her phone. No messages from work, which meant no significant progress. Cottam still out there. And the kids? Dead or alive?

With the wine taking hold she felt her muscles loosen, her concentration blur. She drank more. Put on the twenty-four hour news to see what they were saying. Saw the scant details of the murders scrolling under the current item. When the wine bottle was empty she headed for bed.

It reared up to meet her, a ghost, a blizzard of white. She screamed. Then saw it was feathers, just the feathers from her bloody pillow, a wraith brought to life by the sudden change in air pressure when she'd swung the door open. She sucked in a breath. Then another. Felt her heart pounding. Her face on fire. Thought briefly of the sofa and a sleeping bag but couldn't face that. Got a cushion from the living room, undressed and climbed into bed. The knife under her pillow. Fingers clutched around it. Clenched tight, clinging on for dear life.

Day Two

Day Two

8

Janet didn't often discuss work with Ade. After all these years he had heard most of it before and talk at home, when there was any, centred on the girls and domestic affairs.

But she knew she had to tell him about Geoff Hastings, the fact that she had agreed to interview him. She couldn't keep putting it off. Janet had refused at first when Gill asked. Never wanting to set eyes on the man again. Preferring never to hear his name. Certainly not wanting to be in the same room as him, breathing the same air as him. Gill had emphasized it was Janet's decision, no one would think any the worse of her if she refused. Gill had also let slip, on purpose Janet was sure, that Geoff Hastings was refusing to speak to anyone else. Had asked for Janet specifically. And the thought that if she bottled it they might never know what happened to the women he'd killed ate away at her. Eventually her anger at the possibility that he might escape with less than full

119

disclosure, full punishment, equalled her anxiety at the prospect of encountering him.

Geoff Hastings was accused of killing his sister Veronica, Janet's school mate, and then several other women in the ensuing years. He'd had the perverted audacity to ask Janet to help him by looking into the unsolved case of Veronica's murder. Why? Some twisted desire to play games and test the police? Or had he secretly wanted to be caught? To be stopped?

It had been Rachel who made the leap, seeing a pattern to the other unsolved murders: the women all of a type, their ages consistent with how old Veronica would be if she had not been asphyxiated as a little girl. Then, working out the geographical profile, that all the deaths occurred when Geoff Hastings was working as a lorry driver in the relevant area.

Rachel had rung Janet with her light-bulb moment. Geoff Hastings there, in Janet's kitchen, as she took the call. Reading Janet's face, Geoff Hastings grabbing the knife, Janet fighting, using every ounce of strength of will and energy . . .

She wrenched herself back to the present and buttered toast. Put some down on the table and filled the kettle.

Ade got up for the jam. She waited until he was seated. Choosing breakfast time because if there was a row, and she anticipated at least a few choice expletives, they'd be forced to adjourn for work, whereas if she told him in the evening it could rumble on for hours.

They'd not argued much at all since her injury. First too fragile, then too thankful. Perhaps the new grateful Ade would take a different tack from the one she anticipated.

Janet poured tea. 'Something's come up at work,' she said.

'What, on top of three murders?'

She gave a faint smile. 'I'm going to be interviewing Geoff Hastings.'

His face froze and he put down his toast. 'What? They can't make you do that. They can't, can they?'

'No one's making me do anything.'

'You can't do it, Janet.'

'Ade, look—'

'No!' He began to shout. 'I don't want you anywhere near the man. How can you even think of it?' He hit at the table, slid his chair back, the noise fraying Janet's nerves.

'It's nothing to do with you,' she said, 'it's work.' She felt her temperature rising and with it her temper.

'You're my wife.' He jabbed his finger towards her, proprietorially. 'Don't I get a say?'

'No. This is my professional life. It's none of your business. I'm only telling you—'

'Whose idea was it,' he demanded. 'Yours?'

'I agreed.'

'Who asked you?' he shouted.

'Gill.'

He swung away, clapping his hands to his head. 'Has she lost the plot? You came that close . . .' He held his thumb and forefinger millimetres apart. His face was red with exertion, a blob of spit on his chin. Janet knew she should try to calm him, take some heat out of the situation, but her own ill temper needled at her, pushing her on, avid to shout him down.

'I know! I was there!' she yelled. 'And he asked for me, if you must know.'

He stared. 'Oh, that's priceless.'

Janet shouted over him. 'And because I came *that close* and survived, I will do it for all the others who weren't so lucky.'

'Oh, very noble,' he sneered. 'You don't see, do you? He's playing you, Janet. Some sick little mind game, another way to make you dance to his tune. Just like you did when he first asked you to help.'

'What's all the shouting?' Elise said, coming in, fourteen yet sounding like someone's mother.

'Nothing.' Janet warned Ade with a glare that she didn't want to share this with the children. 'Go wake Taisie.'

'She doesn't need to get up yet,' Elise said.

'I don't care!' Janet bawled, anger boiling inside her. Resisting the overwhelming desire to seize her daughter and shake some sense into her. 'Just do it, Elise.'

'Not if you shout like that. I'm sick of you bossing me about.'

'Do what I tell you to! I'm sick too, sick of you arguing over every bloody little thing.' Janet's throat felt raw.

Elise glared at her, her face reddening, and Janet felt a rush of guilt. What the hell was she doing taking it out on Elise?

Her daughter left the room without a word.

'Nicely done,' Ade said.

Janet couldn't handle it. If she stayed she was scared she'd break something. She picked up her car keys and left, the roar of her own anger still crashing loud in her head and roiling hot in her stomach.

'Right, lads.' Gill called them to attention. 'No ANPR, nothing from traffic cameras or patrols since three twenty-nine yesterday. How come?'

'Laying low, parked up somewhere overnight,' said Rachel.

Or busy getting rid of the kids? 'We are increasing patrols in the Lancashire/South Lakes area and, of course, continuing to examine coverage anywhere close to the two locations, Penrith and then Ribbleton. Mr Cottam is coming in to film an appeal late morning, which should be carried on all lunchtime news broadcasts, and of course headlines thereafter. Crime scene reports are now available.' Gill summarized the substance for them. 'Our initial theory of the sequence is supported by the blood spatter analysis. Time of deaths estimated to be between four and six a.m. Rigor not fully established and factoring in the ambient temperature I think we can be pretty sure that's a solid estimate.'

'Why did he cut Michael's throat and not the others?' Mitch said.

'Didn't like him,' said Kevin.

'No animosity according to the mother,' said Janet, 'though the friend Lynn thought Michael might occasionally have got on his nerves.'

'Well, would you want your brother-in-law living with you, working with you? Especially if he was a bit mental,' Kevin said.

Before anyone could respond to that, Rachel said quickly, 'The body, he was on his side, right? But the girl was on her stomach, the wife on her back . . .'

'Yes.' Gill watched as Rachel spoke. She'd a keen instinct for things, Rachel, a gift that could sometimes lead her astray, trusting her gut feeling, and she could get stuck stubbornly on one track, but on many occasions her contributions were incisive and valuable.

'. . . so if someone's on their side how do you stab 'em? It's all ribs, isn't it? He went for the most accessible and vulnerable spot, so the man wouldn't wake or fight, or the knife get stuck.'

It happened, Gill knew, one of the many surprises that tripped up the novice killer. Those who had not been taught to use weapons. The fact that knives got lodged in bones, or glanced off, or snapped at the tip. That very quickly a knife would become slippery with

124

blood and hard to grip. Same with firearms – mechanisms jammed, a gunshot without a silencer rendered the shooter unable to hear for several hours. The recoil could damage the arm, burn the skin on the hand. Then there was the unbelievable weight and unwieldy shape of a dead body. The immense effort required to dig even a shallow grave.

'Makes sense,' Gill said.

Only Owen Cottam could tell them if Rachel's theory was right. Whether he would, whether they'd find him alive and get the chance to ask him, whether he'd respond, was impossible to know.

'No mention of marital problems, other parties, affairs. No criminal activity. To date our only motive appears to be financial insecurity, the imminent loss of the business and thus the family's livelihood. Cottam remains at large. I want to catch that bastard and I want to nail him. And I want you lot to make that happen. Pick up on your actions from yesterday but stand by for reassignment in case we've any movement.'

It was less than twenty minutes later when Gill called her team back in. 'Sit down, keep your gobs shut and watch this.' Gill ran the CCTV footage. She'd seen the coverage twice already but it still set her pulse racing. Split screen, four cams, showing respectively two views of a petrol station forecourt and two of the inside of the shop, one view of people coming in to pay, the other trained on the counter. A guy there on his own.

'Mr Rahid,' Gill said. 'The station's near Ormskirk, on the A577, twenty miles from our last ANPR hit. Here,' she paused the film, 'we see Cottam arriving. Clock reads seven fifty-four. He doesn't buy petrol so perhaps he's not been riding around all night. He pulls up so.' They watched the Mondeo draw into the bay at the back of the forecourt where there was an air machine. 'Gets out.'

'Same clothes as in the pub,' Janet said. She leaned closer, narrowing her eyes. 'Are the kids there?'

'Yes, according to Mr Rahid, but we don't get a visual. Now . . .'

There was silence as they watched Cottam enter the shop and take items from the shelves, moving from the field of one camera to the other. 'He gets nappies,' Gill said.

'Nappies?' Janet said. 'You don't buy nappies if—'

'Wait, what's that?' Rachel said.

'Bread rolls,' said Gill. 'Then he goes for some bananas and milk and he gets two items at the counter. A bottle of whisky and one of Calpol.'

'Calpol's paracetamol, isn't it?' Rachel said. 'Give the kids enough and he's solved his problem.'

'I don't think one bottle would do it,' Gill said, 'not reliably, two of them.'

'Probably wants to just dope them up a bit,' Janet said.

'As you do,' Gill said.

Janet cut her eyes at her. 'Besides, if he's planning to feed them and change them maybe he's not going to hurt them, maybe he's changed his mind.'

'Or bottled out,' Rachel added.

'Now look,' Gill said. 'As he pays, there's this moment when he flinches, drops some money. It's not clear why but look at the time on the display.'

'On the hour,' Janet said.

'And,' Gill said, 'on the wall behind him is a telly. He's making headlines. His face is up there and a description of the Mondeo. That's when Mr Rahid gets it, makes the connection. Though he's not certain. Cottam leaves.'

One of the cameras picked him up as he walked to the car, opened the driver's side and leant in. 'And Mr Rahid leaves too. Runs out and grabs Cottam.' Gill watched the smaller man grip Cottam by the shoulder, wheeling him round. Cottam shoved him hard, almost decking him, but Rahid regained his balance and moved in again. Cottam swung a fist, a solid blow to Rahid's face, and the man fell. Rahid lunged and gripped Cottam's leg. At this point Cottam stamped down hard with his free foot on Rahid's head. Rahid released his hold and Cottam kicked him hard again in the head, then three swift blows to the abdomen. Rahid by now curled up, trying to protect himself.

'Ouch!' said Janet.

'There he goes,' Gill said as Cottam leapt into the

car, pulled the door shut and drove off at speed. 'So, go see our have-a-go hero,' she said.

Janet went dizzy on the stairs, her vision all spotty, like some sixties op-art design, and an ache bloomed low in her spine. She lost her balance but held the rail and kept moving slowly. Rachel, ahead of her, turned to look up. 'You okay?'

'Cramps,' Janet said, something innocuous to explain her slow progress.

'Time of the month. I've tablets,' Rachel said.

Not menstrual, Janet thought, but didn't say. She had not had a period since the stabbing, one of the things that was off kilter. Not that she minded really. And she wasn't pregnant, she couldn't be, hadn't slept with anyone, either Ade or Andy, in that time. Was that why Andy was so tempting, because there was nothing much going on at home? Ade had made a couple of overtures more recently but she had been tired, drained, and wasn't prepared to just go through the motions. The consultant had explained there might be a range of unforeseen side effects to the trauma and the surgery and Janet reckoned not having her period was one of them. And she wasn't complaining. But the dizziness, the feverish feelings?

'I'll be fine,' Janet said. 'It's going off now.' She didn't want to tell Rachel how she really felt. Not because she couldn't trust her to keep it quiet but because telling someone else would make it more real.

And then she'd really have to face up to it. Come clean. If there were adhesions, that would account for the bloating and stomach pains, but what about the dizziness and the way she went hot and cold, the nausea and the headaches? Did that mean they'd become infected? She shouldn't just keep ignoring it, but when would she have time to see the consultant? She'd be put on a list anyway, wouldn't she? Perhaps she should see the GP first. Even that would have to wait till work was less frantic.

'I know we see all sorts,' Janet said, as she manoeuvred past vehicles queuing for the slip road, 'but this one . . .'

''Cos of the kids?' Rachel said. 'The girl?'

'Partly that, but it's more the whole thing, so methodical. He cashes up the night's takings, wipes down the counter. He sees them off to bed, presumably, prowls about with his bottle. Then, one after another. Cold. Was it cold? Maybe he was weeping, maybe he was crying. I don't know, Rachel. A father. I can't get my head round it.'

'You don't have to. Leave it to the shrinks. That's what we pay them for. All we need to do is catch him.'

Janet frowned, glanced in the rear view mirror then overtook, nudging past a coach, kids with faces pressed to the glass, one lad making a wanking gesture. Rachel flipped him the finger.

'Don't encourage them,' Janet complained. 'But

most men, most fathers, this whole notion of a family being yours, being part of you . . .'

'Is a load of selfish crap,' Rachel said. 'We get it all the time, the bloke who freaks out 'cos the ex has a new fella so kills them both—'

'No,' Janet argued, 'this is different. That's jealousy, crime of passion, though I know that isn't recognized in British law, but there's no passion in this. Despair, more like.'

'Loved them too much, one of the guys said.'

'That's not love. How can that be love?' Janet said.

'A better place?' Rachel said.

'You're confusing love and power. Control.'

'I'm not confusing anything. It's not what I think,' Rachel said baldly.

'Take my dad, or Ade. Never do anything like that in a million years. They didn't "rule" the family . . .'

'Can't see anyone ruling your mother,' Rachel said.

'Precisely,' Janet said. 'Yours probably the same.'

'Yes – so what are you saying?'

'Just . . . that sort of person, the man who's head of the household, the one who wears the trousers, all those trite little phrases, that's seen as normal, isn't it? Acceptable. And that's what everyone keeps telling us: he was a normal bloke, a regular guy, a good provider. But maybe there's something unhealthy in that, having that grip on the family.'

Rachel shook her head. 'You've lost me.'

Janet sighed.

'Look, there's millions of blokes like that, yeah?' Rachel said. 'But only one in a million, less than that, ever goes off his rocker and slays the family. He's an aberration. You'll drive yourself bonkers trying to make sense of it. Most of the toerags we deal with, it's messy, it's stupid and pathetic and grubby, isn't it? *She was shagging my best friend, so I shot her. He hadn't paid me my money back, so I did him. I can't remember. I was bladdered, she looked at me funny, he was a queer, he was a Paki.* It's all ugly, senseless, waste. This too. This is no different. And he's a nutter.'

'Really? So you'd have him in Broadmoor unfit to plead?'

'I'll leave that to the CPS, but think about it. He's all ready, everyone's asleep and what does he do? He lets the dog out. That is mental, that.'

'I don't know – gave him a few brownie points. If he'd killed the dog as well the outrage would be multiplied ten times over.' *The great British public.*

9

Rahid had refused all suggestions from the paramedics that he go to A&E. His wife, summoned from home, had dressed the worst cuts on his hands and face. The effect of the encounter and assault had flooded the man with adrenalin: he was high as a kite, eyes shining, words tumbling over each other as his brain accelerated away from the limitations of physical speech. His nose was very swollen, his speech thick as a result, and from his posture Rachel reckoned his belly hurt like hell. Each time he laughed, he winced. Something not right.

The area where the Mondeo had parked and the attack happened had been cordoned off. Forensics would be looking for any debris that might indicate where the car had been since the last ANPR capture. Rahid's brother served in the shop while they squeezed into the stockroom at the back and Rahid talked them through the incident. Rachel knew the elation would evaporate like so much spilled water, leaving him flat and shaken and probably critical of himself. The sort of self-loathing that comes after a night on the lam. Hangover shame. Because at the end of the day he'd risked his neck and failed. Cottam had driven off. And that's before anyone else put their oar in with observations undermining his actions and saying what they'd have done in his place. But for now he was the man of the moment. His account mirrored the tape they'd watched but now they needed to dig a bit deeper, see what else they might glean.

'Did he appear sober?' Rachel asked.

'Yes. Didn't say much but he wasn't wobbly, like.'

'Smell of drink, or anything else?' Preferably something specific and unusual that would help them track him down.

'I didn't notice. It all happened so fast, you know. Once I clocked who it was, like it was all speeded up, you know?'

'Anything on his clothes or hands?' Janet said.

'Don't remember anything. But he looked a bit rough. He hadn't shaved.' Rahid touched a bandaged hand to his own full, black beard. 'His eyes were bloodshot. They were . . .' he laughed and flinched, 'like cold, you know, dead.' Maybe. Or maybe already Rahid was embroidering the story.

'The car,' Rachel said, 'clean, dirty, dusty?' It hadn't rained since the previous day. That was both a plus and a minus. The rain washed away evidence, obscured traces, but it also made mud which was perfect for collecting tyre tracks and footwear impressions.

Rahid's lips parted and his eyes roamed back, exploring the memory. He laughed. *Bingo*. 'There were bits on it, sticky bits like from trees. I don't know – what is that? Tree juice?'

Not at all funny. Rachel gave him a smile. Being nice.

If any of the sticky bits had been dislodged, left on the forecourt, it could give them something. The forensic biologists or botanists could identify the type of trees. Where they would be found. All over the shop, probably, Rachel thought. Still, it lent some weight to the notion of his being holed up somewhere overnight long enough to have picked up debris from the trees.

'What did you see of the children?' Janet asked.

'Just the one on this side, driver's side. In a car seat. He was asleep, head down. But I could hear crying. The other one was crying.'

'Could you see his clothes?' Janet said.

He shook his head. 'Just the top of his head. I don't remember. By the time I got close he'd started hitting me.'

'Did you see anything inside the car?' Rachel said.

'No, it was all too fast. The way he came at me. I thought he was going to kill me.' He exhaled noisily.

'Did he say anything when you got hold of him?' Rachel said.

'Just swore at me, "fuck off out of it".' Rahid flushed. 'Then he's kicking me. Thought I was done for.'

'You'd better keep an eye on that.' Janet nodded to his hand. Rachel could see the little finger was badly swollen and dark purple. 'If it's broken and you don't get it set right . . .'

'Ribs too,' Rachel said.

'They can't do anything for ribs, can they?' Rahid said. 'Just a corset, yeah?'

'That's right,' Rachel said. 'Bigger problem is if a rib's broken and it punctures something. Like a lung,' she added so he was really clear. 'If you find yourself getting breathless . . .'

'I'll be fine.' He waved their concern away.

'Hey up,' Rachel said as they walked out into the shop. 'The circus is here.' Vans were parked on the far side of the road. A camera crew were setting up.

Rachel impressed upon Rahid that he should not discuss the incident in public or speculate as it could aversely affect any future legal proceedings when he might be called as a witness. 'No Facebook or Twitter. Yeah. The family too.' There was a hint of disappointment as he agreed. It was harder and harder to maintain control of publicity. The force themselves used Twitter as a tool to communicate with and re-assure the general public. Rachel never got all that: waste of time wittering on with strangers.

'Your kids into it? Facebook, Twitter?' she said to Janet as they returned to the car.

'Big time. They all are. Out on a limb if you're not.'

'It's going to hit Rahid before long that Cottam got away in spite of him. He might have more than a bloody nose to cope with when the lights come up,' Rachel said.

'Maybe what we find here will be key to a result. We find him and the kids, then Rahid's done good.'

'You think it's likely?'

'It's possible.' Janet being cautious.

Personally Rachel thought the prospect got more and more remote with each hour. But Cottam's actions were bugging her. 'He bought them food and medicine and nappies. Why do that if he's still going to harm them?'

'Stop them crying. Kids crying – you can't think. There's nothing worse,' Janet said with feeling.

There was a sudden blur of motion, the screech of brakes near the garage entrance. Rachel's heart flew into her mouth and she started, jumping backwards, almost losing her balance. It was another news van.

Janet looked at her and Rachel felt her cheeks glow. 'Just jumpy,' she said.

'Since when?' Janet wasn't smiling, wasn't cutting her any slack.

'Just today,' Rachel said, 'since breakfast, which I didn't have.' She tapped her nose, showing Janet she was prying.

'So it's got absolutely nothing to do with the attempt on—'

'No, nothing. Ready?'

136

Janet laughed, shaking her head.

'What?'

'Not much of an advert, are we? Me with my cramps, you jumping at shadows. They should put us out to grass.'

'Speak for yourself, Grandma, nowt wrong with me. Might get a snack on the way, though. Stop if we see anywhere.'

They found a mini-market and Rachel went in.

'Get me chocolate,' Janet called after her.

'Here you go,' Rachel said when she came back. 'I'm having this.' She unwrapped her food and took a bite, hot and salty.

'What is that supposed to be?' Janet said.

'All day breakfast. It was that or Hula Hoops. Thought you'd approve.'

'I do,' Janet said, 'but open the window, will you? It smells revolting.'

Janet was entering the details of her report on Rahid into the system when her phone went. Her mother, in full schoolmistress fashion. 'Janet, tell me it isn't true. Adrian says you are going to interview that man.'

'Mum,' Janet sighed, getting to her feet, preferring to take this call in the Ladies, away from twitching ears. She would brain Ade when she saw him. A low-down, sneaky trick enlisting her mother.

'Are you out of your mind?' her mother said. 'After what he did to you?'

'It's my job, Mum.'

'Someone else can do it. Let Rachel do it. Or did she put you up to it?'

'Nobody put me up to it,' Janet said.

'You volunteered?' her mother breathed in horror.

'Not exactly.' Janet leant looking into the mirror as she talked. The bags under her eyes looked bigger, the shadows darker. 'I was asked, I thought about it – carefully. And I agreed.'

'Talk to Gill,' her mother said. 'She'll see sense, surely. Even if you can't.' Her mother idolized Gill, saw her as the epitome of what a professional woman could become and was always nudging Janet to be more like her.

'It was Gill who asked me,' Janet said, wondering whether Ade had told her mother that it had been at Geoff Hastings's request.

Stunned silence. But not for long. 'I've a good mind—'

'This is my job,' Janet said. Rachel came into the Ladies as she went on, 'Mum, can you imagine if some detective had tried to muscle in on you when you were teaching? You'd have soon shown them the door.'

'I worry about you. And this seems so dangerous, so wilful.'

Janet looked over to Rachel, who was leaning on the wall with her arms crossed, and rolled her eyes. 'I'll be fine,' she said. 'When it happens, if it happens, we'll be in a secure environment with other officers on

138

hand. He's behind bars, Mum, and I'm going to make sure he stays there for the rest of his life.'

A loud sigh.

'And how are you?' Janet said.

'Not feeling all that great, to be honest.'

Because of this? Janet felt a prickle of guilt. Her mother had always been solid as a rock whenever Janet needed her. But especially after the attack. Janet didn't want to bring any pain or distress to her door. 'What's wrong?'

'Just out of sorts every way. Achy.'

'There's a lot of bugs going round,' Janet said. 'Maybe you've caught something. Taisie had one, Ade as well.' She could hear a forced edge in her voice and tried to rein it in. Hard sometimes to remember that her mother was older now, beginning to need a little help with things after a lifetime of being a competent working wife and mother. Difficult to know how much had changed since Janet's dad died. Her mum had seemed to weather it well but perhaps the strain was only showing now. Loneliness and grief leading to a lack of confidence.

'Maybe,' her mum said, not sounding very sure.

'Have you taken anything for it?'

'I don't really like to,' she said.

'A couple of paracetamol won't do any harm,' Janet said. Sometimes her mother regarded a reliance on medicine as a craven weakness only a step away from crack cocaine or heroin addiction. A stoic edge to her character that could become martyrish if taken too far.

'You will be careful, won't you?'

'Always,' Janet said. 'I'll ring you later in the week.'

'You can always change your mind,' Rachel said as Janet put her phone down.

'I don't want to,' Janet said. 'I want to make him pay. Dig up every dirty detail on what he did to all those other women. They don't get it, Ade, my mum. I could have been the latest on the list. It means we find out the truth for the people, the parents and the husbands and the kids. Truth and justice. That's the point. They don't get it. You get it, don't you? I am making sense?'

'I get it.'

'Good.' Janet picked up her phone and went back to work.

Gill read through the press release while Lisa, the chief press officer, waited in the doorway. *Police repeated the request for the public to be alert to sightings of Owen Cottam, aged forty-five, wanted for questioning in connection with the deaths of his wife Pamela, Pamela's brother Michael Milne and the Cottams' eleven-year-old daughter. Cottam is white, of medium build, six foot tall, with dark hair and a moustache. He was last seen in the Ormskirk area, wearing jeans and a dark green sweatshirt. Cottam is understood to have left the family home yesterday morning with his two sons, aged two and a half years and eighteen months. He may be travelling in a blue Ford Mondeo.*

Police advise the public not to approach Owen Cottam but to contact them immediately on the following number . . .

'That's fine,' she said. The next instalment in the story of the Cottam murder and disappearance, as far as the great British public was concerned, would be the appeal to his son by Mr Cottam senior and the issue of the press release. Gill would conclude the conference by saying they were hoping that the situation could be resolved satisfactorily. A catch-all that equalled no further bloodshed.

'Same photo?' Lisa said. 'Only we have a different one, might help.' She held up a copy. Cottam relaxed, a half-smile. 'It's a similar style top but I'm not so happy about the cap.' A baseball cap. 'What you think?'

Tempting as it was to start debating the merits, Gill was swamped so passed the ball back. 'Your call,' she said. 'Long as we don't confuse them.'

'Everything's ready for the appeal. I've booked the conference room. Dennis Cottam is on his way. Son and daughter-in-law are coming with. The son's happy to sit in. Okay with you?'

'Absolutely,' Gill said.

'See you there.' Lisa left.

Gill went back to her files, reprising the new data coming in from the different arms of the inquiry and considering whether to make any changes to the direction, the strategy, of the investigation.

A knock on her door: Kevin. 'The CCTV that came in – I've found him going into Skelmersdale after leaving the petrol station.'

'Show me.'

In the viewing room, Kevin ran the tape. The Mondeo passing a traffic camera on the dual carriageway. It was clear but not clear enough to see the children. They'll still be there, Gill told herself. He wouldn't have had time to stop the car at any point since making his getaway after attacking Mr Rahid.

'Show me on the map,' Gill said.

Kevin clicked on the desktop and opened a file which brought up a list of exhibits from the Pamela Milne crime scene. 'Shit, sorry, boss.' He closed that and clicked again.

'Centre on Skelmersdale,' Gill said. 'Now zoom out.' Her eyes ran over the map, scanning routes and destinations that Cottam might choose. 'Work up new projections,' she said: 'possible distance travelled, potential locations, other likely CCTV sources. And pass this through to patrols on the ground straight away. Yes?'

'Yes, boss.' He sat there, swivelling in his chair, pleased with himself.

'Now!' Gill said. 'If not sooner.'

Which got him moving.

10

'There's someone downstairs for you,' Pete said to Rachel.

'Who?'

'Don't know. Desk just rang.'

'Can't you deal with it?'

'Said they wanted to speak to you in person.'

'Oh, for fuck's sake!' Rachel pushed herself away from her desk and marched to the stairs.

If it was anything to do with the case they'd have been able to speak to anybody about it, so why her in person? What could it be about?

Nick Savage! The trial? They usually notified witnesses by letter, a couple of weeks beforehand. Gave them a chance to visit the court and have their hands held by the witness service volunteers. Of course she didn't need any of that. Been in court enough times to know the ropes.

Or had Nick been mouthing off? Like a caged rat finding a weak spot to begin gnawing its way out from. That weak spot Rachel. Dobbing her in for lying in court so whoever was downstairs had come to arrest her. Shit! She could feel her heart burning in her chest, as though it was swelling like a bruise. Halfway down she thought she should have hidden in the Ladies, got Pete to say she was off duty, or had left for the day.

She passed Mitch on the way up. 'Have one for me, Sherlock,' he said. He was on the Nicorette.

'Yeah, right,' she said.

Sherlock, her nickname. It stung her, the thought of her colleagues finding out what she'd done. Not only in bed with the barrister but blabbing to him about her daily work, feeding him titbits. Titbits that came back and bit her in the jugular. Forcing her to lie in court. Bastard. Mouth dry now, sweating under her arms, and her hair clinging to the back of her neck where it was damp.

She reached the lobby. Just one person waiting there. A police constable. Suit and shiny buttons, cap in hand. Fuck! Rachel tempted for a split second to run. To scarper rather than stand meekly by while her career and her future were put to the slaughter. Forcing breath into her lungs, registering with some sick irony the poster on the wall behind him: *Have You Got What It Takes?* Did have, she thought, blew it. She stepped forward. 'Rachel Bailey,' she said, her voice sounding like she'd fallen down some well.

'PC Martin Tintwhistle,' he said. Not a flicker of

144

warmth. Rachel could feel the tension in the back of her legs, in her neck, in the soles of her feet. 'Based at Langley.'

'Right.' She watched his lips, waiting for the caution. Aware that the CCTV above the front desk would be filming it all in glorious technicolour. That in half an hour's time the clip of him reading her the caution and snapping the cuffs on would provide a few minutes' rest and relaxation for the officers embroiled in the investigation and the staff in the custody suite. Could go viral. *YouTube*. Except any dickhead did that and they'd be disciplined for unprofessional conduct or prejudicing an ongoing investigation.

'You are related to Brian Bailey, date of birth fourth of November 1950?'

What the fuck had that to do with anything? She wanted to deny it, disown the connection, lie about her parentage, but she just said yes. Irritability a useful mask for the fear drilling through her.

'I'm afraid I have some bad news,' the man said and she saw him draw back very slightly, putting a fraction more distance between them. Worried that she'd what? Thump him? Spit at him? Burst into tears and collapse on him?

Bad news? Bad news wasn't a usual lead-in to a caution on arrest.

'What?' Rachel snapped.

'We were called to an address in Langley earlier today,' the constable said, his voice dull and uninflected.

145

'When the resident did not answer the door we gained entry to the premises.'

Rachel was at sea. Why was he telling her this? She thought of the Cottams, the local bobbies breaking in, calling out, creeping upstairs. One potato, two potato, three potato . . .

'I'm sorry to have to inform you . . .'

She watched his lips. He'd got freckles on his face, one on his upper lip, a light brown stain. His teeth stuck out: no braces at that crucial age.

'. . . but the occupant, whom we believe to be Brian Bailey, was unresponsive and subsequently pronounced dead.'

Oh, God. Fuck. She felt something fall inside, a swirl of pain. Why had they come to her with this? Why not Alison? Alison was the one who still ran up the white flag every so often and mounted a mercy mission. Trying to get the old feller to have a proper wash and some clean clothes, dragging him to the GP or A&E, talking rehab. Pretending there was hope for five minutes until the old man sloped off back to his tins and his baccy and his helpless mess of a life.

Tintwhistle, message delivered, was watching her.

'Suspicious circumstances?' Rachel said.

'No.'

'Right,' she said, 'thanks.' Turning to go.

'DC Bailey,' he said, 'we need you to formally identify the body.'

'No.' Rachel said it without thinking. She didn't want anything to do with it.

'I appreciate that it must be a shock—'

'I've a sister,' Rachel said, 'she'll do it.' Talking over him, not wanting sympathy, not one bloody drop of sympathy. Why should she? She didn't deserve it, didn't warrant it. How long since she had seen her dad? Six years, maybe more. Ran into him one time when she was working sex crimes in the early days, investigating a rape, talking to potential witnesses outside a pub near Langley. The area a black hole disguised with a smattering of shops. Offie, mini-market, nail bar, launderette. Among those potential eyewitnesses, a group of alkies who occupied a bench near the bus stop. And chief rabble-rouser, with what looked like sick down his coat, was her father. Back then Rachel had turned on her heel and told her colleagues she'd talk to the woman in the launderette then try the nail bar. Now she keyed in Alison's number. And got her voicemail.

'I've not really time,' Rachel said but Tintwhistle stood there, batting his cap against his other hand.

'It shouldn't take very long,' he said, 'if you'd like to find somebody to accompany you.'

Fuck no! Janet, who first came to mind, assumed Rachel had a quiet, dull, Janet and John family stashed away somewhere. An assumption Rachel had deliberately cultivated. The prospect of sharing this with anyone was even more sickening than the thought of doing it alone.

She tried Alison again, just in case, got the same message.

Her phone showed twenty past eleven. 'I need to be back here before midday,' she said.

'Yes.' He nodded, and put his hat on.

She followed him to the car park, every bone in her body seething with resentment.

Getting into the car she was struck by the thought that minutes earlier she was expecting to be escorted into the back seat, hand on her head easing her into place, wrists cuffed, wreathed in shame. So it wasn't the worst that could have happened, was it? Not by a long chalk.

'Where was he, then?' she said. 'You said Langley.'

'B&B on St Michael's Road.'

She knew the place. B&B shorthand for dosshouse. Hostel, more or less. Scuzzy rooms at rock-bottom prices, sort of place that welcomed people on benefits. Not the type of B&B you'd see on Trip Advisor. Not a good base for exploring the cultural highlights of sunny Manchester. Full of people who had nowhere else to sleep: alkies or nut jobs, people coming out of prison or heading back in. Breakfast was dished up in a canteen style kitchen. Only meal most of them ate. She knew all this because she had been in places like it countless times for work. Down with the pond life.

The car dropped down the hill among the terraced housing, towards the jumble of dual carriageways that ringed the centre of Oldham. Godzilla had been here earlier with Margaret Milne. Christ, she hoped no one would recognize her from her job. This was personal, nothing to do with anyone else.

How come they knew he was related to Rachel? A question she couldn't get out of her head. Wasn't like she kept in touch or she'd helped him pay his way or anything. What could possibly connect them? She'd severed every tie she could and that didn't take much doing. Leaving home as soon as she got into the police. Alison already married. Dom still there. She hadn't liked leaving Dom and made sure to stay in touch with him, showing him there was a life beyond Langley and the daily grind. Fat lot of good that did. Then Dom pulled his stupid trick and got locked up and she heard from Alison that the old feller had left not long after. Evicted.

Riddled with curiosity and unable to figure it out she finally asked Tintwhistle. 'How did you know to contact me?'

'Cuttings in his room.' Tintwhistle slowed behind a bus.

'Cuttings?' Rachel thought of fingernails and hair. Flashed back to her dad dabbing Brylcreem on his hair and running a comb through it, pocketing the comb, then heading out. How old was she then?

'From the local papers,' Tintwhistle said. 'Features about you, sponsored run for that kiddies' charity. And the half-marathon.'

Rachel's belly turned over as her vision darkened.

Him sat in his chair, studying the paper from front to back, reading it all. News and then the racing pages. She blinked to clear her eyes. Stupid bastard, she thought. Why did he bother? Why the fuck did he bother? Her throat ached and the bus ahead slowed again, needling her with impatience. 'Can't you overtake?' she snapped. 'I haven't got all day.'

Gill met Dennis Cottam, his son Barry and his daughter-in-law Bev prior to the appeal. Lisa had assisted them in putting together a few lines which Dennis Cottam would read out.

There were guidelines to the wording of these appeals, Gill knew, just as there were techniques to be used when negotiating with a hostage taker, which Owen Cottam was at this stage. Nothing that would increase the pressure or exacerbate the tension. Nothing judgemental or punitive. The aim was to start a dialogue, create a breathing space, open a door, defuse the situation as much as possible. To demonstrate understanding and empathy rather than revulsion and incomprehension. There should be nothing in what his father said to panic Cottam, no nugget of criticism to fuel mistrust or paranoia, no bartering or bribery – not yet.

'Stage one is the equivalent of a smile,' she'd heard one trainer say. 'It's a pair of open arms. Until that's accepted we can't build the rapport we need to effect a safe resolution.'

Lisa took her into the little room adjacent to the conference room and introduced her. Gill shook hands with all three of them. 'I'm so sorry for your loss,' she said. 'I want to thank you personally for doing this today. I understand it can't be easy.'

'Keep thinking I'll forget it,' Dennis Cottam said gruffly. A wiry, weather-beaten man with a shirt fresh from the packet and a shaving nick on his chin.

'You don't need to learn it,' Gill said. 'You take all the time you need. I'll be there, and you've got the paper.'

'I'll need my specs,' he said suddenly.

'Here,' Bev said, 'I've got them.' She held out a glasses case. 'I've cleaned them, too,' she said.

'Right, thanks.'

Gill suspected that Bev had bought the shirt as well. She was pretty, blonde, radiated a tense energy probably brought about by the ghastly situation. Some people fell to bits, others grew practical. Gill put Bev in the latter category.

'You'll sit on my left and Barry next to you,' Gill said to Dennis Cottam. 'I'll introduce you and then you read your piece. Try and imagine you're talking directly to Owen. Yes? It will be very quick, no questions. I need to warn you there will be cameras and flashes going off so be prepared for that.'

Dennis Cottam nodded. 'He was never any trouble, you know?' he said, the incongruity of what had happened hitting him anew. 'Not a scrap of bother, was there?' He looked to Barry, who swallowed and shook his head.

'No,' he said.

'Two minutes,' Lisa said. 'Okay? We'll get your microphones on.'

Dennis puffed his cheeks out, exhaled, obviously sick with nerves. While Lisa wired up Dennis Cottam, Gill clipped the lapel mic on to her jacket and checked the power light showed red on her transmitter before tucking it into the waistband of her skirt.

Then it was time. They went through to the larger room and Gill waited by her chair until they were both seated. With Lisa to her right and Dennis Cottam to her left she looked out at the bank of journalists. The case was big enough, brutal enough, to have brought in some foreign crews too. The fact that Cottam was still at large with two youngsters at risk created an extra dimension of human interest.

Some reporters were typing into their iPads or tablets, others tweeting. Around them colleagues wielded cameras of varying shapes and sizes.

'Good morning, ladies and gentlemen. I am DCI Gill Murray, senior investigating officer in this case. I'd like to introduce Mr Dennis Cottam who is here today to speak directly to his son Owen.'

Gill turned to Dennis. The man's eyes swam behind his spectacles as he cleared his throat and began to speak. 'Owen, we'd like you to come in, son. Things have not been easy but there's people can help us sort

152

it all out. You've family here and we want to help. We care for you, you and—' He broke off, face collapsing, on the brink of weeping. He began to shiver, his shoulders heaving, the paper jerking in his grip.

Barry reached over and put his arm round his father's shoulders and took the paper from him. He wasn't miked up but the room was so quiet his voice carried. 'We want you back, we want you and the boys safe. Please come in and we'll be with you.'

'Thank you,' Gill said.

Dennis continued to tremble, his hand over his face now. Beside him, his son Barry, eyes bright with grief, carried on holding him as Gill made her final remarks. Then Gill touched his shoulder and they slowly made their way from the room.

Rachel's arms were shaking as they walked into the mortuary, her arms and hands. She tried to hide it.

'It's just along here,' Tintwhistle said.

'I know the drill,' Rachel told him but her voice sounded shivery and uncertain. They carried on, his shoes squeaking on the floor with each step.

When they reached the waiting room adjacent to the viewing area, he said, 'I'll just go and tell them you're here.'

Rachel's mind skittered around. She tried to concentrate on what she'd be doing when she got back to work but the image of the cuttings, the scraps of paper he'd carefully torn out and saved, him poring over them, remained stuck in the centre of her mind, like a poster slapped on a shop window obscuring everything else. She needed a smoke; she couldn't do this without one.

Getting rapidly to her feet she half ran to the entrance, then along the front of the building, firing up as soon as she could wrestle her cigs and lighter from her bag.

She inhaled, went dizzy for a moment. Closed her eyes. The day was warm and humid and her skin felt moist, almost greasy. She'd only had a few drags when she heard her name called.

'DC Bailey.' Tintwhistle, face like a smacked arse.

'A minute.' Rachel raised the fag between her fingers. He wasn't happy but what could he do? Gave a tight little shrug and went back in the building.

Rachel smoked down to the filter, gazing across at the shop on the corner, the steady trail of customers nipping in for sweets or fags or papers. Only noticed it then, as she made to stub out her cigarette, been staring at it long enough: the sandwich board, MURDER HUNT FOR TOTS in flat, black capitals.

As she turned to go back in her phone rang. Janet calling. 'Where are you?'

'I won't be long.'

'She wants you here now.'

'Tell her I'm on my way,' Rachel said.

'An explanation might help,' Janet said.

She could just go, leave all this for Alison to do

tomorrow. That'd make sense, wouldn't it? She thought of her dad's voice, the way he'd sing if he was in a good mood, *Sunny Side of the Street*, *Spanish Harlem*, *Love Me Tender*, taking the floor at parties before it all began to sour.

How could she explain this? Her mind was blank. 'Make something up,' she said and ended the call.

Once she found Tintwhistle, they went through to the viewing room. Rachel studied the floor, cast her eyes around the ceiling. They'd lowered it at some point. Probably had those high ceilings, fancy plaster-work around the edges, like the rest of the old municipal buildings. Stained glass and frilly bits on the stonework, or the latticed windows, diamond shapes and . . .

'Miss Bailey. You will see there is some discoloration to the face.'

She wrenched her eyes open and looked through the glass to the figure on the bier. Felt something swell, blocking her throat. He was discoloured, his face mottled and dark, smaller than she remembered, and looked older. His hair had grown longer; he used to be clean shaven, always, but this man had a beard and moustache. So for half a second she felt something release inside her, was about to say no, it's not him, but the shape of his face . . . She looked at his mouth, stretched down with disappointment. 'That's him,' Rachel said and coughed. Her stomach hurt. Her eyes were stinging. She bit down hard on her tongue. 'That it?'

'The post-mortem, confirmation of cause of death, they say it was his liver. Apparently he'd spent some time in hospital recently, cirrhosis.'

Rachel nodded. No surprises there, then.

'One of the other residents raised the alarm,' Tintwhistle told her, 'not seen him for a while. Looks like he'd been there a couple of weeks.'

No!

'Drive me back,' Rachel said, *a couple of weeks* banging in her skull over and over like a chant.

'Must have been proud of you,' he said, once they reached his car.

Not so's you'd notice. Not usually, anyway. Rachel didn't reply. Concentrating too hard on hiding everything, not wanting to throw up or burst into tears or faint at the copper's feet. *A couple of weeks.* His own bloody fault really, wasn't it? No one to blame but himself. Silly old sod.

Days when she'd come home to tell him she'd got into the Special Constables or passed her first aid. Half the time he wasn't there to tell, already down the pub. The rest he'd look at her. 'Have you now,' he'd say. Rachel trying to tell if he had a cob on. In which case he'd pontificate about her shortcomings, the fickle way of the world and his own sorry state. *What's it take for a man to make an honest living these days?*

Sobriety would help, getting up and out of the house fully dressed before midday too. He used to do labouring, shovelling and shifting. Nothing skilled.

Then it got so he'd just missed the alarm, or Chalky didn't really need him, or his back was giving him gyp. Till eventually he wouldn't know an honest day's work if it bit him on the bum.

Rachel kept quiet mostly when he began his tirades, lost it now and then with a sarky comment or a direct challenge that earned her a slap. On the better days, no mood on him, he'd be milder. 'Have you now,' he'd say. 'No flies on you, eh? Sharp as a tack.' But still a caution: 'Just remember where you come from.'

What the hell for? Rachel meant to forget where she'd come from as soon as possible. Do a thorough amnesia job on it.

Now with him gone, it'd be even easier.

11

Janet was coming out of the Ladies when she met Rachel running up the stairs. 'What did you tell her?' Rachel said, dragging her back into the loos.

'Said I didn't know. What was I supposed to tell her? Where were you, anyway. She's steaming.'

'I ran out of fags.' Rachel ran water into a sink. Scooped back her hair in one hand and splashed her face.

'Tell me you're joking.'

'Ran out of cash?' Rachel dried her face.

Janet could see Rachel wasn't making any effort to sound plausible. Janet didn't understand what was going on but there wasn't time to try to ferret the truth out of her. 'Come on,' she said.

Gill saw Rachel from her office as soon as they walked in and came to the door. 'Rachel, good of you to join us. Somewhere important to be?' Disapproval etched into every syllable.

'I fell down the stairs, boss,' Rachel said. 'Banged

my head. Thought I'd better get it checked out. Felt sick.'

'Really?' Gill obviously didn't believe a word of it. 'Is it in the accident book?'

'No, boss. Bit muddled, I think. I just went straight to A&E.'

'Who processed you in an hour?' Gill was furious, eyes bright, jaw taut. Everyone knew A&E was an average three-hour wait. Janet felt sick, worried about what Gill might do or say, worried for Rachel.

'Felt better,' Rachel said, 'came back.'

'I was going to allocate you and Janet to the surveillance team. Join our colleagues on the ground. However, if you have suspected concussion . . .'

Oh, Christ. Janet could hear what was coming.

'Please, boss?' Rachel said.

'If you can't be bothered—'

'I can!' Rachel interrupted. Never a good move. Gill glared, nostrils flaring.

'Listen, lady, I don't need officers of mine doing a Houdini on me. What could possibly be more important than working your balls off on a triple murder and missing children? Unless someone died. Did someone die?'

'No,' Rachel said, sounding miserable as sin.

'Boss . . .' Janet tried to intervene though she hadn't a clue what she could say to mitigate Rachel's offence. 'Boss' was all that came out, a bleat that Gill ignored.

'As it is—' Gill continued, then her phone went and

she held up her hand, warning them to wait while she took the call. Eyes flaring with excitement. 'The Mondeo . . . abandoned.' Janet saw the moment's disappointment dampen Gill's energy, but her recovery was almost instantaneous. 'Yes . . . yes . . . agreed.' She turned to them, face alight. 'We've found the car. Woods near Lundfell.'

'Yes!' Rachel's manner changed in a flash, alert and engaged. 'Cottam?'

'He is not with the vehicle but we hope to trace him from there.'

'The kids?' Janet said.

Gill shook her head, 'No.'

That was good, though, thought Janet, no news better than what they might have found. Or had he already killed them and dumped them somewhere?

'Forensics are all over it now and we're getting tracker dogs and a scout.'

'The old Indian bloke,' said Rachel.

'Native American,' Gill said swiftly.

Janet had met him once on a training day. Nice bloke. One of the whole range of experts the police work with, who come in all shapes and sizes, everything from translators to underwater teams, forensic soil scientists and geographical profilers. The scout had the old tracking skills, had inherited a legacy from generations who had hunted their food; he could see where people had walked, changed direction or hesitated by studying the ground and the vegetation.

'How far can Cottam go with two kids?' Janet said. 'The whole country's looking out for him.'

'Stolen vehicles?' Rachel said.

'They're on to it,' Gill replied. 'May need to issue another alert for the area – beds and sheds – but I need to check with the psychs and the hostage negotiator whether that might force his hand. We don't want to panic him into taking action.' Meaning harming the children, Janet knew. The two little ones. Harder or easier than killing his wife and daughter?

'Where's he heading?' Rachel said. She was keen, totally absorbed now, so what had led her to slope off like that, like a kid bunking off school?

'Let's see what the maps tell us and if we can connect the location to anything we've learnt so far.'

The three of them went into the larger operations room where Andy and Pete were working. Janet felt a little lurch when she saw Andy. He had maps of the area up on the whiteboards, map and satellite views. There was a checklist too – the actions currently under way: police officers checking taxi firms, stolen vehicles, train timetables, bus routes, CCTV coverage.

Andy had received the news and entered the co-ordinates. 'Why did he pick here?' he said. 'Gallows Wood, Lancashire.'

'Gallows? You're joking,' said Janet. Some sick irony in the name given what they might find there.

'Cyclist noticed it,' Gill said, 'vehicle smashed through fencing, and reported it to the local police.

Thought it was joy-riders until they got the number plate.'

Andy said, 'Public path and bridleway enter here, and there's a lay-by for parking. Anything from the mother?'

Janet shook her head. Margaret Milne had listed all the locations she could recall that had any significance for the family. Holidays in the Norfolk Broads, Black Rock Sands, Malaga and Minorca. A trip to New York. Weddings of friends in Leeds and Bristol. No mention of East Lancashire.

'I've a list here,' Janet said. 'Nothing fits. He might just have seen an opportunity. Somewhere to hide, or a vehicle he could take. Any CCTV close by?'

'No, nearest is Lundfell town centre – couple of miles away.' Andy moved the pointer on the map, showing her. She studied the map, the village . . . was it too small to be called a town? Small in her eyes, clustered around a central high street, the canal and the railway that ran along the valley bottom. The high street connected to the A road that led in turn to the motorway six miles away. The proximity to the road network presumably responsible for an increase in house building and the open plan estates that ringed the older areas and were scattered along the A road.

Fluke? Or did Cottam know where the cameras were? How clever was he? How collected, given he was on the run and fleeing from the harrowing events of the night before last, from the near miss at the

162

petrol station. Or was he numb, operating on some sort of autopilot? 'How clear is his thinking going to be?' Janet said to Andy.

'Impossible to say,' Gill answered.

'Originally a mining town,' Andy said, 'way back; copper and tin here, quarrying up on the tops.'

'Mine shafts?' Gill asked. 'Somewhere to hide bodies. Talk to the local bobbies, countryside rangers, anyone who knows the area.'

'Nearest railway station has a service every two hours,' Pete said. 'Staffed in the morning when there's most traffic. Commuters travelling to connecting services in Wigan or Warrington. I've requested CCTV footage.'

'Images of the scene should be coming through now,' Andy said.

Janet watched with the rest of them as Andy imported the files and posted them on the screen. She saw the Mondeo, the broken fencing and a shallow bank to the left where the car was, bonnet pointing downwards.

'Accident?' Rachel asked.

'Hard to tell. No obvious blood in the vehicle,' Andy said.

'Could he have left it there to come back to?' Janet suggested.

Gill shook her head. 'After the petrol station, he had to get rid of it, and with two kids on foot he's not going far.' She waved at Andy to change the image.

The second photograph showed the car side on, both doors open on the driver's side.

'He's left the child seats, which might mean . . .' Janet said.

'Doesn't need them any more?' Rachel looked at Janet.

Which in turn meant . . .

'Cordon is being erected now, search parties preparing,' Gill said.

Rachel half rose. 'Boss? Please, boss, me and Janet.'

Gill gestured, moved with Rachel until they were just outside the door but Janet could still hear.

'Can I rely on you, Rachel?'

'Yes, course, I swear.'

A pause. Then, 'Go on then,' Gill said, 'but don't make me regret it.'

'Yes boss, no boss.'

Rachel came back in the room, gave a ghost of a smile and jerked her head at Janet. 'Let's go then.'

'So do I get to know?' Janet asked as they approached the car.

'What?' Rachel said, heading for the passenger side.

'You can drive.' Janet threw her the keys.

'God, you must be peaky. You're not going to faint on me, are you? You getting enough iron?'

Janet ignored her, got in the car. 'Where did you disappear off to?'

Rachel started the engine. End of discussion.

Janet knew better than to push her but it did rankle a bit. Supposed to be best mates, not just at work, looking out for each other, but Rachel had her secrets. *And you don't?* Her health worries. Andy. Janet felt a swirl of nausea and the prickle of sweat across her neck. She wound down the window, letting some air in before they reached the motorway.

On their approach to Gallows Wood they passed two patrol cars, some of the units which were driving around the woods, watching for movement. The tracker guide had the CSIs documenting signs of foot traffic but as the car had been dumped near a public entrance to the area there was plenty of evidence of activity. A talk with the cyclist had told the police that it was a popular spot with local dog walkers too.

The dog handler, Gareth, was looking despondent and when Janet said hello he explained. 'We've tried her with both Owen Cottam's clothing and the kids'. Made a bit of a start up that way,' he pointed along the road to the right, 'but soon petered out.'

Could she trust Rachel? Gill had a sense that the woman was coming apart, this disappearing business not like her unless she had been looking into some-thing to do with the case, working some angle, which she was prone to do, in her time off if need be, and then she'd come running to Gill with the winnings. A cat proudly presenting a dead mouse. But she'd not said anything in her defence and that made Gill doubt it was work-related.

There was something volcanic about her. Some source of steady pressure that built and built until it finally erupted in disaster, or near disaster. Gill had no idea where it came from, the recklessness, the wild side: her background, most likely, but it made her a nightmare to manage and it threatened her future and hopes of promotion.

Brilliance was worth very little if it came bundled with chaotic episodes and sudden meltdowns. As yet Rachel hadn't learnt the lesson that she needed to master and tame that side of her behaviour.

Gill turned her thoughts to Sammy, to the conversation earlier. There was something nagging at her, something that didn't quite gel. Before the stuff he'd said about Alton Towers and the whore of Pendlebury proving to be such a jolly good sport. Open days? Yes, open days – that was it. He'd said it was in hand, he was sorting it out. But shouldn't he have already been to one?

She got her diary out. There it was – *Open day, Leeds*. Last week. One of the four courses he was looking at. She checked her watch and rang him; should be back from sixth form college by now. Would he pick up?

'Hey,' he said.

'Open day last Thursday, Leeds,' she said.

'What about it?' *Buying time.*

'Did you go?'

'No,' he said.

'Why not?'

'Changed my mind.'

'Without even taking a look at the place?' She sounded shrill, tried to modify it. 'Why change your mind?'

'Not sure if I want to go to Leeds.'

'Based on anything in particular?'

'Dunno.'

Give me strength. 'But you'll go to the others?'

'Dunno.'

'Talk to me, Sammy, don't just say dunno all the time.'

'Well, I don't. Dad said you'd do this.'

'What? Do what?'

'Overreact. You just want things your way all the time,' he said.

Her skin felt tight, hot. 'I want what's best for you.'

'No, you say that but you just want me to do what you think is right. That's why I'm here. Emma and Dad, at least they're not on at me all the time. They can chill, right?'

What, with a teenager and a brat to boot? Gill couldn't quite envisage it. 'Leave you to your own devices, you mean?'

'It's 'cos you're never there,' he said nastily. 'You're always at work so you make up for it by bossing me about, making like you care.'

167

The criticism stung. She didn't know if Sammy really thought that or was parroting what Dave and his bit of uniform on the side said. Gill had tried never to disrespect his father in front of him but maybe they were playing dirty.

'See much of your dad, do you?' Dave's job, as Chief Super, carried heavy responsibility. Not as full on as Gill's but more than full time.

'Yeah, like a normal person. But you don't trust me and all you do is check up on me and treat me like a little kid.'

'Well, if you behave like one—'

'Leave me the fuck alone.' He hung up on her.

Trembling, she closed her eyes and took several deep breaths. Nice one, Gill, she told herself. Could you have handled that any more badly?

Issued with high visibility jackets and torches and a map of the search area, carrying protective masks and gloves and evidence bags in case they found anything of significance, Janet and Rachel began. They'd no idea whether this was a crime scene or a wild goose chase. They were looking for people, for disturbance of the undergrowth or the ground, for clothing, for bodies or shallow graves or puppets dangling from a tree.

A helicopter had been raised and was already sweeping to and fro above, using heat-seeking equipment to try to determine if there was anyone hiding in

168

the woods. As well as helping in the search, the police helicopter took film and still photographs of the search area. Again part of the documentary evidence. Analysts receiving live feedback at the station acted as extra pairs of eyes, alert for any signs of activity on the ground that might lead to their quarry. Recorded footage was logged and stored in case it was needed for the construction of case files evidence. No chance of hearing anything when the helicopter was overhead but when it swung away to survey a different quadrant it was possible to listen. To walk and talk with one ear alert to children's cries or footsteps, to the snap of a breaking branch or the rustle of clothing.

The wood was a mixture of deciduous and evergreen. Some had autumn colours but most of those still held their leaves, which made it hard to see any distance. Among the trees were clusters of shrubs, leggy weeds and brambles and nettles.

'Ow! Fuck!' Nettles had stung Rachel through her trousers. How could they do that?

'You okay?' Janet said.

'Nettles.' Dock leaf, he'd tell her, rub a dock leaf on it. One time, she remembered, her almost in tears. It must have been way back when her mum was still on the scene. Renting a static caravan at the coast. Sand in the bed sheets, the sunburn tight across her shoulders and ice creams and wasps and staying up as late as her parents. And shouting. One night them going at it like prize fighters. Another teatime, maybe the same week, Dom getting leathered for nicking another kid's blow-up dinghy. Where was that holiday? She could ask Alison, except their memories never really meshed. Like they'd grown up in parallel realities. Always squabbling about what really happened and who'd done or said what to who.

'Everyone says he's a good bloke,' Janet said, stepping over a fallen tree trunk and waiting for Rachel to follow.

'Bit of a control freak, though,' Rachel pointed out.

'But on the scale of things,' Janet said, 'we have no evidence of domestic abuse, no criminal activity, he brings home the bacon for all these years, never strays that we know of, loves his kids . . . I mean, most of the people we deal with, they're building up to it, aren't they? Known to us, history of violence. Cottam's Mr Normal.'

'You better keep an eye on your Ade.'

'Not funny,' Janet said.

Rachel scowled at her. *Why so touchy?* Usually Janet could take a joke.

'I don't understand how he got from that to this,' Janet said.

'You're not the only one. That's all everyone's on about. It's Jekyll and Hyde, isn't it?'

'Superficially,' Janet said, 'but according to Lee and Leonard Thingy, Cottam thinks this is good, too. That it's his responsibility to take the family with him.'

'Suttee,' said Rachel. 'That thing they do in India,

where the wife is burnt 'cos her husband's died. Or all the poor sods buried with the pharaohs.'

'I'm talking Oldham, Rachel, 2011. We're talking a pub landlord and a woman from Ireland and a learning disabled man and an eleven-year-old just started at secondary school.'

'Hey!'

Janet was being weird. You didn't let it in, didn't let it touch you. You empathized (only if you had to as far as Rachel was concerned), you commiserated but you kept yourself clean and unsullied. Only way to do the job. And Janet had done it for years. Rachel wondered if the stabbing, Janet's own brush with death, had changed that. They'd worked a couple of murders since then and Janet had seemed the same as always. Delayed reaction?

'I'm just . . . bad night.' Janet was red, her face sweaty and blotchy, like she was sick. Maybe she was, gastric bug or something. Rachel needed Janet to be strong, to be calm and level and solid. Holding Rachel steady, like her anchor. Else what might happen? A breath of wind clattered the leaves on the trees and Rachel felt cold inside. Rattled.

The helicopter bobbed low and loud and their radio crackled into life: a positive result on the heat generation. One individual. *One. Cottam on his own. He's done the kids already.* Rachel felt her stomach clench. She and Janet ran to the given coordinates only to find a homeless woman by a makeshift shelter, terrified by the clamour and attention. Once they had calmed her down and reassured her that they were not there to arrest her for trespass, she answered their questions. She had not heard children or seen a man with children in the last twenty-four hours.

They had two hours of walking, looking. The light faded and soon the call came to abandon the search until the following morning. Tired and scratched from brambles and with nettle stings ringing her ankles, Rachel drove back to town with Janet for the end of day briefing. She felt like going out and getting hammered. Finding some feller to flirt with, maybe more if he smiled the right way and made her feel good. But before that there was something she had to do.

'This is progress,' Gill told the team. Aware that they would all be disappointed at not having captured Cottam. 'The finding of the car will provide us with a wealth of information. We are significantly closer than we were this morning. If you are thinking but we haven't got him, we haven't picked him up, then add a word to that thought. *Yet.* Fuller briefing tomorrow, meanwhile some bullet point updates. Andy?'

'Yes, boss – large volume of calls to the incident line. We're checking anything plausible but we've a confirmed sighting yesterday afternoon. Cottam stopped at a roadside snack bar on the A570 and bought two lots of chips as well as tea and milkshakes. Paid cash.'

'Further indication that he was laying low and not travelling far for much of the day. Details of the recovery of the Mondeo being released immediately. How is he travelling?' Gill asked. 'If he's not hiding in Gallows Wood?' Still that possibility, only a third of the area adequately scoured before darkness fell.

'Stolen vehicles being flagged and taxi firms all on board,' Andy said. 'It's two miles from Gallows Wood to the nearest train station at Lundfell, three and a half to a functioning bus route. Support staff have examined the CCTV from the railway station up until six p.m. this evening. Single camera looks out over the platform near the ticket office. Anyone travelling across the bridge for the opposite platform would also have to pass that camera. No sign of Cottam and his children. We'll keep looking,'

'He's not going to be walking that far with two kids, even if he could cover the distance with them. He'd be too exposed,' Janet said.

'I'd want to put some mileage between myself and that area, after the business with Mr Rahid. Cottam knows we'll be all over the place like a rash,' Rachel said.

Janet wasn't so sure. 'He sat there, or near there, all night. I think instead of moving further afield, his new plan involves this area.'

'But if he stays, there's more risk of us finding him, so maybe he'll run again. Start another plan,' Rachel said.

'No one's expecting him to give himself up then?' Gill asked. Rachel compressed her mouth. Lee raised his eyebrows.

'Thought not,' Gill said. 'We have no idea if Cottam is still in the county at all. He could have reached the Scottish border or the south coast if he's got hold of another car and put his foot down. Okay. To your beds, get some kip. And keep your phones on.'

There was a low muttering and the scrape of chairs as people left.

Gill carried on working. Lost track of time until Janet appeared at her office door. 'Gill? You still here?'

'Might as well move my bed in,' Gill said. Her eyes ached. She rubbed at them and groaned.

'You okay?' Janet said.

'Not so as you'd notice.'

'We'll start again in the morning. At least we didn't find—'

'It's not the job,' Gill said.

'What then?'

'Sammy. I don't know what's going on with him, and when I try to talk to him I end up screaming at him like a fishwife. How does that happen?'

'They know how to push our buttons?' Janet said.

'Yeah – but you—'

'Me nothing. I lost it big time this morning with Elise. I'm still working on my apology.'

'You know what Dennis Cottam said about Owen?

Never any trouble, not a scrap of bother. And then –
pow!'

'The quiet ones?' said Janet.

'Maybe we should be thankful that they're kicking
off.'

'But it's us, isn't it? Well, me,' Janet said. 'I was the
one throwing a hissy fit.'

'Sammy . . . he said I was controlling to make up for
being absent so much. Never there when it really
mattered.'

'You were!' Janet protested.

'Should have stayed home like the whore of
Pendlebury up to my armpits in nappies.'

'She still off work?'

'Not sure,' Gill said. 'Think she might have gone
back part time.'

'You know where this is coming from?' Janet
said. 'Dave. Because he never got over your outshining
him when you worked in the crime faculty.
You're a great mum, Gill, Sammy's just testing
you.'

'Know what he said? *Leave me the fuck alone.* Do I
let that go? I can't let that go.'

'Sleep on it. Maybe he'll ring to say sorry.'

'Where was she?' Gill said.

'The whore?'

'Rachel.'

'I don't know,' Janet said.

'If there's something going on that I need to be

175

aware of . . .' Gill didn't want any nasty surprises in her team.

'There isn't. Well, if there is, I'm not party to it either. But she's been fine since. No worries.'

Gill knew Janet was loyal to Rachel, the pair firm friends. Just as Janet and Gill were. A friendship that went way back. Gill saw that this put Janet in the middle, and when Gill had issues with her newest detective constable it must be uncomfortable for her.

'Well, I'm keeping a sharp eye on her, and if there's anything that will compromise her ability to do her job I want to hear about it as soon as.'

'You're asking me to tell tales?' Janet said, folding her arms.

'No, I'm asking you to consider the safety and welfare of your colleague and the rest of the syndicate.'

'Message received,' Janet said, less warmth in her tone now. But she needed to be reminded of what the priority was here. And Gill knew Janet was mature enough, experienced enough, to distinguish between the personal and the professional, to respect and protect her workmates whatever their relationship. One thing they all had in common – police officers through and through.

It was bred in Gill: her parents both officers, though her mum switched to office duties when she started her family. Janet got the call as a teenager. Rachel had the conviction that this was what she was meant to be. But in Rachel's case her temperament sometimes undermined that professionalism. A lack of patience, an over-reliance on instinct and a tendency to leap before she looked had led her into scrapes. Her communication skills were still a weak area, but even so Gill expected her to achieve her sergeant's exam before very long and go on to greater things. Gill wanted to see her succeed and that meant keeping a weather eye open for potential car crashes as they loomed on the horizon. Gill needed Janet as part of that early warning system; she just hoped Janet understood that she was monitoring Rachel more closely for the best of reasons, not the worst.

Like Sammy. Surely.

12

It was after eleven when Rachel got to Alison's, but the hall light was still on. She rang the bell and waited, shivering on the doorstep. A clear night and frost making her nose and fingertips sting.

Alison took her time but finally the latches were thrown back and the door opened. Alison in a candy-striped fleece dressing gown.

'What sort of time do you call this?' Alison said. *Never very original.*

Rachel shot her a baleful glance. Alison huffed and crossed her arms. 'Changed your mind, have you? Thought you'd see sense. Flesh and blood. Do you want to come in? But keep it down, Tony's just gone up.'

Rachel sniffed, stepped over the threshold, arms wrapped about herself, trying to get warm. 'I'm not here about Dom,' she said as they went into the living room. Plastered with photos of Alison's three kids.

Alison turned to study her. 'Are you drunk?'

Not yet, thought Rachel; wish I was though. 'No,' she snapped, ''course I'm not. Why would you think I'm drunk?'

'Well, you don't often turn up here in the dead of night. And when you do, it's because you've had a skinful and can't drive home.'

'Once! I did that once! Bear a grudge, why don't you.'

'Is there a point to this, then? Because I'm knackered and I'd like to get to bed.'

'Yes. The point is—' Suddenly she couldn't say it, her tongue too big in her mouth. She opened and closed her gob a couple of times like a fish gasping its last.

'What?' Alison scowled.

'Dad's dead,' Rachel said.

Alison looked bemused, as if it was a joke and she was waiting for a punch line. 'You what?' she said.

'He's dead. I found out at work.'

'Murdered!' Alison clutched at her throat.

'No, you daft thing, he hasn't been murdered.' She poured scorn on the idea. 'Natural causes – it's his liver. He was found in his room.'

'Bloody hell.' Alison moved backwards, one hand searching for the sofa's edge, and sat down, her eyes never leaving Rachel's face. Rachel didn't want to tell her about how long it had taken to find him. It was like a bloody great flag with *neglect* painted on it. Maybe that was poetic justice. After all, his parenting had been indifferent neglect much of the time. The lure of the bottle and a flutter a far more pressing attraction than the need to put a decent meal on the table or clean clothes on their backs. As for *her*, wife and mother, well her flag would read *abandoned*. Rachel wondered if she was still alive.

Rachel took a breath. 'Nobody had seen him for a couple of weeks,' she said, letting Alison join the dots.

'Oh God.' Alison pressed her fingers to her lips, sudden tears gleaming in her eyes. 'Oh, Rache,' she said sadly, 'I should have—'

'What?' Rachel was suddenly cross. 'Done what? What could you do? He was hopeless.'

'God, Rachel.' Alison had gone white, her face looking years older. She ran her hands through her hair, gripping fistfuls of it.

Rachel shrugged. What was there to say?

'I haven't seen him since January,' Alison went on. 'I was going to go, I meant to go—'

'You've got three kids and a job,' Rachel butted in. No point in her beating herself up about it.

'Yes,' Alison said flatly, staring right at Rachel now. *And you haven't, have you?* The unspoken message, *how come you were never there?*

Alison cried for a minute and Rachel felt awkward, standing like a lemon, so she went and sat in the armchair.

'Cremation,' Alison said suddenly. 'Would he want cremating?'

'I don't know,' Rachel said. 'Cheaper, isn't it?'

'Did he leave a will?'

'A will!' Rachel almost choked. 'Are we talking about the same feller here? He'll have left us a load of debts if he's left anything. Tabs at the bookies and the pub.'

'He was banned from the bookies.'

'When?'

'I told you.' Expecting Rachel to remember every sordid little step in his slide into vagrancy.

'Whatever.' Rachel was eager to go now.

'They'll let Dom out, won't they, to go to the funeral?' Alison's expression quickened. 'We'll have to wait till he can get a pass.'

Rachel said nothing. Couldn't think of a worse prospect than graveside with her dad in a box, Alison blubbing and Dom putting on a brave face.

'That is so awful. God, Rachel, I feel so awful.'

'You weren't to know.'

'At the end of the day, he's our father. We should have known.'

'You know what he was like,' Rachel said.

'I hate to think of it, think of him, on his own and—'

Don't then! 'Look, his liver packed up and he'll have gone quick. The rest he'd not know about, would he. You did your best.' Knowing that she herself hadn't, couldn't. Too angry with him, wanting to get as far away as she could from the mess of his life.

'You need to register the death,' Rachel said. 'Take this to the register office.' She pulled out the death certificate. 'Give them this—'

'Can't you? I've a really busy week.'

'I'm working a triple homicide,' Rachel said. 'Take compassionate leave. They're meant to be big on that, your lot.' Social workers.

'What, and you can't take it?' Alison said.

I'm not feeling very compassionate, Rachel thought.

'We could meet up to go together, at lunch,' Alison said.

Rachel could see Alison was already beginning to try to haul her back into the bosom of the family. 'Don't be daft. I've no idea when I'll get a meal break. It'll take twice as long to do it if we're both arguing about it all.'

Alison had her head in her hands. Rachel heard her make a squeak and realized she was crying.

Rachel sighed. 'If you want me to sort it out then I will, but you'll have to just let me get on with it. You find out when Dom can get a pass and I'll take it from there.'

Alison hesitated. Rachel knew she didn't like handing over control but eventually she nodded her head. 'Okay. Look, the money, it'll take us a bit of time—'

'That's fine.' Rachel thought she had enough to cover it. Never had much chance to spend her salary; on a decent whack for a single person. 'Won't be gold fittings or anything, mind.'

'What about after? Buffet?'

'Pie and pint more his style,' Rachel said.

Alison tutted at her.

'Come on, who'll be there? You and Dom, maybe a clutch of his drinking buddies if they're not too wasted to make it on time.'

'God, you're hard sometimes,' Alison said.

'Just being practical.' If she was hard it was because she had to be. You got nowhere being a doormat, a pushover. 'Sandwiches and crisps and sausage rolls,' Rachel said. 'That place opposite the crem does food, I think. Looks nice enough.'

'The one with the hanging baskets?' Alison said.

'Yeah.'

'Do you think one of us should say something?'

Christ, no! 'Like what exactly? You can if you like. Look, I best get off. Okay. I'll give you a ring, let you know what's sorted.'

'And I'll call you when I've talked to the prison.'

Alison got to her feet and trailed Rachel to the door. 'Do you remember that time he—' she began, warmth and humour in her voice.

'I need to go.' Rachel cut her off, her throat swelling and something like anger tight inside. Alison moved to give her a hug. Rachel bore it, thankful when it was done. And she'd managed not to cry.

Ade was in the lounge watching telly. The girls upstairs. Taisie would be texting her mates, or her boyfriend, rather than actually sleeping, as she should be at this time. Twelve seemed awfully young to be interested in boys. Ade had been Janet's first, at sixteen. When Janet had asked Taisie about it all, she got the idea that 'boyfriend' was an exaggeration. 'We hang together at break,' Taisie had said.

'And that makes him your boyfriend?' Janet said.

'Duh!' Taisie rolled her eyes and waggled her head and that's all Janet got. Janet would check on her soon. First Ade to tackle, then Elise.

'My mum rang,' she said to him, 'not that it'll make any difference. Except she's upset which could have been avoided if you hadn't run to her like a big kid trying to get her on your team.'

He gave a nasty laugh. 'After everything she's done—'

Janet felt rage, raw and dangerous, flash through her. 'Don't!' she said. 'Don't you dare. I know exactly what she's done for me, for us. And what you've done too,' giving him his due. 'But this is separate, this is work. This is me and my job. You don't get to interfere in that.'

She walked out before he could come back at her, taking a few moments to try to rein in her temper before she went to speak to Elise. Her hands were shaking. When did I get to be so angry, she thought? Normally she managed to balance things, to find equilibrium, but these days it felt as if there was a ball of fury in the pit of her stomach just waiting to explode, for a spark to set it off. Was it since the attack? Or longer? Was it simply the effect of being surrounded by two adolescent girls and their raging hormones? Perhaps her body was joining in and she was coming out in sympathy, the way women who live together end up with their menstrual cycles in sync. Or was it to do with Andy, with wanting him and feeling guilty about it?

She didn't like the anger; it threatened to bring her too close to losing control. To letting fly, allowing all her darkest thoughts to escape, and who knew whether she'd be able to push them back in the bottle. And life was so precious, too precious. She did not want to waste any of her time with negative emotions.

Janet knocked and went into Elise's room without waiting for an answer. Elise was at her desk with her laptop open, an essay by the looks of it. Janet could tell she was still in the doghouse as soon as she saw Elise's face, pinched and set, her shoulders rigid, too. Janet said, 'I'm very sorry I shouted at you, Elise, it wasn't fair. I was really cross about something else and I'm sorry. I shouldn't have done that.'

Elise turned to look at her, a sulky expression on her face. 'Why are you so horrible to Dad?'

Christ! Janet's stomach dropped. She felt her cheeks burning. 'I know we argue,' she chose her words with care, 'but some marriages, some relationships, are just like that. People say it clears the air.'

'It doesn't. That's stupid,' Elise said. She had a

point. After one of their rows there'd often be a period of moody withdrawal before the atmosphere improved.

'I'm sorry,' Janet said, unable to think up a better response. 'Your dad and I, we've been together a long time.' *Too long?* Was that why she was tempted to stray?

'I hate it when you shout at each other.'

'Yes.' Janet thought of her own parents. Beyond a bit of low level bickering they'd got on great. Never raised their voices. Not to each other and not to Janet. 'But we're all right, you know,' Janet lied, desperate to reassure Elise. 'We love each other, we love you and your sister.'

Elise gave half a shrug.

'Don't work too late.' Janet nodded at the screen.

'Says you,' Elise sneered.

Janet smiled. 'Walked right into that one.' She put her hand on Elise's shoulder, relieved when she didn't draw away, and kissed her head. 'Night.'

In bed later, Janet couldn't get to sleep, either too hot or too cold. She craved oblivion but the tension in her arms and legs and back wouldn't release her. Tired and drained, she wondered whether to ring in sick in the morning. She had hardly ever taken sick leave, until the knife attack. Not for years. Was this how she would always feel? Would she have to retire on grounds of ill health? She couldn't face the idea of leaving work. She would go bananas if she hadn't work to get her out of bed in the morning, to fill her days. She loved her work. If what Geoff Hastings did cost her her job she'd be another of his victims. She must not let him destroy her like that. She wouldn't let him take that from her. She had come too far, fought too hard – coming back from the dead, recuperating, putting her life back together – to let it all collapse now.

Half an hour after leaving the office, Gill drew into her driveway. Light was peeping out from the house, set on the timer to make it look occupied. Telly on timer too: she could hear advert jingles as she unlocked the door and turned off the alarm.

Once she'd switched the TV off she sat for a moment in the armchair, her mind crammed with fragments of the working day and snippets from her conversation with Sammy. She closed her eyes. It was so quiet out here, even quieter now she was on her own.

Over and over again like a line from a song stuck in her head, Sammy's words: *Leave me the fuck alone*. Well, she wasn't going to sit back and do nothing. If he thought that just because he had moved out she would wash her hands of him and sit back sulking or some other passive-aggressive crap then he had better think again. This – decisions about uni – would affect the rest of his life. Did Dave even know about the open days? About which places Sammy was considering?

The UCAS application had to be in by January, sooner if possible, because then the admissions tutors would have more time to actually read the personal statements and consider the candidates. Come the end of the year they would be swamped, barely glancing at each submission. She'd go round there, much as it sickened her, go round there early before work and talk to Dave and Sammy. So they all knew what the timetable was and what support Sammy needed. Gill was happy to adopt a hands off approach as long as somebody else was paddling the bloody canoe in the right direction.

And she would not refer to Sammy's horrible little comments. She would rise above all that. It would only muddy the water. But now she should eat, eat and relax, get some kip like she told the troops.

She texted Chris: *Long day. Just home. You somewhere exotic? Wish I was there x.* Of course if he'd got a night flight somewhere he wouldn't be able to reply yet. But then her phone bleeped. She read the message, *Not exotic exactly but looking forward to a hot meal and a bottle of vino. Wish you were here too x.*

He hadn't said where. Perhaps he had only been able to get some cheesy destination, Marbella or Faliraki, full of stag parties and drunken Brits and English 'pubs' serving all day breakfast.

Gill put the radio on, opened the fridge and considered her choices. Fancy soup, smoked salmon, bacon and eggs. None of which appealed. In the freezer she had a few ready meals . . .

The doorbell went. Her first thought was Sammy, Sammy forgetting his key. But why would Sammy turn up at this time?

Gill went to the door, peeped through the spy hole and saw Chris. Chris! She opened the door. 'Not today, ta,' she said, keeping a straight face.

'I come bearing dinner.' He hoisted a large plastic cooler box in one hand and a sturdy shopping bag in the other. 'You haven't eaten?'

'No.' She was smiling. 'Come in. How come you're not in Italy or Croatia or somewhere?'

'Prefer this.' He grinned. Put the box and bag down and held up his hands. 'I know you're in the middle of a huge inquiry and you'll need your sleep so you can turf me out whenever you like. I've reserved a room at the hotel on the ring road, in case.'

'Oh, no.' She moved closer to him. 'You're going nowhere, mister.' Reached up to kiss him. He put his arms round her, kissing her slowly, softly, until she was dizzy. Gill was half tempted to skip the food and take him straight to bed but he had gone to so much trouble. And besides, if she ate she'd have even more energy for what would come after.

He began getting things out on to the counter: a hot chicken, croquette potatoes, a mixed leaf salad. Cheesecake, a bottle of white.

Gill's mouth was watering. She opened the wine,

found glasses. 'Cheers. Here.' She fetched a candelabra and lit it. Swapped the radio for the CD player and found paper napkins.

He raised his glass again as she sat down, clinked hers. 'Happy holiday.' Merriment dancing in his eyes.

'Happy holiday,' she echoed. And started to eat.

Day Three

Day Three

13

'Keep your coat on,' Gill snapped as Rachel arrived at work. 'We've a report just in of a stolen car, red Hyundai Accent, registered keeper Mr Howard Wesley at Rose Cottage, Lundfell.' She tapped the map on the monitor screen.

Rachel saw the significance immediately. 'Just down the road from Gallows Wood, where he dumped the Mondeo.'

'Literally. Dogs and CSIs on their way. We've now a mobile incident unit in place at the lay-by near the wood. The search is continuing. Base yourselves there and follow up on the car theft. Any whisper of a breakthrough and I want to know before you draw breath. Yes?'

There was a stiff, brittle way to her this morning. Obviously got the hump. Maybe the toy boy was mucking her about? Maybe it was the investigation. A second night shortening the odds on the chance of a happy ending. Happy being a very relative term, right? Anyway, Rachel read the signs and said the minimum. *Yes ma'am, no ma'am.* Avoided eye contact. Bit like dealing with a wild dog: no direct challenge. Her Maj could be a right cow when she'd got a mood on and Rachel knew she was still in the shit for nipping off yesterday and blagging about the reason.

'Where the hell is Janet?'

'Don't know, boss,' like she was Janet's keeper. Not like Janet to be late.

'Christ! If it's not one of you, it's the other. If she's not in in the next five minutes you pair up with Pete and talk to this Mr Wesley.'

'Yes, boss.' *Please, no!* Pete was okay, a steady copper, but not at all the same as working in harness with Janet.

Janet pitched up within the given time and Rachel said she'd meet her downstairs. She took the chance to make some calls. The pub opposite the crem was straightforward: they could do sandwiches, sausage rolls, tea and cake for five pounds a head. 'Ten of us tops,' Rachel said. Fifty quid the lot. She'd get back to them with a date.

The funeral parlour was more of a shock. 'No, nothing fancy, just the basic package,' Rachel said after she'd told the man it was her father and they wanted cremation. The man started wittering on about options until she interrupted him. 'I don't care if it's chipboard with plastic handles. Just give me a price. Bottom line.'

How long before someone spotted a gap in the market for a budget service? Funerals 2 Go, Deaths R Us?' She had heard of cardboard coffins but reckoned Alison wouldn't like that notion. She was funny like that, wanted to be seen to be doing the right thing all the time as if the rest of Middleton were standing on the sidelines giving the Bailey family marks out of ten for style and execution. You could decorate the cardboard coffins, too. His could have been covered in bar mats, or painted like a giant Special Brew can or plastered with pages from the *Racing Times*.

'In the region of two thousand pounds,' the funeral director said.

'Two grand!' *Jesus!* 'And that's it, no VAT on top? Right. I'll let you know later today.'

'You lashing out?' Janet must have caught the tail end of the conversation. Rachel's mind scrabbled about, mouth open but no words coming out, and then she said, 'New kitchen.'

Janet laughed. 'What for? When do you ever cook? Can't be that old anyway.'

'Don't like the colour. Just getting some estimates,' Rachel said. 'So we going or what?'

It was raining heavily, drumming on the roof of the car and streaming down the windscreen. Lorries sent up great waves of water and visibility was down to twenty yards, forcing traffic to a crawl.

Janet was at the wheel, had offered to drive. Rachel

195

knew Janet still mistrusted her driving in anything but peachy conditions because Rachel liked to travel at a decent speed and because of a small incident when they first met and she had pursued a suspect's vehicle with Janet in the passenger seat. Pranged the car . . . well, okay, rammed it then, but got her man, and Janet acted as though she had driven the wrong way down the M6 or something. So the downpour meant Janet would drive.

Rachel got a call from Alison, let it go to voicemail, then listened: *Dom can get a pass a week on Friday. I thought Friday would be better than Thursday.* Why the day of the week should make any difference Rachel didn't know. *If that's no good let me know. And I've been thinking, you know, I probably will say something, maybe a poem.* Good God, spare me, Rachel thought.

Janet glanced at her. Curious. Rachel put her phone away.

'Did Gill seem a bit off to you?' Janet said.

'Yeah,' Rachel said. 'She was bitching even before she noticed you were late.'

'Wonder what's going on.'

'Search me. I'm the last person who'd know.'

'None of the lads say anything?'

'No.'

'Rachel . . .' Janet said, and just the way she said it, slow, as if she was broaching something, put Rachel on alert, 'you thought any more about seeing someone, talking it through?'

For one God-awful moment Rachel thought Janet had found out about her dad, and all the associated crap – broken home, hand to mouth, sink estate, brother inside – and then it struck her that Janet was on about Nick, about the great betrayal.

'No, I'm fine,' she said.

'You're spooked,' Janet said. 'Yesterday you practically hit the ground, and it's not the first time either. You having flashbacks, trouble sleeping?'

'Now you're a shrink,' Rachel said.

'I'm just saying—'

'I don't need counselling. You didn't have any and you got a lot closer to the pearly gates than I did.' *The terror when Janet had screamed down the phone, the race to reach her, Janet clutching her belly, blood everywhere.*

'That's different,' Janet said.

'How?'

'That was business. Yours was personal.'

'No.' Rachel tried to dismiss the distinction. 'You're talking shite, Janet.'

Janet sighed, said, emphatically, 'I wasn't in love with Geoff Hastings.'

'Not even the tiniest bit?' Rachel joked. Hastings was a slimy tosspot, something deeply creepy in his poor-quiet-little-me act. And that something was a deranged serial killer.

Janet laughed but wouldn't be put off, which annoyed the hell out of Rachel. 'Rachel, he was your boyfriend and what he did was unforgivable. It's too big to deal with on your own. Counselling's not an admission of weakness. And in the long run—'

'I'm fine,' Rachel said firmly. 'Leave it.'

'Really?' Janet said hotly. 'No nightmares, no flashbacks, no overwhelming emotions . . .' ticking off Rachel's symptoms as if she'd been given a list, 'sudden rages, tears, nausea? If you don't address it—'

'Just knock it on the head, will you? I'm okay and coming from you this is a bit rich.'

'How do you make that out?' Janet said, affronted. 'I've told you Geoff Hastings is a stone cold killer and I'm going to get my chance to nail him. Not just for what he did to me,' Janet was suddenly shouting, red-faced, and Rachel was freaked, 'and for what he nearly did to my kids, but for all those others.'

There was a pause, the shush of the rain quiet after Janet's outburst.

'Sudden overwhelming emotions?' Rachel said.

'Sod off.'

'All I'm saying is you're off colour and pretending everything's fine. I'm not the only one.'

'Ah, so you are struggling,' Janet said triumphantly.

'No, I'm not,' Rachel said. 'Pull in at the services.'

'Why?'

'Comfort break. Cigarette. Calm my shattered nerves.'

Janet mouthed *fuck off* but there was a smile tugging at her mouth which meant things were okay again. For now.

* * *

They met the local officers at the mobile incident van now parked up at Gallows Wood, where teams were continuing the search. Janet introduced herself and Rachel. 'Found anything?' she asked, but the officer in charge shook his head. He confirmed that the address for the stolen car was a mile and a half along the road to the north.

'That's the direction the dog went in yesterday,' Rachel said.

'Think it through,' Janet said. 'You've two kids and a car, you want another car, what d'you do? Lug the kids with you to steal the car and risk it going pear shaped? Then you've two kids hampering a quick get-away. I don't think so. I think it makes more sense to leave the kids in your car, lock them in and go off and try to nick another vehicle. If that's a success you can just drive back and pick up the kids.'

'He'd walk it from here in half an hour,' Rachel said. 'Less if he shifted it.'

'Do we know when the car went missing?' Janet said.

'No,' one of the uniformed officers told them. 'I'll take you down there now. You'll want to speak to the owner in person?'

Mr Wesley was mid to late sixties, Janet estimated. A fact confirmed when he gave his full name and date of birth as 1946. Mr Wesley had been working in London the previous day. He was a computer programmer who worked from home so he could care for his disabled wife. Once a month he attended meetings at head office, using a taxi to and from the main railway station in Wigan, nine miles to the east.

The house was a low-roofed cottage, three knocked into one he told them, with a car port at the left reached by the side door. The front door was in the centre of the building and as Mr Wesley had returned home by taxi, in the dark, he had entered by the front door so was unable to tell them when his car had been taken. He only noticed it was no longer parked in its allotted space under the canopy when he glanced out of the window in the side door this morning while making breakfast. Mrs Wesley had heard nothing.

Glass on the driveway showed that whoever had stolen the car had smashed a window to get into the vehicle.

'Are your keys accounted for?' Janet asked him.

'Yes, both sets.'

'Any security devices in the car? Crook lock? Immobilizer? Alarm?'

Mr Wesley shook his head.

'He worked for his father as a mechanic,' Rachel said of Cottam. 'He'd have no problem starting the car.'

'How much petrol was in it?' Janet asked.

'Not very much at all. I was planning to put some in at the weekend.'

'How far would it have taken you?' Janet said.

'Perhaps thirty miles or so. It was low.'

Janet looked about at the stone walls and the carefully trimmed conifer hedging. After the incident at the petrol station Janet couldn't imagine Cottam would want to fill up a new vehicle. But he couldn't travel very far unless he did. Was his journey almost over, or was the new car a stop-gap until he found something better? It certainly wouldn't serve him long now the description and registration number had been circulated to all the neighbouring forces. And with ANPR and CCTV, a car was a lot easier to find than a person. When they did, would Cottam be the one driving it?

The search dogs unit arrived then. Gareth, the handler, said there could be a problem because of the rain. 'Washes the scent away, see?' Janet and Rachel watched while he put the dog through her paces. Giving her a T-shirt of Cottam's to smell, brought from the laundry basket in his bedroom at the inn, before letting her off the lead. The dog ran along the edge of the road, head dipping this way and that, nose close to the ground. She went straight to the main entrance to the cottage then doubled back and went up the side of the house. Under the car port she barked loudly and sat to attention.

'That'll be a yes, then,' Rachel said.

'Sheltered here, see,' Gareth said, stroking the dog and shaking the ruff of her neck. 'Stronger scent.'

Rachel gave a nod to Janet, a smile on her face, happy that they'd got a firm lead.

They waited while Mr Wesley made a list of items that were left in the car, everything from a road atlas and torch to CDs, screen wash and motor oil, tartan picnic blanket, wellies and a cotton sun hat. Where would Cottam go, Janet wondered for the umpteenth time. None of the locations familiar to Cottam were near here. But surely if you were looking to end it all you'd go somewhere familiar, somewhere you knew suited your purposes.

The day had not started well for Gill. She had risen at five thirty. She always was an early riser but today anticipated the alarm, switching it off. Chris stirred as she got up and she put out a hand to cup his shoulder. 'Stay there,' she whispered.

By the time she had showered any remnants of sleepiness had gone and she was feeling more ready to meet the day, buoyed up by the pleasure of Chris's visit: the food, the sex, the intimacy. The fact that he'd chosen to snatch a few hours with her rather than jet off to some island paradise made her glow with pleasure. They spent so little time together, his job even more impossibly antisocial than hers, and she'd worried that the whole thing would peter out, never really get off the ground. She'd almost resigned herself to that and had decided to be philosophical, take what she could while it was on offer. But Chris seemed ever more interested, eager to carve out opportunities to meet, always talking about things they should do together, see together, places he'd like to visit with her. Likelihood was one of them would have to stop work to make even a fraction of it happen. And she was a helluva lot closer to retirement then he was. She found her thoughts running on and yanked them back. Live in the present. Or maybe dwell on last night instead, and the way he'd made love to her.

She left the house at six forty and was on Dave's doorstep by just shy of seven, trying to ignore the fluttering feeling behind her breastbone.

The house didn't look quite as small or as cheap as she had imagined. *Pity.* Dave answered the door, yawning, bleary-eyed in boxers and a T-shirt. She averted her eyes from his bare legs, filing away a flash of Chris's slimmer, more buff body.

He blinked, obviously surprised to see her. 'Now what?' he said.

'Sammy was supposed to go to an open day in Leeds on Thursday.'

'And?'

'He missed it. Did he even tell you about it?'

Dave shook his head. 'No.'

'I don't know what he's playing at,' Gill said.

'Well, ask him,' Dave said.

'That's why I'm here.' *Peabrain.* Gill was striving to be civil against every impulse. 'Get him up,' she said.

Dave frowned. 'He went to your place.'

'What?' Her spine tingled.

'Last night. He had his tea then said he was off to yours.'

'I've not seen him.' She felt cold suddenly, cold and cross and anxious.

'Can you shut the door?' A woman's voice called out, then Gill heard footsteps coming downstairs.

'You'd better come in,' Dave said with a heavy sigh.

Oh, shit. She really didn't want to but there was no way out of it. She stepped inside and saw his floozie, child astride her hip.

Dave flushed. 'Emma, this is Gill.'

'What's going on?' Emma said, barely looking at Gill.

'Sammy never arrived at Gill's,' Dave said.

'Oh, my God!' the woman said melodramatically, making the child glance up at her with concern. 'You think something's happened?'

'No,' Gill said briskly, squashing it, even the thought of it. 'When did he leave?'

Dave looked at Emma. 'Half past seven?' he said.

'Seven.'

'Why? What did he say?' said Gill.

There was a hiatus. The brat seized the chance to whinge. 'I'm hungry.'

'Come through,' Dave said, shifting them all into the kitchen. 'He just said he was going to yours.'

'Why? I'm not exactly flavour of the month.' Gill thought of Sammy's parting words.

204

Dave rubbed at the back of his neck and stared at Emma again. Couldn't he speak for himself? Emma gave him a look which Gill interpreted as *don't ask me* and poured cereal into a bowl.

'He just kicked off,' Dave said.

'You argued?' Gill said.

'He wasn't pulling his weight. We'd asked him countless times to clear up. Then he'd wake the little one.'

Gill hid the little wriggle of relish she felt inside. Petty. Where was Sammy? That was all that mattered. 'So, what, you give him a bollocking and he says he's running home to me?'

'Near enough,' Dave said.

Gill thought quickly. Where would he go? She pulled out her phone and rang his number. He didn't pick up. 'I'll try Josh and Ricky,' she said.

'Ricky?' Dave said.

'Glennister.'

'Right,' but it seemed he'd not a clue who his son's friends were. How could that be, given he was sharing a roof with him? Didn't he talk to him? Wasn't he curious?

'Hello?'

'Josh, it's Sammy's mum, Gill. Is Sammy with you?'

'No.'

'Did you see him last night?'

'No, sorry.' Always polite, Josh, but Gill suspected he was one of the more reckless kids among Sammy's friends. Whether he'd lie to her outright was another matter. 'You see him before I do, will you ask him to call me or his dad?'

'Okay.'

'Thanks.'

Gill felt a little wobble. What if it was more serious? What if he was missing? Not just AWOL but missing?

She tried Ricky. His phone went to voicemail and she had just left a message when he rang her back. 'I've not seen him for a couple of days,' Ricky said. 'I've been off college.'

'Neither of them have seen him,' Gill said to Dave. 'Where can he be?'

'I don't know.' Dave spread out his arms. 'How should I know?'

At the table the child was stirring its cereal round and round and humming some little song under its breath.

'You must know who he's hanging out with.'

'Well you clearly don't.'

'I've not seen him for the last six weeks.'

'And whose fault is that?' Dave said nastily.

'What do you mean?'

'He couldn't stomach it – his own mother—'

Any self-control fled. 'No,' she pointed a finger at him, 'he was fine with it, with me and Chris, me and my younger man.' Determined to call a spade a spade. 'Until you stuck your oar in. You are the one who can't stomach it. Does she know that?' Gill nodded at the

206

younger woman. ' 'Cos it'd bother me, my bloke in a tizzy about his ex's sex life. You can get a younger model but I'm not allowed, eh?'

Dave had gone puce, his teeth gritted. Emma, face set, seized the bottle of milk from the table, flung open the fridge door.

'You should know who his friends are,' Gill said.

'Like you do?' Dave sneered.

'He's probably with Orla,' Emma said, arms folded, plainly brassed off.

Dave and Gill stared at her and spoke in unison. 'Who the fuck is Orla?'

'His girlfriend,' Emma said.

What the fuck? 'How long's he had a girlfriend?' Gill said.

'Ages,' Emma said, something smug sprawling across her face.

A girlfriend! How come Sammy hadn't told her? How come she hadn't known? And Emma had.

Orla lived in a council house on the other side of Shaw. Gill felt acutely uncomfortable as she knocked on the door. A teenager answered – was this Orla? Black leggings, denim shorts that could not possibly be any shorter without turning into a belt, tank top and blouse in neon yellow. Tattoo visible on her shoulder through the flimsy material. Shaggy blonde hair and a nose stud.

'Yes?' she said brightly.

'Orla?'

'Yeah,' less certain now.

'Is Sammy here?'

'Yeah.'

'Can I have a word? I'm his mum.'

'Oh, cool, yes.' She shut the door. A minute later Sammy opened it. 'What are you doing here?' he said, flushed and sounding irate.

'That's my line,' Gill said. 'Get in the car.'

'I'm not going back—'

'I just want to talk to you. Get in the car.'

He'd only socks on his feet but the ground was dry at present so Gill just stood waiting. Sammy leaned back into the house and called, 'Back in a minute.'

She'd been shaken by his disappearing stunt. The prospect, however remote, that he was missing, even hurt, had niggled away and she was trying to shed the sensation now, telling herself that it was all right. Everything was all right. No harm done. Panic over.

They sat side by side, Gill staring straight ahead, trying to ignore the way he was picking at his nails, the clicking sound making her cringe, like chalk squeaking on a blackboard.

'What are you playing at?' she said. 'Lying to your dad. We'd no idea where you were.'

'So?' he said sullenly.

'We're your parents, Sammy. We need to know where you are. Where you're staying at night at the very least.'

208

'Why? I'm seventeen. I could get married if I wanted to.'

Oh, please no, thought Gill.

'Or join the army or leave home. You can't stop me.'

'I'm not trying to stop you doing anything. But sneaking off and lying, running away as soon as things get tricky, that's no way to behave. You want to stay over at Orla's – you let us know. That's all I'm saying. Though I don't think it's a good idea when you've got college the next day.'

He snorted. 'You talk to me about how *I* behave.'

She felt heat in her face. 'Is this about Chris and me? You know what I'm hearing? Your dad. You sound just like him.'

'I do not!' He did not appreciate that comment.

'You were fine with it,' she said. 'You told me that yourself, the first time you met Chris. I mean, I know the thought of either parent having sex is utterly gross but beyond that I have every right to make new friends, start a new relationship if that makes me happy. Your dad might not be able to handle it but you're not an idiot, Sammy. Don't be a stooge for him.'

'It's not just him,' he said.

'What?' Gill turned to look, saw him flinch and turned away again.

'Some people at college. You know what they call it . . . you? A cougar.'

She almost laughed but knew it would be the wrong thing to do. And there was a sting of annoyance that such pettiness was distracting him from the more important things in life.

'Tell them to mind their own business. Jesus, Sammy, you don't need to listen to tosspots like that. In the scheme of things,' she bounced the edges of her hands on the steering wheel, 'with everything that's happening in people's lives, this is just . . . trivia. I love you, kid, you know that, but I'm not going to let either your dad or a load of pimply teenagers with their tongues wagging have the slightest effect on how I live my life. Got it?'

'Yes.'

'Orla seems nice,' Gill said.

'Yes, she is.'

'Good. Right. You get yourself to college and if you're staying here again any time, you tell your dad. And . . .' she held up a hand as he opened the car door, 'if you're not going to talk to me about all the UCAS stuff, discuss it with him. Or Emma,' she said, though it half killed her to acknowledge the woman.

'Okay.'

She watched him walk up the path, stooping slightly, and saw him knock on the door. Then she started the car and drove off. The events of the morning had left a nasty taste in her mouth, and the well-being she'd felt after Chris's visit seemed to have evaporated.

14

The announcement came blaring over the radio, making Rachel's scalp tighten. 'Control to all units, stolen Hyundai Accent, registration sierra, six, one, zero, X-ray, bravo, Charlie, confirmed sighting Porlow.' Rachel entered the coordinates into the map app on her phone.

'That's close, right?' Janet, at the wheel, threw her a glance.

Rachel watched the results load, the red circle showing the location of the car. 'It's a retail park,' she said. She zoomed out to judge the quickest route, then looked out of the window checking that the next street on the left corresponded to what she had on the screen. *Yes*. 'Down to the roundabout, straight over, then second left at the next one,' Rachel said. More details were coming in over the radio. 'All units requested to wait at the perimeter road.' Rachel magnified the image, read the labels aloud, 'PC World, B&Q, TK Maxx, Curry's, Iceland.'

'How far off are we?'

'How fast are you going to go?'

'Ha ha,' Janet said sarcastically.

'Ten minutes, tops,' Rachel said. She studied the screen again, glanced up at the hedges and walls flashing past, the road ahead blurry because the rain was heavy again, a steady deluge that the wipers struggled to deal with.

'It could be a decoy,' Rachel said to Janet. 'He dumps the stolen car, we're all fannying around waiting for him to buy a new mobile phone or a fresh set of threads and meanwhile he's running as far as he can in the other direction.'

'He'd need transport,' Janet said. 'Another car.'

'Train, coach.'

'And how's he get there from here with two kids?'

'Might be on his own.'

Janet swallowed, just as her phone went off. 'Can you get that, see who it is?'

Rachel took the phone and read the display. 'Your mum,' she said.

Janet gave a sigh. 'Leave it,' she said.

Rachel was happy to. Dorothy didn't like her, Rachel could tell; looked down her nose at her. Even the way Dorothy spoke changed with Rachel: she put on a posher voice and acted all headmistressy and disapproving.

'No, answer it.' Janet changed her mind. 'Tell her I'm driving and I'll call her later.'

Rachel pressed the green key, said, 'Hello, Dorothy,' but was cut off by the terrible screaming that came down the line. 'Janet! Janet! Oh, God, Janet, help me, help me! It hurts.'

Janet went white as chalk, shot a look in the mirror and pulled into the side of the road, the tyres skidding on the run-off water. She grabbed the phone. 'Mum? Mum? What's wrong?'

'Oh, God, oh my God,' Dorothy moaned, 'I don't know, oh, it hurts.'

'I'll call an ambulance,' Janet said. 'I'll be there as soon as I can.' She hung up. 'Oh, fuck, Rachel.'

'Ring the ambulance,' Rachel said, 'then you go. Maybe she's fallen.'

'She's not that old,' Janet said as she dialled, 'not falling down old. God, the way she screamed.' The operator answered and Janet spoke precisely. 'I need an ambulance to 6 Waterfield Lane, Middleton, M24 7AP.' The operator began to ask the routine questions but Janet cut in. 'I'm not with the person, but she's my mother, she's just rung me in extreme distress, in great pain. I've no idea what's wrong or even where she is in the house. I'll try to get someone round to open the door. You may have to tell them to break in.'

That wouldn't be easy. Her mum had solid UPVC doors, high quality locks. She thought quickly. There was a phone in the living room, another in the kitchen and one upstairs. Given they were cordless her mother could have been anywhere.

'Can I give you the number,' she said, 'and you can try to ring her back.' She reeled it off.

'Has she any health problems?' the operator asked.

'No, not really. Look, I've no idea what's wrong. Please, just send the ambulance.' She thought of the previous day, her mum feeling tired, off colour. Janet had dismissed it as a minor niggle. Oh, God. 'You have my number,' she said, 'this number. Please make sure someone informs me when the paramedics reach her.'

'Was the patient conscious?'

'Yes, but I've no idea if she is now.'

'Is she taking any regular medication?'

'Erm . . . statins and thyroxin, I think.'

'Please hold the line.'

'No, I need to get moving,' Janet said sharply. 'Just send an ambulance, now.'

'The ambulance has been dispatched.'

'Right. I need to see if my husband can get round there with a key,' Janet said. She hung up. She knew there were sound reasons for the operator sticking to the script but on this occasion there was nothing Janet could tell them and she judged it more important to sort out access to the house.

Ade didn't answer so she left a message and then rang the school office and spoke to Claire, the administrator, who had been there nearly as long as Ade. 'Family emergency,' she said, after introducing herself. 'My mum's collapsed at home; there's an

214

ambulance on its way. I need Ade to go round there straight away with the spare key to let them in.'

'Certainly. I'll find him now.'

Janet put her phone down and took a deep breath.

'You go,' Rachel said. 'Just go.'

'What about you?'

'Drop me at the lights. If you turn left you can get to the motorway that way. I can walk from here. Bum a lift back later.'

Rachel walked along the dual carriageway towards the retail park, wishing she had an umbrella or a hooded coat with her. By the time she'd come in sight of the turn-off to the stores, the rain had crept down the back of her neck and her hair was plastered to her head. She hurried on. Whatever lay ahead she did not want to miss it.

At the entrance to the complex she could see two men in high visibility jackets, nothing to show they were police. They turned a car away, and as she got closer she heard one of them say to the next motorist, 'Sorry, security operation under way, no access at the moment.' And caught the replies to the ensuing questions. 'Can't say at the moment' and 'I'd leave it till tomorrow, if I were you.'

Rachel reached the men as the car drove off and showed her warrant card. 'Who's in charge?'

'Sergeant Ben Cragg,' one of them said, and pointed. The man leading the operation was in plain clothes and was standing by a white van, the back doors open as though he was loading up. To the unobservant there was little to show that there was a significant police presence at work in the retail park. No squad cars or police motorcycles, no marked vans. All designed not to panic Cottam and increase the risk to the general public.

'Are we sure it's him?' Rachel asked Ben Cragg after she'd introduced herself.

'No. We've just got the car there.' He nodded. The stolen vehicle, the red Hyundai with its broken driver's window, was next to a silver Daewoo in the middle of the parking area outside B&Q. 'Patrol making a sweep of the retail park called it in. The plan is to identify and apprehend the suspect as he reaches his car. Plain clothes officers already in situ. The Daewoo's ours.' Through the rain Rachel could just make out four figures inside. 'And we've another unit on the park. Green Honda outside PC World. Squad cars around the back in the delivery area, out of sight.' Cragg nodded towards TK Maxx. 'Hostage negotiator is on his way, and a firearms unit. We've put down a spike strip close to this exit in case he does try to drive away. Other vehicles leaving will be diverted to avoid it.' As he spoke she watched a bloke in dungarees and a work-stained coat speak to a woman leaving PC World, gesturing with his arms to show her how she should leave the complex. He was obviously a plain clothes officer.

'So we've no idea if the kids are with him?' Rachel said.

'That's right. Where's your vehicle?'

'My partner was called away – domestic situation. Said I'd make my own way.'

Each time anyone emerged from any of the five stores ringing the car park Cragg stilled, gathering himself for action. Rachel watched, shivering slightly, the damp stealing through her. 'Do we know where he's shopping?' she asked.

'No idea. I'm hoping he's like the rest of us, picked the nearest parking space.' He nodded towards the DIY outlet. It was a huge store, the sort that had a garden centre and a section with heavy duty building supplies as well as a café and toilets.

'If we can ID him, we wait until he reaches the vehicle, then block him in.' The radio crackled. He spoke into a headset, said, 'Your ETA?' Frowned.

What would they do if Cottam came out of somewhere before the armed unit arrived? Rachel had started to ask Cragg when she saw the automatic doors open at B&Q, but it was only a couple with a child. Grandparents by the look of them, grey-haired, the man pushing a trolley stacked with paint tins and a long item, one of those rollers for doing the ceiling. They were parked in the first row of spaces. The woman took the keys from the man and walked quickly to a black Fiat, the child trotting at her side to keep up. The woman opened the car boot. The man in the dungarees walked over and spoke to the old man, giving him directions for leaving the car park.

A gust of wind sent rain splattering against the van, drenching Rachel even further. She shuddered.

'If you want to get out of the rain you could join one of the squad cars,' Cragg said.

'Miss all the action?'

'Thought you'd be equipped for it,' he said. 'Mancunian.'

'We've webbed feet and all,' Rachel said. She liked the banter, liked the look of him. In different circumstances she might be tempted to take it further. Sound out his availability.

'I could go and buy an umbrella,' she suggested. 'See if I can spot him. B&Q do brollies?'

'You are joking,' he said.

'Worth a try.' As if they'd let someone wander around solo in the midst of a sensitive police operation like this.

The toddler with the couple wanted to help, raising its arms for the paint tins, but the old man, no doubt concerned about the situation, was hurrying to load the car. Then the toddler was shouting, crying, kicking at the trolley. A tantrum audible even in the rain.

Two women came out of TK Maxx and a single man emerged from PC World. 'No,' Rachel said. 'Too young. Wearing a suit.'

The toddler was now flat on his back, on the wet

ground in the rain, kicking up as the woman bent over him.

Movement at the DIY store caught Rachel's eye. Her heart gave a kick. 'He's there,' she said. Owen Cottam coming out of B&Q, jeans and a bottle green sweatshirt. A khaki hat on his head, the sun hat from Wesley's car. Moustache visible. 'That's him.' A carrier bag in one hand. No children with him. The toddler kept screaming.

'Suspect in sight.' Ben Cragg was speaking into his radio. 'Stand by. Prepare to apprehend. Taser him if we need.'

Cottam walked steadily towards his car, his head slightly lowered. Rachel heard the sound of a car engine start over to her right. Presumably from one of the other units. She was counting beats in her head, counting her pulse, her mouth dry as Cottam came forward.

'Wait for it,' Cragg said into the radio.

Rachel watched Cottam; only ten yards now to the Hyundai. Beside it, the windows of the silver Daewoo were steamed up. The car rocked gently. Someone in there must have moved.

Without warning Owen Cottam veered to his right and back towards the store.

'Shit!' Rachel said. 'He's spooked. He's on to us.' She set off after him. She expected him to go back into the shop but he ran towards the old couple, yelling as he reached them.

'Keys! Give me the keys.'

Rachel covered the ground quickly, wet hair whipping at her face, breathing hard. She saw Cottam push the older man over and turn on the woman. The child on the ground stopped crying, the wailing snapped off as though a switch had been thrown. Behind her Rachel could hear engines firing, vehicles moving.

Cottam snatched the keys from the woman and ran round to the driver's door of the black Fiat. The old man climbed to his feet shouting. Rachel pushed herself on, reached the car, running round in front as Cottam gunned the engine. Voices raised behind her, too confusing to take in.

She slammed her hands on the bonnet, looking directly at Cottam. His face clenched, eyes blazing. She banged on the car with her fists, yelling, 'Police! Stop the car. Get out of the vehicle.'

He thrust the gear into reverse and drove back at speed, the boot still raised, clipping the trolley, which crashed over. Rachel lost her balance and tumbled forward, breaking her fall with her hands, jarring her joints and scraping her palms raw on the wet tarmac. *Bastard!* She scrambled to her feet. Watched Cottam reverse the length of the DIY outlet, ignoring the barrage of outrage coming from the old couple.

Two cars were moving up towards the Fiat. The silver Daewoo and the green Honda. From the back of the parking area two squad cars squealed out, ready to box him in. With squad cars ahead of him and the Daewoo and the Honda approaching behind, Cottam swung the black Fiat round to the left and shot forward, heading for the exit. The Fiat hit the spike strips and travelled a few yards before the tyres collapsed, making the vehicle hitch like a bucking bronco.

Cottam got out and ran back towards the shop, still clutching the carrier bag. Rachel saw that the shutters were coming down, almost closed. Someone had had the foresight to instruct the retailers, who would have been alerted to the threat to public safety, to seal up all the units. Cottam whirled round. He switched direction. He was going back to the Hyundai, must be. Equidistant, Rachel ran, intent on beating him, struggling for breath.

He got there first, started the car, drove forward. She ran to intercept him but he never wavered, forcing Rachel to leap out of the way. She pelted after him and he increased his speed, the engine whining, two wings of spray fluting up on either side of the vehicle.

As the patrol cars raced in pursuit, one of them skidded and ploughed straight into a parked car. The other one swerved but not in time and ploughed into the rear end of the first. Instead of turning towards the other exit, Cottam swung the car right, towards the back of the shops. The delivery area. Rachel followed on foot, her heart thumping painfully, her windpipe sore. He fishtailed as he turned and then revved the engine. The Hyundai leapt forward with a

221

snarl as Rachel rounded the building. The delivery area was empty apart from some recycling bins by the steel fencing on the left perimeter. Along the right was the back of the superstore and at the far end facing them a brick wall right across where the building supplies section was housed.

He increased his speed and she saw. She knew. She yelled and hared after him. Watching as he accelerated, the noise of the engine climbing, howling, and the car smashed into the end wall. A clanging, crunching sound, the scream of metal on brick, a cloud of debris hurled in the air.

Rachel reached the car and yanked at the door. The bodywork was crumpled, the door frame buckled. Petrol fumes stung her eyes. She pulled again, then put her foot up on the wheel arch to increase her leverage and rocked the door to and fro until it swung open. Cottam's eyes were shut, blood all over his face and on the airbag.

Ignoring shouts from the people running to join her, she reached in and worked her hands under his armpits and dragged him clumsily from the car. His heels snagged on the seat and she had to tug and shake him to release them.

She fell back and landed with him partly on top of her and wriggled out from underneath. On her knees she straddled him and slapped his face, oblivious of the blood and the rain. 'You bastard, you fucking, fucking bastard,' she shouted at him. She thumped his chest, hearing only the roaring in her own head. 'You call yourself a father? Call yourself a father? Where are they? Where?' She hit his chest again and again, desperate for a response, shaking and white hot with an anger she could not contain. 'Where? Tell me, you fucker, where are the kids? The boys, Theo and Harry? Where? Where?'

Then hands were on her, pulling her back, and she clawed at them, trying to resist. Knew they were shouting, but the words had no meaning. They were half carrying, half dragging her, one of her legs trailing on the ground. Others lifting Owen Cottam, moving, shouting, so much shouting. There was a great thundering sound and the air was sucked away and a ball of fire exploded above the car, burning her face and searing her airways. It began to snow. Hot black flakes that scorched as they touched her cheeks and her forehead, and sizzled as they singed her hair.

15

Spectres crowded in Janet's mind as she drove towards Oldham. What if it was too late? What if those agonizing screams were her mother's last words? If a heart attack or haemorrhage had taken her? Janet wasn't ready yet, not halfway ready. Losing her father had been hard. Her dad, a lovely man. But her mum? The thought of life without her filled Janet with dark panic. Her mum had been there for her in the worst times, in the wilderness days after she and Ade had lost their first baby to cot death, when Dorothy had cleaned and shopped and cooked and nurtured them, both of them, until they began to function again. And after Janet had been attacked she had done the same, and, more important, given the girls the love and reassurance they needed when it was uncertain that Janet would survive, and then that she would fully recover.

And Janet had imagined she would in turn look after Dorothy as her strength waned, as she became older and less independent, frail even. She had always imagined there would be years ahead, with all the stress and worry of ensuring proper care and all that, but what if this was it? The prospect made her throat ache and she wanted to cry. She couldn't give in to that. She had to drive safely, get there in one piece and deal with whatever she found.

Would a heart attack make you scream like that? People talked about a crushing pain, a fist squeezing their chest in a vice, and that would make screaming impossible, surely? And a stroke, a stroke was sly, sneaky, silent, wasn't it? A headache or a numb sensation, one side of the mouth not working right, but not the sort of physical event that had you howling in pain. What, then? Had Rachel been right? Had she fallen and broken her leg, her arm, her shoulder? Or cut herself? *Oh, God!* Been doing some little job, gardening or cooking, a moment's lack of concentration and she couldn't stop the blood, blood everywhere, making her scream with panic.

Janet tried to shut off this line of thought but there was nothing big enough to distract her. Even when she thought about Cottam, about how they were drawing closer, her mind slid back to pictures of her mum dying alone and frightened. If she dies, Janet thought, I don't know how I'll cope. I'll go under myself. Knowing it shouldn't be about her and feeling awful for being selfish. This was about her mum, her mum's life, the fact that she should enjoy another ten, fifteen years. Janet drove on, her back rigid, her hands clamped to the steering wheel and dread heavy in her chest.

Rachel wanted them to just leave her alone. To leave her alone and let her go. But they wouldn't. She had to give her account when she could barely string two words together and she kept drifting off, her mind wandering all over the shop.

She knew she looked a right mess if she was anything like the rest of them, oily black smears on their faces, cuts and burns. A car bomb, in effect, that's what Cottam had made of his vehicle. Mind you, he couldn't have relied on it going up in flames – though as a former mechanic he must have known there was a chance of that. All he would have been thinking about was that brick wall. Oblivion.

'Is he dead?' she kept asking. But no one knew, or if they did they wouldn't tell her. Put her off, said, 'If we can just complete your statement first, while it's fresh in your mind.'

Fresh? It wasn't fresh, more like frazzled, bitty, broken. She could smell his blood on her. Blood and smoke. The burning rubber fumes caught at the back of her throat. He hadn't responded after she pulled him from the wreck. Not a flicker.

'He drove straight into the wall?' the officer taking her statement repeated, as though he couldn't quite believe her. Christ, he only had to look at the scene. At the wreckage.

An ambulance had taken Cottam away, a second

one had left with a uniformed police officer who had broken his leg in the explosion and an ambulance car had transferred another officer with cuts to his face.

Rachel had been checked over and almost got carted off as well. One of the paramedics said her responses were a little slow and there might be some concussion. *I fell down the stairs.* The lie she'd told Gill yesterday. *Banged my head.*

'I'm not going in,' she said, 'I refuse. That clear enough for you? I'm fine.'

Someone had wrapped a space blanket round her and she caught snippets of words from the other officers, *who is she, disaster, firearms unit were late, total cock-up.* Ben Cragg wasn't talking to her, his face white with tension, a little sneer of disgust each time he looked her way. For what, for fuck's sake? Showing some initiative?

She saw the elderly couple and the kid being escorted into a squad car. Her hands were hot and sore, the heels of her thumbs, the edges of her palms and her fingertips scraped raw. She flexed her fingers, hoping the stinging pain might cut through the fog and jumble in her mind and help her concentrate.

'You pulled him from the vehicle,' the officer said, 'and tried to revive him.'

The slap. The blows. 'I tried to get him to talk.'

'How did you try to revive him?'

'Smacked his face, hit his chest.'

227

'CPR?' He frowned. 'Had you checked for signs of life?'

Rachel shook her head. She'd skipped that bit, checking the airway, looking for the rise and fall of the chest, feeling for his pulse. Jumped straight in. She'd wanted to pound the truth out of him. She'd lost it, deserted procedure, but the guy probably knew that.

'Not exactly. I wanted him to wake up, to tell me what he'd done with the kids, where they were.'

'Did he respond?'

'No,' she said, feeling flat. She looked away to the burnt-out car where CSIs were examining the ground. A bird, a big black bird, a crow, landed on the brick wall close by. She felt unsteady, the same feeling as before, when she had almost been run over and had realized she was the target. Then her stomach had lurched with this same sick feeling, revulsion and a dreadful fear.

'And what happened next?' the guy said.

She wrenched her attention back. 'Sorry?'

He repeated, 'What happened next?'

'They pulled us clear,' she said, nodding to the other officers. 'Then it blew.'

He wrote it down. 'Anything you want to add?'

'No. I need a lift back,' she remembered, 'to Manchester. Could you sort something out?'

They put plastic on the back seat of the car, the way they did when someone was likely to vomit or worse.

The driver hadn't been at the retail park and knew no more than Rachel about the fate of Owen Cottam.

The boss would know, wouldn't she? Rachel got out her phone, saw the screen was cracked, the display milky. She pressed at it, trying to get some response, but nothing worked. The thing was buggered.

She got dropped off at her flat, peeled off her clothes and showered as quickly as she could manage with her stinging hands. Towelled off her hair but didn't bother drying it, just pulled it back into a ponytail. Under the layer of grease and soot her hands and face were pock-marked with cuts and burns. On the back of her left hand a smear of something blue had melted on to the skin. She rubbed antiseptic cream on it, found some co-codamol in the kitchen drawer and took two of those. She opened the window, lit a cigarette and blew out the smoke in a steady stream. The wind blew it back into the room.

She called a cab and got it to stop at a mobile phone shop on the way so she could replace her phone. Luckily the SIM still worked fine. Several missed calls. The boss. One from Janet. With a swooping sensation Rachel realized that she hadn't thought about Janet and her mum at all. Hadn't thought about anything but Cottam. If he hadn't survived how would they ever find the kids? She thought of them starving, growing listless. Thirst would kill them in the end. Dehydration. But maybe they were dead already. Smothered and left down some mine shaft or strangled

229

and buried. Gallows Wood was still being searched. With Cottam dead how would they ever find them, dead or alive? They could be left undiscovered for years.

She didn't ring the boss. What was there to say? Best to face the music in person. She could imagine it already, a ferocious tongue-lashing, occasional dollops of sarcasm. *And you physically assaulted a man we need to speak to? Repeated blows? How does that help us, DC Bailey? Accusations of police brutality could undermine charges against a man who we believe has killed three people. Are you out of your tiny little mind?*

The boss was a stickler for rules and regulations and it wouldn't be the first time Rachel had had a strip torn off her, but she did worry that this might be one time too many. She didn't know if there were cameras covering the delivery area, if they'd captured her actions on film. She imagined that clip being played at inquiries and special committees, leaking on to *YouTube*. Joining the ranks of all the infamous examples of heavy-handed police tactics. But this wasn't some innocent caught up in a sweep and detained by mistake, or a student kettled or someone in the wrong place in a riot. This was a multiple murderer and Rachel had after all been trying to get him to give her information that might prevent further loss of life. She had! She turned deaf ears to the little voice inside mocking her. *Not that clear cut, Rachel. You lost*

230

control. You'd have beaten him to a pulp if they'd not dragged you off. If he had sat up and spoken, told you what you wanted to hear, would you have been able to stop? No way. You wanted to hurt him. Because he was a murdering bastard. Because he'd nearly run you over, like before; because your own father had lain rotting for two weeks in a dosshouse and you didn't even give a shit.

'Fuck it,' Rachel said aloud and the taxi driver glanced into the rear-view mirror at her, probably thinking he'd picked up a nutter. She caught his eye, gave him a look, a cold stare that she hoped would make him think twice about trying to get shot of her, and then turned to look out of the side window.

The desks in the main office were empty, as was the boss's lair in the corner. And the door to the briefing room was closed. Should she interrupt? Join in as though all was well? Or wait out here for them to finish? She put her bag on her desk, then picked it up again, but before she had a chance to move the door to the briefing room swung open and they came out. Andy first, then Pete and Mitch, Lee, Kevin and finally Her Maj, a pile of reports under one arm, phone in the other hand.

A quiet descended as people moved to their desks. Lee looked over at her and seemed to be about to speak, but Godzilla's voice cut through the air. 'Rachel.' Cold, taut. 'My office.'

Rachel complied. The boss put her folders down and shut the door, drew the blinds. Rachel's hands itched, and she felt a buzz of static in the back of her skull.

The boss stood behind her desk. She wasn't as tall as Rachel but still had the ability to make Rachel feel small just by the way she stared at her.

'Where do I start?' she said. 'With you charging at a moving car as if you're a fucking rhinoceros instead of a serving police officer? Or should that be with you diving into a road traffic incident without a second's hesitation or giving a flying fuck for your own safety?'

'Ma'am—'

'Don't ma'am me, lady. Don't you say a word, not a word, until I am done.'

Rachel swallowed, looked at her shoes.

'Force guidelines,' the boss went on, 'at any incident – safety first. Remember that, DC Bailey? Say it.'

Rachel said it.

'Drummed into every recruit, reiterated at every opportunity. There for a fucking reason,' she thundered. She had a loud voice for such a petite woman, and her face was red with exertion.

Rachel looked back to her shoes.

'I cannot imagine a situation where any officer would disregard such a basic principle of police work. One designed to protect them and their colleagues and the wider community. An unbreakable golden rule.' Thumping her fist on her palm with each phrase.

'Have you got a death wish?' She cocked her head to one side.

Rachel didn't know if she was expected to reply, but the boss carried on. 'Not satisfied with the real and present danger inherent in all our work, with the scumbags and tosspots we have to deal with, you go off like a high wire act without a safety net. Some sick thrill, is it? Or are you just suicidal? Because if that is the case you are out on your ear for the duration.'

She still hadn't got round to Rachel thumping Cottam. Rachel knew that when that was added to all the personal safety stuff the boss would probably have no choice but to discipline her.

'Your actions not only endangered yourself but put your fellow officers in harm's way. Two of them had to attend hospital, yes? Ben Cragg is livid. Would you have behaved as you did if Janet had been there? Or is it only officers that you've not worked with before that you have no loyalty to? No basic human concern for? No professional respect for?' Ducking her head as if she was pecking at the questions.

'I never meant—'

'Quiet!' she barked. 'You expect to progress to your sergeant's exam when your behaviour is that of an irresponsible child. You expect to stay in this team when you don't know the meaning of the word? If you want to be the Lone Ranger, DC Bailey, buy a mask and a pony and fuck off to the wild west, but don't do it here. Not in my syndicate, not on my watch.'

Rachel's face was burning; she could feel sweat under her arms. She couldn't bear not knowing any longer. She was obviously fucked any which way even before Godzilla got to the assault. 'Is he alive? Cottam? Please, boss? No one has told me.'

The boss laughed, a nasty, humourless sound. 'If you think that in any way mitigates your cavalier—'

'Is he alive?' Rachel shouted.

'Yes!' Godzilla matched her.

Oh, thank fuck! Rachel felt something inside fly from her. If he was alive they might get him to talk. If he talked they might save the children. And see him punished for the murders he'd committed.

'Thanks to your stupid stunt dragging him out of that vehicle and your CPR routine, his heart, which failed in the collision, restarted. He is conscious, being monitored, and we are waiting to talk to him as soon as he's anywhere close to fit.'

CPR? She had been belting the prick, not trying to start his heart. Hadn't even known his heart wasn't beating. Only that he wasn't responding.

'But that is not a trump card.' Her Maj poked a finger towards her. 'Your primary duty was to ensure your safety and that of your fellow officers and the general public. Saving Owen Cottam was way down the list. You know that. Now get out.'

'But—'

'Go write your report, hook, line and sinker, while I consider what action to take. And it won't just be down to me, I'll be taking Ben Cragg's view into account.'

'The kids?' Rachel said.

'Out!'

Rachel left.

In the main office, only Lee and Mitch were at their desks. Both of them looked up at her, though neither said anything. She broke the silence. 'The kids?'

Lee shrugged. 'Nothing in Gallows Wood,' he said. 'They may be calling it off. Appeal's gone out for the county as a whole.'

'They could be anywhere,' Mitch said. 'Andy's done the map and timeline. You've only got to look at it.'

'But he'd not much petrol,' Rachel reminded them.

'Unless he talks to us . . .' Lee said, letting the sentence hang.

Rachel sighed. Then the thought struck her. 'What did he buy?' Remembering the carrier bag clutched in one hand as Cottam had come out of the shop, wearing Mr Wesley's hat, in an attempt at disguise. 'At B&Q?'

'Rope,' Lee said. 'Nylon rope.'

Oh, God. He meant to string himself up. She rubbed at the blue plastic that had burnt her hand.

'And bin liners, heavy duty,' Lee added.

Oh, Christ. Bin liners were not good. Bin liners were bodies or body parts, they were the ghastly plastic shrouds of murder victims, the makeshift coverings for the abominations found in hastily dug woodland

235

graves or landfill sites, in skips and on wasteland. In car boots and cellars and storm drains.

As far as Rachel was concerned, the prospect for the kids had just got a whole lot bleaker.

16

Janet reached the Oldham exit, thankful that the rain was slackening off. She was close to making bargains with some higher power that she didn't even believe in: let Mum be all right and I will be good, I'll raise my kids and rub along with Ade and do my best to forget about Andy.

She'd had a message from Ade. He had arrived just in time to stop the paramedics asking the police to force entry. 'Your mum's in the Royal,' he said. 'They're assessing her, still no clue what it is. I'll wait for you here. Drive carefully.'

Oh, Ade, so steady, so thoughtful. She felt a trickle of relief in every pore. Mixed with guilt. There were times when she wanted to throttle Ade, when he was being boring, when his glumness was sucking oxygen from the air, but any crisis and he was there, completely dependable.

After finding a space in the car park and getting a ticket, she made her way to the accident and emergency department. It was a familiar place. The job brought them here at times, wanting to talk to victims who'd been attacked or suspects or witnesses. Not as much as in the days when Janet had patrolled in uniform and her night and weekend shifts were awash with drunken fights. She looked about and saw Ade just down the corridor at the drinks machine.

'Still no news,' he said. He pointed to the machine and Janet nodded.

'Water. Where was she? Did you see her? Was she conscious?'

'She was in the kitchen. I don't think she was conscious: her eyes were closed and she didn't answer any questions.'

But no blood. He hadn't mentioned blood. That was a good thing, surely?

They found seats.

'She'd not fallen downstairs, then,' Janet said. She drank some water, trying to quench the raging thirst she had. 'Did they give her oxygen, anything like that?'

'Not at the house,' he said. 'They got her into the ambulance pretty sharpish.'

Janet felt tears sting the backs of her eyes. 'Oh, Ade.'

He put his arm round her, gave her a hug.

'Do you want to go?' she said.

'No, I'll wait with you.'

'The girls?' she asked.

'I texted and explained, told them to sort out something from the freezer if we're not back.'

Janet shivered. Watched a new group arrive, a teenage boy being helped to walk by two mates, one trainer off, his foot a mess. Janet looked away. There was a young woman in a sari on her own, head bowed, every so often dabbing at her eyes with a tissue. Janet wondered if she was hurt or if she was waiting for someone: son, daughter, parent. Janet thought of Margaret Milne, could barely imagine the desolate landscape she was inhabiting. Her son and daughter, her granddaughter, all dead.

'Mr Scott?' A nurse stood there.

'Yes.' Ade cleared his throat.

'You are next of kin?'

'Janet is – my wife. She's Dorothy's daughter,' he said.

The nurse nodded. 'We've done some initial assessment and it looks like a burst appendix.'

Janet gulped. That could kill you.

'We're prepping her for theatre now but we need you to sign some consent forms.'

'Yes,' Janet said, 'of course. How is she?'

'She's very poorly, but we'll know more in theatre.'

Janet couldn't speak, just nodded her head.

'If I could go through her medical history with you, allergies, that sort of thing.' The nurse sat down and Janet answered all the questions she could, the practical task almost a distraction from the fear gnawing inside her.

She elected to wait even though the nurse could not

tell how long the operation would take, but she insisted on sending Ade home. 'There's no point in us both being here, and it'd be good to have someone with the girls. They'll be upset.'

'Ring me as soon as you hear anything,' he said.

She nodded, close to tears.

'Hey.' He bent over and hugged her.

'Thanks,' she said.

'Don't be daft.' He kissed her gently on the forehead.

She'd been mercifully unaware of anything when she'd been in here herself back in April. Lost two weeks of her life as her body concentrated on fighting the massive physical trauma of having her abdomen sliced open. Hopefully her mother's suffering had stopped when she lost consciousness. Worries prowled around Janet's mind: what if the operation failed? If her mum didn't wake up? If there were complications?

Time crept by. She was hungry but didn't want to eat; just the thought of food brought a wash of saliva into her mouth that nauseated her. She had nothing to do, nothing to read. There was a shop somewhere where she could have bought a paper or a magazine, but she didn't want to leave the waiting area in case she was missing when news finally came.

She was daydreaming, memories of a holiday with her mum and dad when the girls were small. An apartment in the south of France. There had been some little niggles between the adults, not used to different routines, but most of the time the four of them got on well enough and her mum had come into her own, speaking fluent French at the market and in the restaurants. English was her subject at school but she had kept up her French and went to conversation classes before the trip.

'Janet.' Gill sat down.

'What are you doing here?' Janet said.

Gill gave her a look: daft question. 'How is she?'

'In theatre,' Janet said, 'burst appendix.'

'Oh, God.'

'You shouldn't be here – with everything . . .'

'I can spare ten minutes for a mate,' Gill said.

Janet tried to smile. 'Thanks.'

'So what happened?'

Janet told her the story, from getting the phone call to the diagnosis that the doctors had made. 'She said yesterday she was feeling off.' She shook her head.

'You weren't to know,' Gill said. 'She obviously didn't.'

'If she'd just got it checked out.' Janet thought of her own health, how she had been ignoring whatever her body was trying to tell her. That was one promise she could make. Or a bargain. She *would* carve out the time to see the GP and get it sorted out. If it was adhesions then the sooner they were treated the better.

'And work?' Janet asked.

'You've not heard?' Gill's eyes danced.

'Nothing,' Janet said.

'We've got him,' Gill said quietly, clearly not wanting anyone to overhear. Before Janet could ask about the kids, Gill said, 'Just him. Drove his car head-on bang into a wall when he was cornered, but we got him.'

'Is he saying anything?'

'Still waiting for him to be declared fit to interview. It'll be morning at least.'

Another night. 'But the kids . . .'

'We're still searching.'

'Needle, haystack,' said Janet, suddenly angry at the impossible odds.

Gill stiffened then and Janet followed her gaze and saw Rachel at the end of the room. Rachel looking uncomfortable.

'I'll leave you to it.' Gill got up. 'Let me know, yeah?'

'I will. Thanks.'

Gill walked out past Rachel without any communication.

Rachel came and took Gill's seat. Janet saw her face and her hands, cuts and blisters and angry marks. 'What on earth happened to you?'

'How's your mum?' Rachel said, ignoring the question.

Janet told her. 'So what's going on?' she said. 'The state of you, and you and Gill?'

'She's got her knickers in a twist,' Rachel said

242

dismissively. 'You don't need to worry about it.'

'You say that and of course I'm going to worry about it. Is it serious?'

'You've got enough on your plate.'

'It *is* serious! What have you done, Rachel?'

Rachel opened her mouth as if she was about to protest and then shut it again, did some facial contortions. 'Reckless endangerment. She says I was reckless.'

'Gill?' Janet checked.

'Yeah, the Queen of Sheba – and the local officers,' she said, sounding mutinous. 'I wanted to catch the bastard. So I went for it. Then he piles into a brick wall. I'm supposed to let him lie there and go up in a fireball? Yeah, right!'

'The car was on fire?' Janet said. She could just imagine it.

'Not then, after.' Rachel shrugged. 'So I got him out and then some of the lads came and pulled us back away from the car. And *then*,' she stressed the word, 'the car blew up.'

Janet didn't know what to say.

'So I'm getting earache off Her Majesty but what everyone's forgetting is that if I hadn't got the bastard out he'd be toast and we'd have no chance at all of finding out what he's done with the kids. I saved his life.'

'And put everyone else at risk,' Janet said.

'Now you sound like her,' Rachel grumbled.

Janet began to laugh. In spite of herself, in spite of everything that was going on. Laughing with a feeling of hysteria bubbling in her chest. Laughing with tears leaking out of the sides of her eyes.

'What?' said Rachel. 'What's so funny?'

'You,' Janet said, gasping, 'you, you stupid fruit-loop. You could have been killed.' Thinking, then what would I have done? What would I do without you?

Close to ten o'clock, the doctor came to find her. Her throat closed as she tried to guess what was coming, to judge from his posture and body language whether it was good news or bad.

'The operation's been a success,' he said. 'We'll want to monitor her for a couple of days, make sure everything is as it should be.'

'She'll recover okay?'

'All being well,' he said. 'Good job she got here when she did.'

Janet nodded. 'Can I see her?'

'Just for a minute. She's in post-op – very groggy.'

Her mother looked both familiar and strange. Hair hidden under a protective cap, face slack, the wrinkles around her eyes and under her chin etched deep in the artificial light. Janet took her hand. 'Mum,' she said quietly.

Dorothy's eyelids fluttered and the blanket rose and fell as she took a full breath.

'Mum? Hello.'

Dorothy opened her eyes and gave a small smile, though the frown on her forehead deepened.

'You've had an operation,' Janet said, 'to remove your appendix. You gave us quite a scare. How do you feel?'

'I'm tired,' she said, slurring the words.

'You rest,' Janet said. 'I'll see you tomorrow.'

Her mum closed her eyes, but the frown remained. Janet gently withdrew her hand and turned to go, thanking a nurse waiting close by.

'You know your way out,' the nurse said.

'Yes. Oh, what ward will she be on?'

'Acute medical, either A or B.'

'Thanks,' Janet said.

'No worries.'

Janet made her way to the car park. Bone weary, she still had to drive the works car back to the station and pick up her own before going home. 'That's all right,' she said aloud. 'Everything's going to be all right.' And she started the engine and wound down the window so the chill on the night air would help keep her awake.

Day Four

17

Police officers had guarded Cottam's hospital bed
overnight. Gill spoke to the doctor who was treating
him, who told her that Cottam was fit to be
questioned. Given that he hadn't been wearing a seat
belt and had piled into a brick wall at forty miles an
hour, he had had a miraculous escape. The impact of
the crash had arrested his heart. Initial blood results
had been indicative of heart failure and further tests
detected arrhythmia. He might well have not been
aware of the condition, if the story of his never seeing
a GP was true.

Gill sent Lee and Mitch to make the arrest. Cottam
was moved at seven in the morning in a high security
vehicle. The custody officer had done a risk assessment
and flagged Cottam as a suicide risk. That surprised no
one. While in his cell Cottam would be visited every
fifteen minutes. His clothes and shoes had been
collected in an evidence bag at the hospital and sent
straight to the forensic science lab. One of his

shoelaces was missing; it hadn't been found yet at the retail park. At the police station he was provided with a disposable paper suit and flip-flops.

Gill made sure the family liaison officers assigned to both Margaret Milne, now staying with her daughter's friend Lynn, and Dennis and Barry Cottam were fully briefed and could inform the family of the latest development. Gill also told the FLOs that detectives would be talking again to the family to try to unearth any significance for Cottam in the Wigan area. Had he been there before, and why? A brief press release would state that police were questioning a forty-five-year-old man on suspicion of murder at an undisclosed location in Manchester.

Questioning could begin as soon as Cottam had been booked in. Gill wasn't sure yet who would begin the interview. She would have liked to use Janet but thought that Janet might well be off work with her mum in hospital. A solicitor was en route. Gill had almost everything in place by eight thirty, when Janet turned up.

'How are you?' Gill asked. She didn't look great; face puffy as if she'd not had enough sleep, no doubt awake all night fretting about her mother. But Gill knew Janet had a resilience that served her well in times of crisis.

'I'm okay,' Janet said. 'I'm better keeping busy, but I want to take an hour after lunch to visit the hospital. If that's going to be a problem—'

'It's not a problem. We've got Cottam downstairs. I can always ask Lee to take it.'

'I'll take it,' Janet said. 'Really, I'd like to.'

Gill smiled. Janet shied away from promotion whenever Gill raised the question, but she had as much ambition as anyone else in the syndicate when it came to interviews. Interviews were the nuts and bolts of the work, and Janet was highly skilled.

'Okay,' Gill said, 'if you're sure. I'll put Lee in with you.'

'What about Rachel?' Janet said.

'No,' Gill said. She wasn't sure how much Janet knew about Rachel's antics the day before but was not about to discuss it. And she certainly wasn't going to reward Rachel by letting her in on the interview. Besides, this was tricky territory and it could be muddied by Rachel's previous encounter with Owen Cottam. 'The doctor says Cottam is pretty withdrawn. It's not going to be easy getting him to talk. I think it would be good for you and Lee to sit down with the hostage negotiator to plan the approach.'

'Fine,' Janet said. 'Anything from the search?'

Gill shook her head. 'We've finished at Gallows Wood. Nothing. The vehicle was stolen in Lundfell and Cottam was finally seized at the retail park in Porlow, which is ten miles away, near Wigan. We're now patrolling the area in between and asking householders county-wide to check their premises. Can't do any more searching on foot until we know where to look.'

Once the solicitor, Hazel Pullman, arrived, Gill went through to brief her, making it clear what the grounds for arrest were and that the police were treating the situation as life threatening. Given that the preservation of life was their highest priority, the initial interviews would focus on the whereabouts of the children.

'We would appreciate your client's cooperation,' Gill said.

'Of course,' the solicitor said. 'No brainer.'

The hostage negotiator, Stephen Lambton, was a slight, balding man with a big grin and a thick Geordie accent. He met Janet and Lee in one of the small interview rooms.

'Given his need for control it's going to be a delicate balancing act. He'll be aware that he's lost control, that we've taken his liberty, and with it his ability to act. And now we're going to be asking him to give us information and he's not going to want to share it with us. It's the last vestige of control he's got, so we need to undermine that view. The conversation needs to take him to a point where he accepts that concealing the children's location no longer gives him any advantage. We need to persuade him that it's game over.'

An unfortunate turn of phrase, thought Janet.

'Our disadvantage is not knowing whether the children are still alive, but I think we can use that. What is crucial,' Stephen emphasized, 'is that we do not challenge the central tenet of his world view: that he acted in the interest of his family. If there is any hint of condemnation, anything that paints him as a villain, he'll probably switch off completely. There's an element of narcissism in this personality; the only perspective he accepts is his own. Everyone else is wrong. There is likely to be a great deal of anger and frustration that he's not achieved his objective as it is. If he sees an opportunity to vent that, then we're likely to lose him.'

Janet knew that in most situations there was a clear pattern to the interviews. Three stages. At first, encouraging the person to tell their story, at their pace, and with their choice of emphasis. Making them feel comfortable. Janet's role to listen and absorb, apparently accepting everything that was said. The second stage, moving on to develop the account, building greater details, filling in gaps. And finally, if there was a mismatch between the account and other evidence acquired (from witnesses, CCTV, forensics and so on), going through each element, laying out for the suspect each flaw, every lie, any inconsistencies, and asking them to explain. All of which depended on the person being prepared to comment in the first place.

Stephen said, 'The drive will be for him to remain master of his own narrative, to not have anyone misinterpret his actions, and that could work in our favour. Key to this is to remember he loves his family.'

* * *

Janet was surprised that her first thought on meeting Owen Cottam was that he looked a bit like Ade. If Ade were taller, fitter, fifteen years younger and had grown a moustache. He'd a similar pleasant but unremarkable face, a thickset build. Nothing extreme, no disturbing features. No mad eyes or twisted mouth to betray the killer inside him. The right side of his face was bruised and she could see little red burns about his hands and face, like the ones Rachel had.

His eyes were slightly unfocused when she said hello and he glanced at her, remote, as though he wasn't really present. She wondered where he was in his head, and what he was thinking of. The long night at the inn, the flight with his sons, the crash?

She began the formalities. 'My name is DC Janet Scott. Also present are DC Lee Broadhurst and duty solicitor Hazel Pullman. Please give me your full name and date of birth for the tape.'

'Owen Cottam,' he said quietly, 'fifth of August, 1966.'

'There are some points I need to make clear to you. You are under arrest on suspicion of the murder of Pamela Cottam, Penny Cottam and Michael Milne. And on suspicion of the attempted murder of Theo Cottam and Harry Cottam. You do not have to say anything, but it may harm your defence if you fail to mention, when questioned, something which you may later rely on in court. Anything you do say may be given in evidence. Do you understand?'

'Yes,' he said. His voice sounded dry, rusty.

'This is your opportunity to tell us what happened, Mr Cottam. Before I ask you any questions, is there anything you want to say?'

'No,' he said. The fact that he had spoken at all gave Janet some hope.

'There are several matters we will eventually wish to talk to you about, Mr Cottam. For now, I want to concentrate on where your children, Theo and Harry, are. And that is all I will be asking you about this morning. Do you understand?'

'Yes,' he said again.

There was no desk between Janet and Cottam, no furniture to his right or left. The layout of the space was deliberate, designed to make the suspect feel exposed and vulnerable. There was nothing to hide behind, no table edge to fiddle with, no table legs to kick a foot against. No barrier, no support, no prop. Nothing to focus on for displacement activity. The interviewee was spatially isolated, so that the only interaction was with the interviewer opposite.

Janet knew she had to set aside the wider picture, the crime scene photos of Cottam's victims, the acres of press coverage and speculation, the frantic hunt for the missing boys, her own troubles, and focus in on Owen Cottam. Ignore as much as possible the solicitor at his side, Lee behind her right shoulder taking notes, and the winking of the video camera. She must create a magic circle around herself and Owen Cottam. Undivided attention, endless patience, bottomless interest. Engineering it so that Cottam and what he could share was the only thing in her view, and similarly making Cottam feel that all there was in his world now was the woman opposite.

'Can you tell me where they are, your boys?'

He didn't respond and Janet let the silence play out.

'Can you tell me why you took Theo and Harry from home on Monday morning?'

He gave a half-shrug.

'We have a witness who saw you with the children later that day at ten past four when you stopped on the A570 to buy food and drink. The following morning, according to a second witness, the boys were with you when you stopped at a petrol station and were confronted. Where are they now?'

He didn't meet her eye but looked up and past her.

'Are they safe?'

'It's none of your business,' he said. A gleam of something, perhaps hatred Janet thought, in his eyes.

'It is my business,' Janet said. 'The preservation of life is my highest priority. Are Theo and Harry together?' When he said nothing, she went on, 'I think they are. I think they are together and they are waiting for you to come and get them.'

Cottam shuffled, but didn't speak. 'Your boys,' she said, 'you can't be with them. No one's with them. Will you help me find them?'

She saw slight movement, his hand tightening.

'The reason why we are here,' she said, 'my duty as a police officer, is to protect people. Your sons need protection. You can't protect them any more, you can't go to them, and I think as their father you will want to see them safe.'

He closed his eyes momentarily.

'You bought some rope yesterday,' Janet said. 'What was that for?' No answer. 'Shall I tell you what I think? I think you got the rope because you wanted to take your own life. I think you wanted to take the boys with you, too. So you'd all be together.' Janet's voice remained neutral. She could have been talking about a trip to a theme park or seats on an aeroplane rather than wholesale slaughter. But she could sense the tension mounting, see his knees pressed together, his facial muscles tighten as she described the failure of his scheme. 'Now that can't happen. You can't be together, but they still need your protection. Theo and Harry need you to tell me where they are so I can get them to safety.'

'It's too late,' he said.

Janet's stomach fell. 'Why is it too late?' she asked, wanting him to spell it out.

No reply.

'Please can you tell me what you mean by too late?'

'It's all too late,' he said, 'everything. They'll be dead.' Janet noticed the phrasing. They *will be* dead. Not they *are* dead. The syntax gave her a surge of hope.

'What happened?' she said. Having said they were dead, he should find it easier now to volunteer some details. But he was quiet for a long time.

'Perhaps it's not too late. If you help us get to Theo and Harry, we can bring them to safety.'

'Not if they're drowned you can't,' he said swiftly.

Janet looked up towards the video camera that was recording the whole interview. The word *drowned* should alert the team to avenues for the search. Lakes, canals, rivers, sewers. She remembered what Andy had said about mines and thought there might be shafts with underground water too.

'How did they drown?' she said.

He made fleeting eye contact with her, animosity plain in his expression.

'Can you tell me how they drowned?'

Again nothing.

'Can you tell me where they drowned?'

He took a slow breath in, didn't answer.

'I can't verify what you told me unless you give me some more information,' Janet said. 'If it was true then help me prove it.'

His face was impassive, and he looked away and down. Absented himself as much as he was able.

'Mr Cottam, I can't take your word for it and I'd be failing in my responsibility as a police officer if I didn't pursue this and bring your children back, even if it is too late.'

He continued to look at the floor.

'You wanted everyone to be together, your family. Is that right?'

He didn't respond but she saw his jaw twitch and his lips thin as though he'd seal them up if he could. And she saw how his fingers sought his wedding ring, no longer there – it had been confiscated with the rest of his belongings, a white band marking where it had been.

'But at the moment your boys are on their own, not with you or their mum or their big sister.'

A tremor passed over his face and she watched his Adam's apple move. She sensed he was uncomfortable and knew she had to be very careful not to alienate him. 'It might be difficult to talk about these things, Mr Cottam, but everything I have heard about you tells me you were a family man, a good father. I think a good father would want to see his family reunited. Where are they? Tell me where they are and we can get someone to go and fetch them.'

His mouth worked and she thought he was about to speak then, but instead he cleared his throat and shifted position.

'This – everything that's happened over the last three days,' Janet said, 'I don't think you wanted any-one to suffer. Am I right about that?' Silence. 'But what if the boys are suffering now? You can help us put an end to that. Will you do that? Will you help them?'

'It's too late,' he said brusquely. Then he glared at her, pent-up energy leaking out. 'Too late.'

'If that is the case,' Janet said, 'let me fetch them back. They should be with the rest of the family. This isn't what you want for them, is it?'

He didn't answer. Janet waited for a moment, then decided to deal in some hard facts. If Cottam would not speak, she would have to keep going.

'The day before yesterday you bought nappies for Theo and Harry, you bought food and drink and Calpol. What was the Calpol for? Was one of them poorly? Margaret says Theo gets earaches, is that right?'

He squirmed, that was the only word for it, and colour flushed his neck and cheeks. He did not like the new tack she was taking. Janet carried on, alert to the risk that she'd take a step too far and he'd shut down on her completely. 'That was just after eight o'clock in the morning. Theo and Harry were alive then and you were looking after them, making sure they were fed and clean. What happened after that?'

He remained silent.

'I know you left your car at Gallows Wood and I know you stole a vehicle close to there, a red Hyundai which you drove to B&Q yesterday to buy the rope and some bin bags. What were the bin bags for?'

He swallowed but didn't speak.

'You can still be a good father. A decent man. You can do this for your own father, for Pamela's mother. For your boys.'

He closed his eyes. A refusal. Janet felt a flood of

impatience, felt too hot, itchy in her skin. All of which she had to conceal. 'Talk to me,' she said simply. 'Tell me about yesterday. Where did you leave Theo and Harry?'

The silence went on and on. Janet sat, her body as relaxed as she could make it, her eyes on him.

Silence isn't golden. Not in an interview room. It's oppressive. The silence seems to gain in weight as the seconds tick by. Janet sat it out, aware of the rhythm of her breathing, the smell of Cottam's pungent male sweat reaching her. Darker and stronger than the talcum powder scent the lawyer gave off.

Janet watched Cottam and was disconcerted to see his tension gradually ease off, his hands relax. He scratched at his throat and closed his eyes. She was losing him. It was going to be a very long day.

18

Every item of interest from every path of the investigation was fed into the HOLMES database. At the click of a mouse, Gill could call up forensic details, witness statements, crime scene photographs, biographical information on any of the victims. The pool of information grew by the hour. As SIO she was the one person expected to have a complete overview. And to develop new lines of investigation as a result of studying the disparate elements.

Cottam's assertion that his children would have drowned prompted Gill to plan a new strategy for the hunt. Lundfell and the Porlow retail park were taken as two fixed points to delineate a search area of some fifty miles diameter. Until one looked at an aerial view it was hard to imagine how many stretches of open water littered the landscape. In that zone alone there was a reservoir, a river with tributaries, a canal and two lakes as well as numerous smaller meres and streams. Gill did not have unlimited resources, even given what was at stake, and could not dispatch under-water search teams to all those locations.

In consultation with the POLSA, Mark Tovey, a police search adviser, she set out to establish an order of priority. Which sites were easiest to access from a vehicle? As they had no link for Cottam to the immediate area and he had not used his phone at all, they had to assume that he had found a site by chance, spotting something as he drove, or from a road atlas (a copy had been recovered from the Mondeo and there was one listed by Mr Wesley in the contents of the Hyundai – now so much ash).

The reservoir was secured by high, locked gates and monitored by CCTV so they ruled that out. Of the two lakes one was part of a country house estate, now used as a wedding and exhibition venue and not open to the public. The other, Kittle Lake, was a popular beauty spot. The river and canal were more problematic, with multiple access points at road bridges and in Porlow country park, and webbed with a network of public footpaths and bridleways.

'At best it would be a scattergun approach,' Mark Tovey said. 'A body of water the size of that lake alone could take several days to cover. Meanwhile, if the bodies are in the river they're getting moved down-stream. We're dealing with small bodies too, so that's an additional factor to consider.'

Gill understood. 'Harder to find. I'm not interested in a PR exercise,' she said. 'I'd rather hang fire and use you wisely. And all we've got to go on is his claim that they've drowned. He's refusing to back it up with anything at all.'

'What about forensics from the cars or his clothing?' Tovey said.

'Working on it. The Hyundai's likely to give us less than we might have hoped for because of the fire. I've been promised results on the Mondeo today. Cottam's footwear and clothing are being fast-tracked now.' Gill had got the forensics lab to pull out all the stops, which meant paying extra, but if anything could tell them where he had come from to the retail park, his shoes were probably the best bet. 'Soon as I get anything on that, we'll look at this again, yes?'

He agreed.

She saw him out, then turned back to look over the map. An area of almost two thousand square miles. There have to be some clues somewhere, she thought. We've got to find them.

Everything was in the system but now it was a waiting game.

Cottam was taking his statutory break and Gill had pulled together the team for updates. 'Gallows Wood gave us nothing, except the Mondeo,' Gill said. 'No sign he even entered the wood itself. We have increased patrols and we are repeating the appeal to the public throughout the Lancashire area to look in their garages and outhouses.'

'When he took the car it was low on petrol. He didn't fill up anywhere,' Mitch said.

'That we know of,' said Kevin.

'There are only four petrol stations in the area,' Gill told them, 'and all have been visited and alerted. So, yes, it's more likely he kept his mileage low. Holed up somewhere like he did on the first night. Nevertheless, we are keeping the net wide in terms of public assistance. Today is day four, over forty-eight hours since the children were seen by Rahid. Forty-eight hours since he bought provisions. Janet's just gone three rounds with him. He's been less than cooperative, yes?'

'He's implied repeatedly that the children are dead,' Janet said, 'and that they drowned, but I'm interested in how he put it. The first time he said *They'll be dead*, and the second *Not if they're drowned*. Conditional. He was not making a definite statement.'

'It means the same thing, though,' Rachel said.

'I'm not sure,' Janet said. 'I think they might still be alive and he's stalling because he doesn't want us to find them. He doesn't want us to save them.'

'But the bin bags,' Rachel said. 'Whether he's killed them by drowning or strangled them with the missing shoelace or whatever, the bin bags point to him having something to get rid of.'

'If they are still alive he might have been planning to drown them,' Pete said. 'Drown them in the bags like you would kittens.'

'Isn't it usually sacks?' Mitch said.

'Water wouldn't fill a bin bag as quickly,' Andy agreed.

'Suppose it'd still do the job,' Rachel said, 'if you weighed it down with a brick or stones or whatever, tied it up, chucked it in. Maybe the air runs out before it fills with water. Either way the job's done and it'll take months for the bin bag to rot so no nasty surprises for a while.' Rachel pragmatic as ever, Gill thought.

'He's not worried about surprises,' Janet said. 'He's not been trying to escape detection. He didn't expect to be around much longer anyway so he's not been planning long term.'

'Okay,' Gill said, 'we're speculating. We don't know if the drowning is fact or fiction but it's all he's given us. If it is, or was, his intention and if he's remained in the area as we think, these are the places where he might accomplish it.' Andy pulled up a satellite view of the area. 'We've ruled out Lundfell Reservoir and the smaller lake at Groby Hall House. That leaves Kittle Lake in the west, the River Douglas near Wigan in the east, and the Leeds & Liverpool Canal. Several small meres in the north.'

Gill heard the various sighs and murmurs from the team as they reacted to the sheer scale of potential crime sites. 'I'm in touch with a POLSA. Until we narrow it down, I can't call out fire service search and rescue,' she said, 'but if we reach a point where we can focus our energies that's what I intend to do.'

'But the rope,' Rachel said. 'The rope must be so he could string himself up.'

'Or to tie up the bags—' Kevin began.

'No, listen,' Rachel interrupted. 'Everyone's saying that he wants to die and he wants to take the family with him. So we want trees, don't we, or something else with some height.'

Gill almost reprimanded Rachel for barging in but the point she was making was valid, so she let her continue.

'And I bet he'll want them to be together, the three of them, so he'll do it next to the kids if they're dead already, drowned or whatever. If they're alive he'll hang them with him.'

'Not easy to hang a child, not enough weight,' Mitch said. His army experience had given him a breadth of knowledge beyond that gained in the police.

'We know that; he might not,' Rachel said. 'All this talk of drowning – I think he's trying to throw us off the scent. We fart around in wet suits and the kids are in some forest somewhere. It's bollocks.'

'I'll be the judge of that, DC Bailey,' Gill said, irritated that Rachel dared to criticize her strategy. 'Janet, you and Lee go prep for your next interview. The rest of you, actions as follows: Pete talk to Dennis and Barry Cottam – any link, however slim, to the area. Rachel – same with Margaret Milne and Lynn.

Mitch, work with Andy on any sightings, timeline, CCTV, ANPR. Go.'

Rachel had been sent to ask Margaret Milne and Lynn about the location. Any ties they could think of. Pete was asking the same questions of Dennis and Barry Cottam. Rachel thought it should have been the other way round, since she had already met the Cottams and continuity was always thought to be an advantage in liaison with the families and victims. But given that Godzilla still had her on the naughty step she wasn't going to quibble.

She had briefed herself before driving over, read through Janet's report on the Margaret Milne interview, revisited what Lynn had told them.

Lynn's house was in Moston, north Manchester. A council house but in one of the better parts of the area where the tenants were more likely to be in work and some had exercised their right to buy and set up home watch schemes and the like. Red-brick semis, three bedrooms and a garden.

One of Lynn's teenage lads answered the door, nodded at her request to see Lynn, moved to fetch her, then appeared to think better of leaving Rachel on the doorstep and invited her in. She could smell pizza or something similar and her stomach growled with hunger.

Lynn, a scrawny black woman, came through from the kitchen at the back, wiping her hands on a tea towel.

'Rachel Bailey.' Rachel showed her warrant card. 'Did the family liaison officer explain?'

'Yes,' Lynn said, unsmiling. 'You want to talk to Margaret as well?'

'Please.'

'She's been trying to rest,' Lynn said. 'We'll go in here. I'll let her know.'

Rachel waited in the front room. The television was on mute, showing some chat show. Rachel had no idea what it was. She watched precious little television and never in the afternoon.

Margaret Milne looked wretched, broken. Hair flattened at one side of her head, face a sickly grey, no make-up. She shook hands with Rachel and her hand felt cool and limp as though there wasn't enough blood pumping round her veins any more.

'As you know,' Rachel began when both women were seated, 'Owen was detained yesterday.'

'There's still no news?' Margaret said slowly, her eyes painfully bright in contrast with her dull complexion and sluggish manner.

'No, I'm sorry,' Rachel said. 'Can either of you think of anywhere in Lancashire that Owen has a connection with, perhaps near Porlow, or Wigan? I've brought a map to help you see exactly where we're talking about.'

Rachel's hand stung as she unfolded the map, a large-scale one, which made it easier to see the towns, villages and natural features in the area.

'This,' she touched the map south of Lundfell, at the edge of Gallows Wood, with the wrong end of her pen, 'is where Owen's car was found. Over here,' she tapped the retail park over to the right at Porlow, 'is where he was apprehended. That's a distance of ten miles. You can see these are the main towns.' She named them: Ormskirk to the west, Wigan to the east, Skelmersdale between them, Parbold and Lundfell in the north. 'Anything?' She looked from Margaret to Lynn.

'No,' Lynn said, and Margaret shook her head.

'He was working at the pub nearly all the time,' Lynn said. 'It was hard for them to get away. They had to get cover.'

Margaret nodded. 'It wasn't like he had a social life or a gang of fellers he'd be going off with,' she said. 'You *are* still looking?' Fear trembled in her eyes. 'There *is* a search going on?'

'There is, but it's a large area and we'd be more effective if we could narrow it down,' Rachel said.

'But there might not be a link,' Lynn said. 'Owen might never have been there in his life before. That's possible, isn't it?'

'Yes,' Rachel agreed, getting ready to leave. And if that is the case, she thought privately, then we really are buggered.

She had just opened the car door when Lynn came rushing down the path. 'I've just remembered,' she said. 'When Owen took Michael fishing, I think they went somewhere over that way, going towards Liverpool. That's the right direction, isn't it? I don't know if that helps.'

'Why go all that way to fish?' Rachel said. 'Surely there's fish nearer?' She remembered kids in Langley heading off down the cut with makeshift rods. Anything they pulled out of there would be toxic, but no one bothered.

Lynn shrugged. 'I think it was one of the regulars put them on to it, went with them at first. Perhaps he had a ticket thing, the thing you need.'

'Fishing licence,' Rachel remembered from training. You could be fined for fishing without one. Bought them at the post office. 'You know who he was, the feller that took them?'

'No,' Lynn said.

'Might Margaret?'

Lynn shrugged. They went back through to the lounge, where Margaret was sitting staring into space. She hadn't moved since Rachel had left. Rachel wondered what she was thinking about, or if she'd escaped into some blank vacuum away from her sorrow. She asked her about the fishing, about a pub regular who introduced Owen and Michael to it, but Margaret just gave a small shake of her head.

From doing the house-to-house, Rachel had a clear tally of the regulars in her mind. There weren't many: the pub had been on its way out. She drove back to the

271

Larks estate. The inn was still cordoned off and a couple of CSI vans were parked on the roadside as the investigators continued to work at the scene. Floral tributes lined the grass verge.

Rachel followed one of the crescents round to the house where the birthday boy lived. He had been celebrating his thirtieth at the pub on the night of the murders. One of the last group of customers to be served by Owen Cottam.

'You've arrested him?' he said, looking concerned.

'Yes.'

'Still hard to believe.' He was shaking his head, looking for her to respond. After a murder everyone they came across wanted to go over it with them, pick apart the reasons, relive the shock of hearing, speculate on how close they'd been to the horrific event. But once the police had taken initial statements they simply didn't have time to stand around chewing the cud.

'I don't need to come in,' Rachel said. 'I wanted to ask you about Owen and Michael going fishing. If you knew of a regular at the pub who took them with him?'

'That'd be Billy,' he said. *The neighbour, the one whose dog Cottam let loose.* 'Billy Dawson. He was from Ormskirk originally – think he was in an angling club that way. He's in hospital now. Cancer.'

Rachel had no idea whether Billy knew anything about events at the inn but presumably Tessa would have had to tell him something to explain why his dog Pepper was no longer being looked after by the Cottams. And unless Billy was comatose he'd have heard about the murders from the news and the papers and the gossip swirling round the town.

Rachel rang Andy before she set off. Avoiding too much one to one with Her Maj till things blew over.

'The dog, the one from the crime scene, who's got it now?' she said.

'Not sure, hang on . . .' Before she could object she heard him say, 'Gill, where did the black Lab end up?'

'Who wants to know?' Rachel heard the boss ask.

'Rachel,' Andy said.

Rachel's heart sank. There was a clatter, then, 'Rachel?' Godzilla's voice came on.

'I might have found a connection to the area,' Rachel said, 'but I need to talk to Billy Dawson. If he asks about his dog I wondered what to tell him.'

'Neighbour's got it. Tessa,' Godzilla said and hung up. No pretence at civility. Stuff her, thought Rachel. She can't keep it up for ever. Though it felt like a life-time already. Because the boss was everything Rachel wanted to be, in the professional sphere. She led the best syndicate in Manchester. Ninety-nine per cent of the time she was solid, giving support and encourage-ment in equal measure. But when she wasn't, when she went off on one, it was fucking horrible. And it always seemed to be Rachel on the receiving end. Sometimes Rachel wondered if Her Maj was jealous, of Rachel's youth, perhaps, or of how much easier it was to progress in the twenty-first century. But then she felt a tit for thinking like that. The boss had no need to be jealous of anyone.

Billy was tucked up in his hospital bed. A ward of four. Three old blokes and a younger man who was sitting up, his eyes closed and earphones on.

With his wild white hair and full beard, Billy looked like an old seaman. Just needed a pipe and a stripy jumper. And a monkey or a parrot.

'Mr Dawson, I'm DC Bailey,' Rachel said.

'Been a naughty boy, have I?' he said. 'Got the handcuffs, have you, ossifer?'

Great! He's a joker. Rachel didn't laugh, didn't even crack a smile. *Stupid old fart.* She drew the curtains round the bed to give them a semblance of privacy. 'I want to talk to you in connection with a serious incident at Journeys Inn.' She moved the bedside chair to face him but not too close to the bed. His face straightened and he gave a stiff nod.

'Shocking,' he said. 'When you find him he wants stringing up. I'd do it for you if you're short-handed, like.'

'You used to go fishing?' Rachel said.

'That's right.' His eyes gleamed. 'Always was a good man with a rod.'

Oh, for fuck's sake. You got all sorts, Rachel knew, but she did wonder if his illness had addled his brains

274

a bit, so that he didn't know what was appropriate any more. Or was it simply that after a lifetime of taking the piss and saying everything with a nod and a salacious wink it was impossible to abandon the habit.

'And you accompanied Owen and Michael Milne sometimes?'

'I did, before all this.'

'Where did you go?'

'Kittle Lake. Lundfell Anglers have rights there. They've a few pitches round thereabouts.'

Rachel felt her heart thump. 'Thank you.' She closed her notebook.

'Is that it?' he said. 'You're not going to ask me what we caught?'

'No, I'm not.' She pulled the curtains back. 'That's all I need to know.'

Still he spoke, determined to play his game. 'I caught a whopper, naturally. Hah!' He gave a laugh, but then his tone changed as he said, 'He was a good lad, you know.'

'Owen?' Rachel was aware that not only could the other patients now hear the exchange, they could see it too. She edged closer to the bed, masking Billy from the room.

'No, Michael,' he said. 'Slow like, simple, born before his crust was done, they used to say.'

'How did he and Owen get on?'

'Fair enough,' he said.

'But they gave up the fishing?'

'They went a few times after but they didn't stick it. Not got the staying power,' he winked, 'if you get my drift.' He licked at his lips. Rachel felt like throwing up. 'Why're you interested in all that?'

'I can't say.'

'Go on,' he said, 'I can keep a secret, if you can. Strong silent type, I am.'

Gill was working her way through the latest reports when Mary Biddulph from the forensic science lab called her up. 'I'm emailing you our reports on the Ford Mondeo,' she said, 'but I wanted to tell you what we've got in person. Something that might be of use. Material from the tyre treads on the Mondeo includes a significant proportion of guano.'

'Bird-shit,' Gill said, her mind running ahead.

'Just testing. Canada geese.'

'Which gives us?'

'Open water. Bird reserve, lake, canal, river. Several sites with colonies in your area, according to my bloke at the RSPB.'

'What about his footwear?'

'Still being examined.'

Gill sighed. 'I wanted that done as a priority. That was what I asked you to do.'

'Going as fast as we can,' Mary said sharply. 'As well as the bird droppings, we have material from a number of native trees, willow, oak, beech and alder, suggestive of mixed woodland. A lot of that in your area but the willow also suggests a location close to water.'

When Rachel phoned through the news about the fishing trips, that coupled with the forensic material from the Mondeo was enough to focus attention on Kittle Lake. Gill instructed CSIs to make an initial assessment. Within twenty minutes of their reaching the lakeside, word came back that tyre tracks matching the Mondeo had been found in a shaded area of the car park used by visitors to the lake. Gill immediately got back on to Mark Tovey from POLSA and contacted the fire and rescue service to plan a search of the lake. Local uniforms were drafted in to cordon off the area.

Gill sent word to the team so everyone would be up to speed and asked Kevin to look for anything in the exhibits that might be pertinent to the new line of inquiry. She felt hopeful that they were getting closer. She did not want to dwell on the possibility that the children were already dead. Drowned in the lake. Time would tell. Time and their best efforts.

19

Janet had placed a small table at her side in the interview room. On it were a pile of photographs requisitioned from the exhibits. Some were framed. She had also asked for the family photograph album and had a selection of pictures from that at the ready.

'I'd like to show you something, Owen.'

'Mr Cottam,' he said. 'You call me Mr Cottam.' Still trying to master the situation, control what he can, thought Janet.

'Of course, Mr Cottam. Here, for the purposes of the tape, I am showing Mr Cottam a framed photograph, exhibit KL41.' She held it so it was square on to him. 'You and Theo and Harry, just after Harry was born. Tell me about this picture.'

He shook his head.

'You look very happy. Your father told us you always wanted boys. Is that right?'

'A man likes to have a son,' he said.

'Why is that?'

If she could just get him talking, keep him talking, unpick his mute resistance, she'd have a better chance of getting the crucial information they wanted.

He shrugged.

'It felt different from having Penny?' she said.

'Yes.'

'How?'

Another shrug.

'Tell me about them. Theo – what's he like?'

No answer.

'He looks like you,' she said. 'Am I right?'

He rubbed at his forehead and sat back in his seat.

'It's confusing for us,' she said. 'People say you're a good father, there looking out for your kids. Is that true?'

'Yes,' he said.

'But now your boys are on their own, no one to protect them. Doesn't that bother you?'

He looked torn between the desire to respond and the wish to conceal the facts from her.

'You can't be with them. You're stuck here. They must feel you've abandoned them.'

'No,' he said vehemently. 'No, I've not.'

'Not intentionally, but I need to make it clear to you that you will be held here and probably charged and it is almost inevitable that you will be remanded in custody. You have no chance whatsoever of getting back to them. The only way they can be reached is if you tell us where they are.'

His left fist was clenched, bumping on his chin. The tension in him was palpable.

'A good father,' Janet said. 'What would a good father do?' She put down the photograph and picked up another: Theo on a bouncy castle. He was sitting near the edge and looking at the camera. Perhaps someone had called his name. He wasn't grinning or mugging for the camera as so many children do in that situation, but his face was bright and open as though a smile might follow.

She held the photograph up, facing Cottam. 'Theo won't go to sleep on his own. One of you has to stay with him. He's just a little boy – your little boy. Please, Mr Cottam, tell me where he is.'

He was trembling, the muscles under the skin of his face flickering, but he said, 'I can't.'

'You can,' Janet said. 'Tiger, that's his nickname, isn't it?'

'Don't you—' He didn't like the intimacy. 'Don't.' Didn't like where it was taking him, she suspected.

'You can help him, you can let us fetch him and his brother back. If they're alive—'

'They're not.'

'But they are alone. You don't want that. To leave them alone.'

'It's . . . it's done,' he stammered, which made him sound less sure than he might. Was there uncertainty there? Could she exploit that?

'How do I know you're telling me the truth?'

'I am.' He turned his face to the side, pinched his moustache. Hiding his mouth, hiding the lie, Janet wondered?

'If that's the case, if Theo and Harry are dead, then why would you care about what happens now? Why not just let us recover them? You're an intelligent man.'

'No,' he said, which was no answer at all.

'I think you're letting them down.' Janet wanted to provoke a response but there was a risk that the provocation might make him refuse to answer, which would be disastrous. She said, 'If they are dead, shouldn't they be with their mum and their sister? And if they're alive surely they'll be frightened. They might be cold and hungry and thirsty. Is that how you want it to be? You know what people are saying about you? They're saying you didn't care.'

Janet heard a tiny explosion of air from his nose, a snort of derision that he tried to mask.

'People are saying you betrayed your own family.'

He stood swiftly, roaring, 'They are my kids, mine. You don't tell me what to do. You don't.' Rage made his face red, thickening the veins in his neck and on his forehead, but Janet remained calm. At least on the outside.

'Isn't it about time you accepted your responsibility for them, then? Acted like a man? Like a decent man?'

He stood for a moment, shaking, then sat without her needing to ask.

'Where are Theo and Harry? Look.' She held up a picture of Harry crawling, one that had been on the living room table at the inn and had Cottam's prints on it. Had he been looking at it while he waited to begin the killings? 'He's only eighteen months old, Harry – he's the cheeky one, into everything. He's not old enough to understand why you've left. He can't ask for help and he might be crying. Crying for you. There could be a ground frost tonight. Harry, he'll be at risk of hypothermia if he's not somewhere warm. He'll be confused. He'll be shivering. He might be thirsty, too. But he's too little to find a drink for himself. Did you leave him a drink?'

He glared at her, then away.

'Mr Cottam, I will sit here asking you these questions all day and all night for however long it takes. My duty as a police officer is to preserve life, to prevent crime. I'm committed to saving the lives of two tiny little boys who, through no fault of their own, have been abandoned. I hope Theo and Harry are still alive. I'm not prepared to accept otherwise unless you give me proof. So I will continue to act as if they *are* alive. I'm asking for your help. You can do the right thing, as a loving parent would do, and end this now. Tell me where to find them.' She sat and let the silence swell to fill the room till the pressure in the air seemed to alter, making it dense and oppressive, but still Owen Cottam sat impassive and unyielding.

* * *

282

A cordon had been erected preventing public access to Kittle Lake and a dive team from the fire and rescue service were preparing to search. Gill had spoken to Mark Tovey, who told her that the biggest problem would be limited visibility. It always was with water. The lake was not particularly deep but silt would soon cloud the water and the search would be as much a tactile as a visual exercise. They had three hours of daylight left, at best. Only enough to cover a fraction of the area. She wanted someone from her team down there, a direct conduit, able to shortcut questions if the divers found anything.

She called Rachel into her office. 'If I task you with attending the search at Kittle Lake can I trust you not to turn it into some extreme sports event? You won't try and join in? No misguided heroic stupidity?'

Rachel had the grace to flush. 'You can trust me, boss.'

'Have you completed your written report on the Porlow incident?'

'Yes, boss.'

She chewed at her lip, stared at the floor.

'Sometimes you act like you're bullet-proof, Rachel. You're not; none of us are. You saw what happened to Janet. I thought that might have taught you a lesson. Stab us and we bleed. In this job we need three hundred and sixty degrees thinking. A situation like that, there is you,' Gill demonstrated with her hands, 'and there is the suspect. You,' Gill pointed at her, 'you think in a straight line, like a dog after a rabbit. But if that dog is running through a minefield then it's boom! Pedigree Chum. Three hundred and sixty degrees; not just your target but what's either side. Who's behind you. Who has your back. You have to think of other people. Impact assessment. Risk assessment. Not there for fun or because some wanker with a set of shiny pencils wants to make life harder. There for a reason. How do I drum it into you?'

'I know, boss, I'm sorry. Have you decided what—'

'No. When I have you'll be informed.'

'Yes, boss.'

The lake was reached by a narrow track from the car park, where a sign told visitors that the fishing rights belonged to the Lundfell Angling Association and gave a phone number to ring.

Rachel met the man coordinating the search, Mark Tovey, who took her to see the tread mark which a simple cast had proved to be a match to the front nearside tyre on the Mondeo.

The extent of the lake was visible from the shore where she stood, larger than she'd expected and oval in shape. At the far end the land rose up and was covered in trees and the right bank above the car park was wooded too. But the left-hand side was bare scrubland. A path circled the water and small wooden platforms here and there marked fishing spots. A large flock of Canada geese, maybe twenty, seemed unruffled by the activity and continued to peck at the fringes of the lake and the grassland around and leave curds of greeny-brown shit everywhere. There were some sort of seagulls too, squawking away. The sky felt low. Fat grey clouds moved overhead, pushed by the wind that sent waves rippling across the surface of the water, breaking up the reflections there.

Rachel watched from the lakeside as the dive team went about their work. There were no buildings in sight, which was an added attraction if you were looking for somewhere to dispose of a body, or two. Rachel kept coming back to the bin liners. If the children had already drowned, why buy bin bags? Unless he'd drowned them in very shallow water and now had two corpses to dispose of. It only took a couple of inches, didn't it? Toddlers drowned in the garden pond, in the bath. As a beat copper, way back, Rachel had once been sent to exactly such a scene. A grandmother it was, babysitting, and the granddaughter playing in the bath. 'Two minutes,' the woman kept saying over and over, 'I was only out of the room two minutes, to answer the phone.' The phone call had been the child's mother, calling to check if everything was all right, to say night night. Away with friends at a hen party. Two minutes. And the child was dead.

Mark Tovey told Rachel it would be a slow, methodical operation, and after watching for a while longer she decided to wait in her car, out of the cold. There she'd be out of sight of the lake itself, so she asked him to come and get her if anything turned up. She spent some time working through her notebook, then phoned the funeral home. When the man answered she said, 'I spoke to you yesterday. Bailey. You quoted two thousand pounds for a basic cremation, fees and the coffin and everything. We'd like to go ahead, next Friday if you can.'

'We can do ten thirty,' he said. 'Would you want extra cars?'

'No, just one, to the crematorium.' She gave Alison's address.

She rang Alison at home, expecting to get the answerphone with it being office hours, but instead got Alison herself.

'Oh, hi, it's me,' Rachel said. 'You skiving?'

'Don't be stupid,' Alison retorted. 'Little one's been throwing up all night. Playing nurse.'

'Right, it's all sorted, set for ten thirty a week to-morrow. Car will come to yours about quarter past. Buffet after.'

'Okay,' Alison said. 'I've been trying to think if there's anyone else we need to tell.'

'Such as?' Rachel said.

'His mate Henry. Do you remember Henry?' Alison said.

'No.' The name meant nothing to Rachel.

'I don't know if he's still around.'

'What's his surname?' Rachel said.

'Don't know, he was always known as Big Henry.

286

Look, maybe Dad had an address book in his room. Is his stuff still at the B&B?'

'Not sure,' Rachel said. She'd a hazy memory of Tintwhistle saying that the B&B wanted the room clearing.

'We should find out, see what there is,' Alison said.

We again. Trying to rope Rachel in. 'I don't think there'll be anything there,' Rachel said. 'You can always tell them just to get rid.'

'Without even going through it?' Alison said.

Rachel thought of the cuttings. Her stomach twisted at the idea of Alison poring over those, where that might lead, lectures about how much he cared really and loneliness and favouritism and whatever else.

'Leave it with me,' Rachel said. 'If I find Big Henry or anyone else, I'll let you know. I just wanted to tell you about the funeral. And it's all paid for.'

'Thanks. What do I owe you?' Alison said.

Rachel told her.

'Bloody hell!'

'There's no rush,' Rachel said.

'Right, okay.'

'Got to go,' Rachel said. 'See you later.'

Her phone rang immediately. Godzilla. 'Boss?'

'Rachel. No news, I assume?'

'Nothing. They've not been in long, though,' Rachel said.

'We've soil analysis from Cottam's footwear, different make-up from that found in the Mondeo tyres.'

'Well, he had been driving around in the Hyundai, hadn't he, different places, to the retail park and that,' Rachel said.

'Swan-shit,' Godzilla barked.

'Say again.' Rachel thought she'd misheard.

'Swan-shit, shit from swans. Big white birds,' irritable still and making Rachel feel thick. 'There *are* still some traces of the geese waste, but there are also seeds from different plants which our forensic scientists tell us is likely to mean he spent time at another waterside location after he was at Kittle Lake. Can't be any more specific than that. Can you tell Mark? See what his take is on it.'

'Yes, boss. Has Janet got anywhere?'

'Not yet,' the boss said.

Rachel got out of the car and walked up to the lakeside. She was passing on Godzilla's message when a signal came from one of the team, a diver with his arm raised in the air. Rachel's pulse gave a jump and she hurried around the shore. The diver pulled off his mask and spat, then said, 'Bulky object wrapped in plastic.'

They had special equipment for retrieving anything, a hoist which they set up in the shallow water. The sling was lowered and manoeuvred around the discovery. It seemed to take for ever with the men in the water stopping every few minutes to make adjustments. Rachel wanted to scream at them to get their bloody fingers out.

'We have to take it slowly. Could be very fragile after being in the water,' Mark Tovey explained, probably sensing Rachel's impatience. 'We puncture or rip the outer layer and we could corrupt everything and destroy potential evidence.'

The bundle when it finally emerged in the dying light, trailing weeds and ropes of water, was about four foot long, roughly rotund. The covering, dull black sheeting dappled with green slime. Not a bin bag; perhaps some sort of building material?

The hoist swung the thing slowly round, still streaming water, and over the shore, where it was lowered on to a large plastic sheet designed to contain any evidence and prevent anything from leaking away into the ground. The sling was carefully removed.

Mark used a camera to document the find from all angles before taking a pair of large scissors to one end of it. Pond liner, Rachel thought; the covering was like pond liner. Mark cut along the shorter edge. Then knelt, angling the scissors, and sliced along the length of the plastic. She braced herself, trying to prepare for whatever she might see. Without looking up at any of them, in silence, Mark pulled at the plastic sheeting and peeled it back.

'Oh, fuck!' said Rachel, taking in the long, yellow teeth, the sodden, matted fur, the glimpse of bones.

Mark sat back on his heels. 'Dead dog,' he said unnecessarily.

'Alsatian, be my guess,' a diver said.

'Barking up the wrong tree there,' said the one who'd first alerted them to it. And the tension was released in an explosion of laughter.

Mark looked up at the sky. 'That's us for today, lads.'

Turning to leave, after agreeing that Mark Tovey would liaise directly with DCI Murray, Rachel realized that it was nearly full dark. Her torch was in her car so she used her phone to light the way back, almost stumbling on the uneven ground.

She wondered if there was more in the lake, if tomorrow's find would be grimmer, or if tomorrow would be as much of a dead loss as today had been.

20

'Boss.' Kevin stood at Gill's office door.

'Kevin?'

'The fishing thing.'

'No joy at the lake. Tomorrow's another day,' Gill said. Wondering if it would be a day too late – or if they were too late already.

'Yes, I got that, but the techs – they've come up with some pictures on the computer.'

'Pictures?' Gill thinking for a moment of pornography, which she got to see far too much of in her line of work.

'Snapshots, a couple from a fishing trip.' Kevin waved printed copies her way. Gill beckoned for them. Kevin passed them over. The first was an out-of-focus snap of Owen Cottam, a box of fishing tackle at his side, stooping to pick something up and looking back at the camera. A straight edge to the bank near his feet, a corner of dark water beyond.

'The date fits,' Kevin said. 'Last year, summer,

291

fishing season.' His face bright with satisfaction.

Gill swapped the photos over. The second showed Michael Milne standing, his fishing rod upright in one hand at his side, like a picture of some warrior with his spear, or a safari hunter with his blunderbuss. Behind him at some distance a road bridge.

'I think this is a canal,' Gill said quickly. 'Look, the bridge, and here, the edge is completely straight. It's not the lake.' She thought of the latest from forensics, the combination of material found on Cottam's shoes. An indication that Cottam had been at a different waterside location. This one?

'There's some numbers or something here.' She pointed to a rectangle on the brickwork of the bridge, a metal plate. 'Get this magnified, enhanced if necessary, and sent through to our contact at the waterways. We want to know where that bridge is. My money's somewhere on the Leeds & Liverpool Canal. Is Rachel back?'

'No, boss,' Kevin said.

'Okay.' Gill called Pete through and showed him the pictures. 'Cottam and Michael fishing last year, a canal. Find out if the Lundfell Angling Association have any rights on any canal and whereabouts they are.' Should she rethink the search? Hang fire on the lake and concentrate on the canal? Based on what? Two photographs and the rather generalized biological profile from Cottam's footwear? She decided to ask Mark Tovey. She needed his advice.

'Nice one, Kevin,' she said, and watched him preen with pleasure. 'There's hope for you yet.'

'I know you're up to your eyes,' Janet said, 'and now's probably the worst possible time . . .'

'What?' Gill took her glasses off. She looked as tired as Janet felt, her eyes narrow, frown lines on her forehead.

'Quick drink?'

Gill hesitated. 'Oh, go on then,' she said. 'Have to be over the road?'

'Yes, fine.' Janet wasn't going to put it off any longer. She owed it to Gill to tell her that she might need more time off, that her health was iffy. Seeing her mum had brought it home to her big time, like a shovel in the face. And there were wider repercussions. Gill might need to bring someone new into the syndicate, find someone else to interview Geoff Hastings. Janet was the most experienced interviewer on the team and Gill would want to find someone of a similar calibre to replace her, or choose one of her existing staff members to develop. Lee would be good, and Rachel was improving. But if Rachel got her sergeant's ranking she would be tangled up in all the managerial stuff that came with it.

In the pub, Janet bought a glass of white wine, turning down the offer of a bottle. She'd be driving home later. Gill stuck to cola.

'How's your mum?' she asked.

'She's fine,' Janet said. 'She's going to be okay. They want to run some more tests, but she was lucky. Another half an hour . . .' Janet shook her head. 'Out of the blue. And how're things with Sammy?'

Gill rolled her eyes. 'Spent the night with his girl-friend after telling Dave he was going to mine.'

'No!'

'I kid you not. Apparently they had a barney, Dave and Sammy, so Sammy slung his hook, then lied about it,' Gill said.

'Not everything in the garden's rosy then?' Janet knew how much Gill had resented Dave's pretending to play at happy families, in the wake of breaking up his marriage.

'I met the whore of Pendlebury.' Gill clapped her hands lightly together.

'Gill! And?' Janet said.

'Wish I hadn't.'

Janet jumped in before she could get cold feet. 'There's something I've got to tell you.'

'Okay,' Gill said slowly.

Janet had the glass in her hand, something to hold on to. She took a swallow of wine. 'I'm not well.' Her throat tightened on hearing it aloud. 'I'm sorry. They said there was a risk, after the surgery, that I'd get adhesions. Which means operating again.'

'Oh, God,' Gill said.

'And I might have to go on the sick, long term. Or even retire.'

Gill looked shocked. 'Janet. Does it hurt? When did you find out?'

'I've not seen the GP yet but I will as soon as I can. But I looked it up; it's all there. I can't control my temperature, I get fever, headaches and nausea, bloating – that's a main symptom. My digestion's gone to pot, which is making me irritable . . . oh, I don't know. I've been such a bitch at home. I'm so pissed off.'

Gill didn't say anything for a moment but there was an odd look in her eyes, as though she was weighing something up. She had a drink, then said, 'The fever – it comes on suddenly?'

'Yes.'

'You sweat at night?'

'Buckets,' Janet said.

'What about your periods?'

'Irregular. Well, non-existent at the moment,' Janet said.

'You daft cow,' Gill said.

'What?' Gill was laughing at her when she was potentially facing the end of her life as a detective, about to be pensioned off, sick. 'It's not funny,' she said angrily, feeling the heat bloom through her again and the irritation prick like thorns. 'Christ, Gill, I expected a bit of bloody sympathy.'

'It's the menopause, you daft bat,' Gill said.

'What?'

Gill held up a hand. 'Hot flushes, night sweats,'

ticking off a finger with each symptom, 'bloating, headaches, mood swings.'

Janet was stunned.

'Classic,' Gill said. 'You're going through the change. It's a bloody nightmare but a few years and you should be fine.'

'Years!'

'It varies,' Gill allowed. She lifted her glass. 'I'd still check with your GP to be on the safe side, but if I'm wrong you can sue me.'

Not adhesions? No surgery? No enforced retirement? Janet covered her eyes, embarrassed and hugely relieved, close to tears.

'You'll have to do better than that to pull a long-term sickie on me,' Gill said.

'So . . . you?'

'Got off lightly so far. Can see the light. Now . . . I hear the flooding is probably the worst. You might want to invest in rubber sheets. And then there's the depression, of course.'

'Spare me,' Janet said, feeling giddy now. A reprieve. A big, fat, bloody wonderful reprieve.

The vacuum cleaner wasn't picking up properly. Rachel did her best but there were still feathers stuck fast to the carpet when she was done. She half expected the people from the other flat to complain, but when else was she going to get a chance to hoover? Six a.m. wouldn't be any better. It was going on for eleven and she couldn't settle. She tried channel-hopping then switched the TV off and got a book she'd been reading, an American true crime tome about the development of forensics, but she couldn't concentrate on that either.

'Fuck it!' she said aloud, and decided she had to get out. It took exactly twenty minutes for her to shower, throw on some slap, get dressed. The taxi took another five minutes and she was at the bar before midnight, ordering a vodka tonic. It was busier than she had expected and the people who'd been there longer were partying now, some of them rowdy. It was a club that the police knew and used, so it was unlikely that any-thing much would kick off bar a fist fight between two coppers shagging the same woman. Or man. There was always a lot of shagging around in the police service, whether because of being thrown together in sometimes dangerous situations, or being in one big gang, or something to do with the effect of wearing uniforms, Rachel had no idea. She wasn't here looking for an affair, not even a one-night stand, but a bit of attention, a bit of company, a bit of a laugh would hit the spot.

His name was Graham or Greg and he worked in IT, he said. Which could mean anything. She was about to get her second drink and he'd come to the bar, just behind her, making eye contact in the mirror and then asking if she was on her own and could he buy her a drink. He was Welsh, from Cardiff, and a few times she had to ask him to repeat himself so she could work out what he was saying. He was attractive in a sort of baby-faced way, with puppy-dog eyes and tousled hair. Rachel told him she worked in personnel. No need to confuse matters with her real identity. He was in Manchester for a conference at Manchester Central. It was hard to hear him above the music and when he suggested a dance she was happy to oblige. The drinks kept coming, the tunes kept playing. Rachel let the noise fill her head, let the dancing loosen her limbs and make her breathless, ignoring the ache in her battered muscles.

Graham or Greg leant in close and asked if she'd like to get some air. Not particularly, she thought, but a fag'd be good. She nodded and they set off for the exit, and he caught her arm and gestured. Her coat, she was forgetting her coat.

Her ears were ringing and the air was cold but dry outside. 'I'm only just round the corner,' he said, 'if you fancy?'

Rachel began to laugh, which made lighting her cigarette very difficult.

'Here.' He took her lighter from her, used it and handed it back. 'What's happened there?' he said. 'Your hands?'

'Skating,' Rachel said. *On thin ice.*

He raised his eyebrows. 'What d'you reckon then?' he said.

'All right,' she said.

The street was cobbled, which made walking particularly challenging, but he took her arm and they made it to his hotel without her breaking her neck.

He kissed her in the lift, his breath coming quickly, groaning when they reached his floor and he had to stop.

His room was at the front, looking out over the city centre. Rachel had a sudden, sickening flashback to Nick's flat, not far from here, and her at the window gazing out at the lights, him nuzzling her neck and begging her to come back to bed.

Rachel swung round and almost fell over. 'Whoops!'

'Steady, man, you'd better sit down,' Greg or Graham said.

'You got a minibar?' Rachel said.

'Sure. What's your poison?'

'Brandy,' she told him. She sat on the edge of the bed, pulled off her shoes. Watched him fix the drinks. He brought hers over. Took off his shoes and jacket. Joined her on the bed. Kissed her again, one hand going round her back, the other stroking her breast. Rachel felt a rush of excitement, imagined him on her, inside her. She felt for his crotch, felt him hard.

She pulled back. 'One minute.' She went to the bathroom and emptied her bladder. Looked in the mirror, grinning to herself, and feeling dizzy, wanton. Savouring the sensation.

'All right, kid?' Her father, in the mirror, grinning back, happy-drunk, a rollie in one hand, can in the other.

'Fuck off!' she said, the room tilting.

'You okay in there?' called What's-his-face.

Rachel closed her eyes but that made her feel worse. 'You will not fucking ruin this,' she told her father. 'You ruined everything else, well you can fuck off back to the mortuary.' She ran cold water over her hands, pressed them to her cheeks. Went back out.

'You were swearing,' Taffy said.

'Stubbed my toe,' Rachel said. And then it came over her, like a wave, sadness as if someone had snapped the lights off, stopped the music. Filling her mouth and throat, her belly. Even as he held his hand out to her, his shirt open, belt gone.

I can't, she thought, I can't. 'I'm sorry. I can't— I've got to go.'

'Aw, no, man!' he said. She wondered if it was a Welsh thing, the *man*, or if he was trying to be down with the kids (though round these parts they all said bro or bruv these days), or if his parents had been New Agers. 'What've I done?'

'Not you, sorry, not you,' Rachel said. 'Just a bad idea.'

He looked crestfallen, sat and sighed. 'Get you a cab,' he said.

A good bloke. She was surprised, had anticipated nasty words, *prickteaser*, *slapper*, maybe something physical.

'Reception'll get me one.'

He gave a little nod.

She pulled on her shoes, the earlier elation now a sour sort of misery, an ache in her guts.

'Take care then,' he said at the door, with no hint of hostility. Somehow it made her even sadder. It might have been easier if he'd bitched about being led on, let down. His understanding made her feel even lousier. Not only was she fucked off with her wastrel of a father and her posh knob of an ex-boyfriend but now she felt guilty for messing the Welsh bloke about.

She felt sober and sick when she got home but she was still stumbling about. She threw up in the lavatory, drank a pint of water with some painkillers. In bed the room swayed and there was a drone buzzing in her ears, but eventually she slept.

She dreamt of the lake, her bed floating on the lake and a dog barking at the water's edge and her father fishing. She was looking for something but could not remember what it was. She knew that something terrible would happen if she didn't find it but how could she find it if she didn't know what it was? She kept pulling at the duvet and the sheet as the bed spun round and round, searching, hunting for a clue, anything to help her recall what was lost. But there was nothing there, just her bed turning and the wide black water.

Day Five

Day Five

21

Chris had spent the night at Gill's again. Which meant she got even less sleep. It was his last night. He was moving on to spend the rest of his leave with friends who lived on Skye.

'Oh, whisky and peat fires,' she said, 'windswept beaches. Take me with you.'

Before they'd gone to bed, she'd talked to him over a ridiculously late dinner about the deadlock in the case. 'Janet's the best we've got, but he's withholding. It's the only power he's got left.'

'Do you think he'd be any different with a male interviewer?'

'No, or perhaps even more entrenched if that was possible,' Gill said.

'What's the psychologist say?'

'Same old. Be polite, stay calm, we're playing all the right strokes.'

'Can he keep it up indefinitely?' Chris said.

'I don't know. I think the way she's appealing to him

as a man with a moral code, acting as though he's still responsible for the family, I think that's right. And I think if anything will break through the barrier that will, but so far – nowt.' Gill shook her head.

She didn't talk to Chris about Sammy, preferred to keep that quiet. Of course, Chris knew Sammy had moved to Dave's and that Gill had been dismayed when he left so suddenly. But she didn't want to share the latest developments, especially given the implicit criticism of their relationship by Dave, which was being aped by her son.

Chris got up in the morning when she did, wanting to start his journey north while the roads were quiet. She kissed him goodbye outside the house. It was still dark, the sky just beginning to lighten in the east, the air still and misty and everything drenched with dew.

'It was great,' she said, 'even though I was at work most of the time.'

'Quality,' he said. 'Good luck with it all.' He kissed her again. She had to stand on tiptoe to reach him.

'Do you know where you'll be next?' she asked him.

'No idea. Soon as I do I'll let you know.'

Gill felt a pang; she'd miss him. It could be weeks before they'd have a chance to meet again, especially if his next case was far from Manchester.

'One for the road.' He smiled. She could see his breath, a mist in the cold of the morning.

They kissed, a kiss to remember, one to savour. At last she drew away, said goodbye and got into her car.

He followed her over the edge of the moors and down the hill to the main road, where they went their different ways.

And Gill wondered, as she did each time he left, if she would ever see him again.

It had been agreed the previous evening that while the search continued at Kittle Lake, an initial assessment visit would be made to the canal to consider the best approach to a search there. Rachel was due to meet Mark Tovey on site first thing.

Rachel suspected Her Maj was keeping her away from Cottam, away from the heart of the inquiry, but if that meant getting out into the field looking for some clue, something, anything, to lead them to the missing kids, then that was fine by Rachel. Way better than sitting on her arse wallowing in reports, which she might have been told to do.

Fog was forecast and Rachel set off early in case of delays. Idiots piling into each other on the motorway, ignoring the hazard warning signs, FOG SLOW DOWN. Still going at seventy and then bleating when it all went tits up. If they'd still breath to bleat with.

Her hands were scabbing over but any time she did anything the skin opened again, and she needed to use her hands for practically everything. The itching sensation was worse and her shoulders and knees and ribcage ached from the impact of slamming into the ground when she was trying to stop Owen Cottam.

She'd dosed herself up with painkillers and coffee to deal with that and the residue of a hangover which lingered at the back of her skull as though someone had cuffed her too hard on the head.

The good news was that the bridge had been identified as Dobrun Lane on the Leeds & Liverpool canal between Wigan and Lundfell. The bad news was that the local angling association had fishing rights on extensive stretches of the canal and there were many other access points to the waterway in the area. A snapshot of Michael Milne and Owen Cottam's reference to drowning were the only tenuous links to miles of water.

Rachel arrived half an hour early and parked as directed on a rough patch of land shy of the Dobrun Lane bridge. The site of a pub in times past, now razed to the ground.

She had brought maps of the area with her. North of the bridge there was a scattering of houses and farms on either side of the canal, the properties few and far between. To the south it was mostly farmland.

It was cold sitting in the car and Rachel did not want to put the heater on and risk the battery. She decided to make use of the time by having a walk along the canal. She took a torch with her, as it was still dark. She did not want to end up in the drink herself.

Sound was distorted, she noticed, as she walked up to the bridge: her footsteps were harsh against the gravel but sounds beyond that, birds and a distant motor, were muffled. She took the steps down to the towpath carefully. They looked worn, wet and slippery in the light from her torch. Once she was on the path she lit a cigarette and smoked as she walked along. The fog, thick yellow-grey, smothered the place.

Dead or alive? If the Cottam boys were dead, the police would have to try to find and recover the bodies. From the water somewhere if he'd drowned them. She didn't know much about canals but she did get that they were still water so there was a limit to how far the bodies would travel with no currents or tide to move them further afield. Finding them in the canal should be relatively easy, then, if they only knew which part to look in. If they'd been killed some other way, strangled or suffocated, then buried, they could be in any of the surrounding fields or woods. And if they were still alive they must be contained somewhere.

Rachel heard a splash by the bank, but no other noises followed. She swung her torch over the water but could barely make out the surface through the fog, let alone see anything else.

She retraced her line of thought. Alive equalled contained because you couldn't just leave little kids somewhere; they'd wander off. That's why people had playpens, used reins. So they had to be inside somewhere, shut in, or tied up. Another car perhaps, or an abandoned building: an outhouse, or a shed or a garage. Farms, like the ones on the map, would have loads of hiding places. Rachel thought back to Grainger, the geese, his miserable bugger-off attitude.

She imagined most of the landowners in the area would have made a search of any obvious places after the first appeal to do that was made. But since? Would they have repeated that search? Because there was every chance that Cottam had found somewhere to conceal the kids in the meantime. If Mark Tovey did agree to work up a strategy for this area, Rachel would chuck that in. Make sure that any appeals stressed the need for people to look again.

Light began to spread over the land and the fog seemed to rise from the ground in ragged shreds like some special effect from a horror movie, though it stayed hovering close to the water. Soon she could switch off her torch.

A row of houses on the opposite bank had gardens that reached the water's edge, but there was no towpath on that side so they wouldn't be easy to access for a stranger. That made her wonder how far he could walk with the children. A fair way, she assumed. He was a strong man; with one on piggyback and one in his arms he'd not be particularly hampered. Though he would be conspicuous and that might limit how far he'd travel on foot.

She decided to continue to the next bridge, which she could just make out, a smudge on the horizon, and then retrace her steps to the rendezvous with Mark.

The world was beginning to stir, traffic zipping inter-mittently along the narrow road over the Dobrun Lane bridge behind her. The side of the path was thick with brambles and tall weeds, gone to seed most of them, dried out now, shrivelled and wispy. It wouldn't be hard to conceal bodies in there. Though dogs being walked along the canal would soon sniff them out. But if they were right about his motivation, Owen Cottam wasn't a murderer who wanted to escape detection and run free. All he'd wanted in his manoeuvres over these last days was to buy himself time to complete his plan – the mortal destruction of his family and himself.

Rachel carried on, walking more briskly now she could see the way. A pair of ducks at the far side of the water made quacking sounds and drifted in and out of the mist, dipping their heads down now and again. She looked ahead to the bridge. There'd been less traffic crossing this one, only a couple of cars. Betty Lane the road was called, according to the map, one of a warren of small lanes that ran by the farms and up to the B road.

Beyond the humped shape of the bridge, she could see some low-lying structure: huge horizontal bars, black and white, and railings. She glanced down at the map: a lock. The canal was littered with them. She walked under the bridge where it was dank and smelled of earth and the stones glistened wet, and up to the lock.

Here the canal banks widened a little then narrowed

again for the lock itself. The black and white paddles, a pair at either end, were attached to the great lock gates. The paddles were used to swing back the wooden gates. She'd a dim memory of doing it in primary school. Sections of the canals had been built at different levels, and the locks were the way of transporting boats from one stretch to the next. The boat would enter through the first set of gates, which would be closed behind them, and then underwater sluices would be opened to allow water to flow in, or out, and raise or lower the craft. When it reached the correct level the second set of gates would be opened and the boat would be able to resume its journey.

At the edge of the lock she stared down into the chamber. The walls were covered in green mould and streaks of orange. With the huge gates at either end they formed a great box, water in the bottom. A long drop. The notion hit her like a punch, made her guts burn. The rope. To hang himself. She looked at the backs of her hands, at the biggest blister where the blue plastic had fused to her skin. He'd need a long drop to do it. Somewhere like this would work just as well as the woods, better really, since you'd not have to scale a tree. All sorts of places to attach the rope to, here. Okay, he might not be completely free hanging, might hit the walls, feet scrabbling for purchase, but most hangings it was the drop that killed you, the sudden wrench as you reached the end of the rope, which broke your neck and severed your spinal cord.

When it went wrong, when the body was too light or the drop not far enough, quick enough, then the person strangled slowly.

Rachel's heart was hammering in her chest, racing, and there was a buzzing in her ears. She scanned the land beyond the verge: no dwellings close by. Looking ahead, further down the canal, just before a bend, she made out an old barge, the first she'd seen.

Boats. Somewhere else to search along with the farms and sheds. Another angle to cover. Unless Cottam opened up to Janet and saved them all the aggro. Rachel wondered if there were more boats parked further round the corner. Parked wasn't right. Moored, that's what they called it. There was still a pall of fog suspended over the water as she went on to look.

A ripple of dark shadow on the path ahead brought her up short. A rat, sleek and silent, slid over the edge of the bank and disappeared. Rachel swallowed and walked on. Something dark and fearful growing inside her. Just a rat, she told herself, millions of them all around, everywhere. Knowing that the fear wasn't from the rat. She saw the lock gates, she saw Owen Cottam and his rope. And the bin bags. Why the bin bags?

By the time she reached the barge, she could see round the bend. There were no other boats there. Just this one. Ancient by the looks of it. Rotting into the water.

A car slowed and stopped in the distance; perhaps Mark Tovey arriving for the meeting? Above her there was a strange sound which had her ducking instinctively. Making her temples thud with pain. A cormorant, large and black, soared overhead, the beat of wings loud and powerful in the still air.

The barge was desiccated. It had once been black but most of the paint had peeled away and bare wood showed through silvery grey. Fragments of pink and green lettering decorated the prow. Some sort of fungus, a canker, sprouted lumps of ginger here and there. The cabin was partly covered by an old tarpaulin, faded and ripped in parts. The roof, splashed with bird-shit, dipped in the centre where a mush of skeletal leaves was trapped. Shuttered windows were thick with cobwebs. No flowers or fancy watering cans or signs of habitation. At the back, where the door was, lay a number of old plastic containers, cracked and dappled green with mould. Rachel looked at the door, rickety as everything else, crumbling. An old padlock hasp secured with—

Gorge rose in her throat and her knees went weak. There. A scrap of black cord. A shoelace.

The world shrank around her. The canal, the farms beyond, the lock and the road bridge faded as she focused on the boat, the door.

The boat rocked alarmingly when Rachel clambered on board. Water pooled on the deck underfoot. With trembling fingers she worked at the knot, her nails slipping and the scars on her fingertips starting to bleed. Finally it came loose and she pulled the shoelace free and opened the narrow double doors, which made a squealing sound.

The interior was pitch dark, only the small flight of steps leading down into the cabin illuminated by the daylight. She could barely see a thing,

But she could smell. The brackish odour of the canal and the mushroom scent of decay, mixed with the high acrid stink of shit. Her chest tightened. There was a thudding in her temples as she switched on her torch and climbed down the steps, one hand braced on the edge of the door. When she stepped into the cabin the boat rolled in the water, the timbers creaking and moaning. Rachel played the cone of light over the space, picked out bench seats with their torn and faded foam cushions furred with white mould, tattered curtains spotted with mildew, and then, on the floor, a tartan blanket and next to it two small forms, pale-faced and utterly still.

Oh, fuck. Something dark and cold crawled up her spine. The torch juddered in her hand. Her eyes hurt. The stench caught at the back of her throat and she retched but fought the reflex. She stepped closer and the boat lurched. Rachel almost fell, flinging her arms out for balance. She knelt down. The floor was wet, soaking through her trousers.

Struggling to breathe, she bent over the boys. Theo in his tiger pyjamas, the garments grubby, smeared with marks, was curled towards his brother. Harry lay flat on his back, one arm above his head, his legs splayed outwards. Shit had soaked through his all-in-one, staining the legs toffee brown. Tear tracks had dried leaving salty trails on his cheeks. The only movement came from the boat rocking on the cold water.

Rachel reached out a hand and touched Theo's neck to see whether rigor mortis had set in. Knew that if it had the child's body would feel dense, leaden, every muscle rigid as wood. And cool. She placed her fingers across his neck, below his ear. Felt the faintest residue of warmth there. So close! If they'd only searched here yesterday instead of the lake.

She felt her throat clench and tears burn behind her eyes. 'Fuck it!' she said aloud. Theo's eyes fluttered open. 'Daddy?' he said huskily. Beside him Harry startled, his arms jolting as though something had bitten him, and began to wail, a thin, reedy, faltering sound that drilled into Rachel's head.

She jerked back, gasping for air, frantically hitting keys on her phone, summoning help. The child's cry filling her head and Theo's plea scalding her heart. *Daddy? Daddy? Daddy?*

22

Janet was about to go in to interview Owen Cottam when Gill appeared, her eyes shining, fizzing with energy. 'We've got the boys. Alive!'

'Oh, God!' Janet stared at her. 'Where?'

'A barge on the canal. Rachel found them.'

'Alive?' Janet checked. *After all this time.*

'Dehydrated, hypothermic, dosed up with paracetamol but they should be fine. Taken to Manchester Children's Hospital.'

Janet swallowed. 'So now what? You don't want me to interview yet?'

'No. Give me an hour. I'm going to see the CPS to run through what we've already got. Wait till I'm back and we'll discuss it then. Might let us go straight to charges.'

'Be better to see if we can get a confession to the murders first,' Janet said. Then she thought that if they did move on to questioning Cottam about the murders it might be hard for her to get away later.

So she said, 'Is it okay if I nip to the hospital now?'

'No problem,' Gill said.

Dorothy was sitting up in bed and looking almost normal.

'The scan they did, well, apparently they found a growth on my uterus,' she said.

Janet's stomach contracted. 'Oh, Mum.'

'No, listen. They're pretty sure it's just a cyst but the womb's enlarged so they think, at my age, it's best to take the whole lot out.'

'Hysterectomy?'

'Yes. It's a big op. Take me a few months to get back to normal.'

'You'll stay with us,' Janet said.

'If you'll have me,' her mum said.

'Course we'll have you. You got any better offers?' Again that wash of relief, that she was sitting here joking with her mum instead of grieving.

'Not yet, but I'll let you know if I do,' Dorothy said, a gleam of merriment in her eye.

When Janet got back to the station, she saw Rachel in her smoking spot, clutching a large coffee. Janet went over. 'Hey, well done you. Amazing.'

Rachel looked peaky, her face drained of colour, her lips pale.

'You're a hero,' Janet said. 'Wait till word gets out.'

'I don't want to be a hero.'

'Why not? Looks good on the old CV.'

Rachel looked away and released a trail of smoke. 'I thought they were dead,' she said flatly. She bit her lip, blinked.

Janet wasn't sure what to say, what Rachel needed from her. 'A shock?' she ventured. It wasn't like Rachel to get bound up in a case, to let it get to her like this. True for all of them, really. To do the work well you needed resilience, a way of detaching yourself so that you could concentrate on the facts of the investigation and not get damaged emotionally. Of course some cases were harder, poignant or downright sad, especially those involving kids, but Janet had never seen Rachel respond like this. If anything she demonstrated a lack of empathy verging on the autistic.

Janet felt a wave of concern for her friend. Something felt wrong. Had done for days. It would be simple to turn a blind eye, gloss it over, pretend all was well, but Janet wouldn't let herself take the easy option.

'What's really going on?' she said directly.

'What d'you mean?' Rachel scowled at her.

'We're supposed to be mates,' Janet said. 'Talk to me.'

'What about?' Rachel said scornfully. 'There's nothing to say.' She dropped her cigarette, crushed it underfoot. Irritation flickered through Janet, and she was tempted to tell her to pick the tab end up and bin it. Have some consideration for once. But she resisted getting sidetracked.

'Look, it's not just this case or those little boys. I don't know if it's to do with Nick Savage or—'

'Not that again,' Rachel said.

'You tell me,' Janet said. 'What's the point of being mates if it's a one-way street? If I'm the only one putting the effort in.'

'You tell me,' Rachel echoed. Her face set, mutinous.

Janet wanted to clout her, or hug her. Instead she said, 'You shut me out. I know there's something up and you won't talk to me about it. Don't you trust me? Do you think I'll go running to Gill, telling tales?'

Rachel put her hand up to her head, clutched her ponytail, closed her eyes. 'I'm fine,' she said.

'You're not fine,' Janet said crossly. 'You're a long way from fine. And I don't know how to help because you won't let me in.' She felt close to tears. *Bloody hormones.* 'Have you done something stupid, is that it?'

'Oh, thanks!'

'Well, I don't know, do I? Unless you tell me, I'm imagining all sorts. It's like dealing with a bloody teenager.'

'Yeah, you're imagining all sorts, and that's all it is – your imagination. I'm not telling you anything because there's nothing to tell.'

Whatever was going on, and Janet was even more

convinced there *was* something going on, she could see that Rachel was not going to tell her. The friendship had boundaries, limits, set by Rachel, and Janet either put up with that or walked away. Rachel was proud and stubborn and Janet knew she would not bend. For all her flaws and fuck-ups, Rachel was too big a part of Janet's life to lose. Janet resigned herself. Let the frustration leak away. Drew her coat tighter and closed her collar.

'Have it your own way, then,' she said.

Rachel raised her drink. Janet saw that her hand was shaking. 'When did you last eat?' she said.

Rachel didn't answer, just shook her head with impatience.

'Right,' Janet said decisively. 'When we're done tonight, we'll go out. Italian, yeah? Break from all this.'

'I don't need—'

'Maybe I do,' Janet said. 'Not exactly been a cake-walk for me, this last couple of days, my mum and all.' Pulling a bit of a guilt trip.

Rachel opened her mouth. Janet expected her to refuse, but then something softened in her eyes and she gave a nod. 'Sorry. Okay, you're on.'

When Rachel walked into the briefing room, everyone applauded, Gill included. Rachel looked taken aback at first, as if it was a practical joke that couldn't be trusted rather than a genuine and spontaneous response to her success. Then she relaxed and sketched a half-bow but held her hand up too, asking them to stop.

It struck Gill that Rachel's success had been a solo number yet again. Through circumstance perhaps, rather than Rachel's heading out alone with a mission in mind, but it was a familiar pattern. On the one hand, Gill valued her DC's flair, her passion and tenacity, the drive that led her to be out on that canal before dawn. But on the other, she worried that results like this undermined her efforts to get Rachel to improve her teamwork skills.

'Well done, Rachel,' she said, as the clapping died down. 'The press office want to see you after this.'

'Poster girl!' Kevin said.

'No way,' Rachel said quickly, then visibly flinched as she heard herself refusing to do something. Disrespecting Gill.

'I think you'll find that's *yes ma'am, three bags full, ma'am*. Clear?' Gill said crisply.

'Yes, ma'am,' Rachel was quick to answer, some colour in her face now.

'Oh, and both Margaret Milne and Dennis Cottam want to thank you in person.'

Rachel closed her eyes. It didn't look as though that idea appealed either.

'Doesn't have to be now,' Gill said. 'Let the dust settle, wait until the children are given the all clear. Right – we have a lot to get through. Forensics from the barge show Cottam's fingerprints all over and on the pack of nappies and the Calpol from the filling station. Items we can link to him. Another few hours without fluids and the children would have died. CPS have read the triple murder case file and believe we have strong enough evidence to warrant charges, but we've not yet spoken to Mr Cottam about the murders so we have agreed to do that and see how he plays it. A confession would be nice.'

'He's not given us anything yet,' Pete said.

'True,' Gill agreed, 'but now we've found the boys and prevented their deaths he may feel he's nothing left to lose. Lee?'

'Yes,' Lee said, 'though he might refuse to cooperate if our success makes him angry.'

'Timeline, forensics and crime scene reports all hang together,' Gill said. She talked them through the evidence on the electronic whiteboard. 'CCTV from Journeys Inn. Eleven forty our last sighting of Pamela and Michael. Eleven fifty-two – Pamela texts Lynn. No activity on anyone's phone or computer after that. Three ten a.m.' Gill indicated the time in the frame. 'Last sighting of Owen Cottam on CCTV with a whisky bottle. CCTV then switched off. Blood spatter analysis and analysis of blood samples on the victims and at the crime scenes confirms the order of attack. Pamela, then Penny, last Michael. Knife with finger-print evidence from Owen Cottam and blood from Michael also carries blood traces from the previous two victims. Microscopic traces recovered from Owen Cottam's jeans and top link to Michael and to Penny. At six thirty a.m., Cottam was spoken to by Tessa returning the dog. Six forty-five car seen leaving by neighbour Grainger. Subsequent movements we know from the investigation into the missing children, though we still have some gaps. Updates on inquiries so far. The marriage? Either of them shagging around?'

'Nothing,' Andy said. 'Not a whisper. Her phone, the computer, friends and acquaintances. They were squeaky clean.'

'No evidence of domestic violence, no rumours either,' said Mitch.

'And the children?' Gill said.

'No concerns,' said Lee. 'Penny was thriving at school, health visitor never had any worries about the younger ones.'

'Happy families,' Gill said. 'So our motive remains financial. Did Pamela know the situation?'

'According to Lynn,' Janet said, 'she knew things were tight but that's all.'

'He kept spending,' Pete pointed out. 'He dealt with all their finances.'

'Didn't she have her own bank account?' Rachel said, sounding horrified.

'She did,' Pete said, 'but it was peanuts. Only thing going in was her child benefit and she used that to clear her credit card when she'd bought something. All the bills, the direct debits, are on his account. He'd several credit cards and taken out payday loans. He wasn't profligate . . .'

Gill noticed Kevin blink, not familiar with the word.

'. . . just living beyond his means.'

'And he can hide the debts from her,' Gill said, 'until he gets word that the brewery are pulling the plug.' She paused a moment. 'How long before the murders was that?'

'Nine days,' Kevin said.

Nine days. Gill wondered at what point in that period his idea of a way out had come to Cottam. And how long till it had crystallized into a plan? Had he counted down to that Sunday night, choosing it for some reason known only to him, or had the decision been made on the day itself? Some comment of Pamela's or a remark from one of the customers the spark that lit the fuse.

'Okay,' she said, 'any loose ends, any callbacks you need to do, try and get them cleared. I'd like to hope we can press charges later today, and the more comprehensive our case file is the better.'

Gill concluded the briefing and asked Rachel to stay behind a moment. When they were alone she said, 'I've persuaded Ben Cragg that your actions at the retail park were as a result of over-enthusiasm and, given that both of his officers are expected to return to work without any problems, he's willing to accept that.'

Rachel dipped her chin in acknowledgement.

'But you came close, Rachel. No one wants to work

with you if you're a liability. This lot tolerate you, just about, but word gets out you're impulsive, thoughtless, that you're a potential booby trap, and it could derail your career. You understand?'

'Yes, boss.'

'I'd rather not have this conversation again. Got it?'

'Yes, boss.'

Why am I not convinced, Gill thought as Rachel left. Why am I really not convinced?

Janet faced Owen Cottam and took a steady breath in and out. He looked blank, absent, his unfocused gaze directed at the far wall over Janet's shoulder.

'Mr Cottam,' she said, 'I have some news for you.'

His eyes wandered to her, though his eyelids were low, wary.

'I'm pleased to say that we have found Theo and Harry and they are safe and responding well to medical treatment.'

'You're lying!' he burst out.

'No. I don't tell lies. That wouldn't get us anywhere. I only tell you the truth and I would like you to tell me the truth.'

'Where, then?' he said, his voice agitated. 'Where were they?'

'In a canal barge on the Leeds & Liverpool canal near the lock at Betty Lane bridge.'

A spasm flickered across the lower part of his face as the hard fact of the matter hit home.

You would have let them starve, Janet thought, die from thirst and hypothermia rather than give us the location. Die like trapped animals, helpless. She waited until the moment's antagonism she felt subsided, then said, 'In our earlier interviews, I've been asking you about the boys, trying to establish where they were, but now I want to move on to talk to you about the murders of your wife, Pamela, your daughter Penny and your brother-in-law Michael at Journeys Inn on Monday the tenth of October. Do you understand, Mr Cottam?'

'Yes,' he said.

'Can you tell me what happened, Mr Cottam?'

He swung his head, closed his eyes.

'When did you last see your wife Pamela?' Janet said.

His eyes remained shut.

Janet said, 'Please – open your eyes.'

He complied.

'When police entered the premises, Pamela was found, fatally injured, dead in bed. What can you tell me about that?'

'Nothing,' he said, with little inflection.

'Do you know how she died?'

He shook his head, touched the tips of his fingers to his moustache and pressed.

'Can you answer out loud?' Janet said. 'We need it for the recording.'

He let his hands fall. 'Don't know,' he said, a weak response but not an outright denial.

'Penny was in her bedroom. She was dead, too. How did that happen?'

'Don't know,' he said again, strain twisting his features.

'A knife was recovered from a third bedroom, Michael's bedroom. A knife consistent with the weapon used on the victims. This knife carried traces of blood from Michael and both Penny and Pamela. And this knife had your fingerprints on it. Can you explain that to me?'

'No,' he said tightly. Janet could hear that his breathing had altered, the pattern faster and ragged. He'd begun to sweat, a sheen on his forehead, and a drop ran down the side of his face, past his ear and under his chin. The sharp smell of him was rancid in the room.

'Mr Cottam, your clothes were taken for examination on your admission to hospital. We have found traces of blood from Penny and Michael on them. How did that blood get on to your clothing?'

'I don't know,' he said.

'That evidence suggests that you were present at the scene when the murders were committed or afterwards. How do you account for that?'

He was silent. He lifted his head to the ceiling, the pulse in his neck jumping again and again. Sweat, in rivulets now, snaked down his face. He made a noise in his throat, a hitching sound.

'Pamela and Penny and Michael,' Janet said. 'Tell me what happened.'

He raised his hands and rubbed at his face, at his hair, like someone emerging from a pool or a shower. His breath was choppy, uneven.

'Did Pamela know what you planned to do? You'd been together eighteen years, married, working together. Three children. Through thick and thin. What changed?' Janet watched and waited. After a few moments she spoke again. 'Penny had just started high school. She was doing well – she'd made friends, joined the netball team.'

Something moved in his cheek, a tic he couldn't suppress.

'What did you do, Mr Cottam? The early hours of Monday morning? We have film of you drinking whisky. We have very persuasive evidence that tells us you were there, that you handled the weapon. Tell me your side of things.'

He sat there on the chair and touched his knuckles together, sniffed loudly a couple of times. He had resisted appeals to his better nature and seemed almost oblivious of the evidence presented. He really didn't care, Janet understood. He still wanted to die and nothing else mattered any more. All along Janet had played the game, pandering to his world view, never challenging his actions. She had nothing to lose now.

'You can refuse to cooperate,' she said, 'and we will

question you for as long as the law allows and then we will, in all likelihood, charge you with murder and attempted murder. After that you will be asked to plead. If you continue to withhold information you will have to plead not guilty and that means there will be a public trial. Witnesses will be called to give evidence, not just experts but people close to you and Pamela and the children. You will be in the dock and your family will be the subject of intense debate and speculation. Your life, your actions, will be picked apart in full public view. You're entitled to a trial. Is that what you want?'

He twisted his head to the side, as though the paper suit was too tight at the neck.

'I don't think you did discuss it with Pamela. She'd never have agreed in a million years. They didn't stand a chance, did they? Fast asleep, defenceless. Are you ashamed of what you did?'

He shuddered. She felt she was getting to him, piercing that shell of pretend indifference.

'You failed,' she said. 'We saved the boys. You've lost your whole family but you're still here. Are you ashamed? Is that why you won't talk to me?'

'No,' he said, eyes blazing, fists hitting his knees. 'No! I did what I had to.'

'What was that?'

'I killed them,' he said softly, and every hair on Janet's skin stood up. Ice ran through her spine. He sat back in his chair and closed his eyes.

'You killed them,' she echoed, hoping to prompt more from him.

'Yes,' he said, and rubbed at his forehead.

'Tell me, from closing up the bar, everything you can remember after that.'

His eyes met hers then and for the first time she saw vulnerability there, distress and fear. 'I don't want to,' he said, his voice hollow.

'It's difficult,' she agreed. 'A step at a time. You cashed up, then what?'

'Went upstairs. The others went to bed.'

'The others?'

'Pamela, Michael.' He coughed.

'And the children?'

'They were already asleep.'

Janet nodded. 'Go on.'

'I went down, had a few drinks.' His fingertips were tapping together, a tattoo, a dance of dread. 'Then I got the knife.' He screwed up his face, gave a sharp exhalation. He hadn't mentioned the dog yet but Janet didn't want to interrupt him. She could ask questions later.

'You got the knife from where?'

'The kitchen. The sharp knife, that's what we always called it.'

Janet nodded. Every household had something like that, didn't they? The only knife that cut bread properly or sliced through meat like butter. She and Ade had one, a wedding gift. The handle was burnt on

331

one side but they never considered throwing it out. 'Go on,' she said.

'I, erm . . . I had some more to drink and then I went into our room.' He bowed forward, pressing his lips together. 'I stabbed Pamela,' he said quickly. 'She barely made a sound.' He looked at Janet intently. 'Like she understood? Then Penny, with the knife. And Michael . . .' He swallowed, fingers curled, clenched now, something in that memory appearing to distress him more. His mouth worked. 'He . . . I stabbed Michael . . . the sound . . . he woke up . . .' Cottam stuttered and gasped. She saw tears in his eyes. At last. Had he wept since? As he drove frantically up and down the motorway, those noises fresh in his ears? In the car park by the lake during the long, cold night with his sons, his plans in tatters? Or when he woke in hospital after crashing the Hyundai to find himself very much alive and remembered all that he had done? Or was he the sort of man who never cried?

'What happened next?' Janet said. All the cross-checking, all the elaboration – *how many times did you use the knife, where on the body, where did you stand* – still to come.

'Someone was at the door. It was this woman, Tessa, with the dog. I'd let the dog out.' He shook his head, Janet wasn't sure whether at his own folly for letting the dog out or at the woman's action in returning her. 'And she said the farmer had called the police. So I got the boys and we went.'

Tessa's comment had just been a warning, but in the midst of the murders Cottam interpreted it as a much more definite and imminent threat. If he hadn't thought the police were about to arrive might he have gone on killing undeterred?

'If she hadn't come with the dog, what did you intend doing?'

'Kill the boys, then myself.' His voice was close to breaking.

'How?'

'The knife. Cut my throat.'

'Why?' Janet asked.

His shoulders rose, then fell. 'For the best,' he said. 'It had all gone to shit. We were losing the pub, the bank was on my back, bleeding us dry. Better off out of it,' he said, quietly emphatic. Not a scintilla of doubt there that Janet could discern, but complete belief that the path he had chosen was the right one. For some killers, along with the confession came guilt and grief and expressions of sorrow for what they had brought down upon the victims and their families. There was none of that with Owen Cottam. No remorse at all.

'Are you sorry?' Janet asked him.

'Sorry I couldn't finish it,' he said, regret heavy in his voice, but not malice. 'If you hadn't stopped me—'

'You'd have done what?' Janet said.

'Gone with my lads.'

'Why did you wait?' Janet said. 'Once you'd got to Lundfell?'

He blinked slowly as though it was a stupid question. 'I had to do it right. The three of us.'

'Do what?'

'Drown them, hang myself. Together.'

'That's what the bin bags were for?'

He nodded. 'There were some stones near the lock, to weigh them down. We should have gone together,' he said. 'We should all have been together.'

'The deaths at your home, the pathologist tells us they were very quick. The victims would not have suffered for long, if at all. Yet you were prepared to let Theo and Harry die of thirst and dehydration, left them alone and unprotected from vermin, predators, cold and thirst. Can you explain that to me?'

'That's your fault,' he said. 'The police, you lot interfering. You messed it all up.' His eyes were flinty. 'That wasn't meant to happen. You made that happen.'

Shifting the blame. And you sat there and allowed it, Janet thought. Thank God they had saved the boys. How much more grotesque would it have been if they'd lain there undiscovered, imprisoned in the old barge until they died.

'You cared more about yourself, about seeing your plan through, than the suffering of those children,' she said.

'I love my children,' he said dangerously.

'No,' she said.

'I love them,' he insisted, but there was bitterness in his eyes and the edges of his lips were white with tension.

'That's not love,' Janet said.

She had it – his confession. *I killed them.* It must be enough to pass the threshold test, meaning the case was likely to result in a successful prosecution, but she had to get the say-so of a solicitor from the Crown Prosecution Service before she could charge him.

Cottam was taken back to his cell while Janet completed her case summary and then sought out the CPS solicitor. She gave her the written file and waited while she read it.

'That's good,' the solicitor concluded. 'Happy with that.' And she signed the form.

Janet took it through to the custody officer and waited while he typed up the charges.

When everything was ready, Owen Cottam was brought through.

Janet relaxed her shoulders, waited a moment before she spoke. 'Owen Cottam, you are charged that on the tenth of October 2011, at Oldham in the county of Greater Manchester, you did murder Pamela Cottam contrary to common law. You do not have to say anything, but it may harm your defence if you fail to mention now something which you may later rely on in court. Anything you do say may be given in evidence. Do you understand?'

'Yes,' he said, a single word, the slightest tremor in his voice. He was trembling, the muscles shifting under the skin on his face, but his expression was bland, empty. Janet had no idea what was going on in his head.

Janet went on to the second charge. 'Owen Cottam, you are charged that on the tenth of October 2011, at Oldham in the county of Greater Manchester, you did murder Penny Cottam contrary to common law. You do not have to say anything, but it may harm your defence if you fail to mention now something which you may later rely on in court. Anything you do say may be given in evidence.'

As she continued to read out the charges, Janet thought that this was what it all led up to, all the speculating and hunting for information, all the accumulation of evidence and typing up of reports, all the hours of careful questioning and testing. To this. The moment when she could charge someone with the crime. And when those left devastated and bereaved could begin to see the prospect of justice.

She got to the fifth and final charge. 'Owen Cottam, you are also charged that between the tenth of October 2011 and the fourteenth of October 2011 at Wigan in the county of Greater Manchester you did attempt to murder Harry Cottam, contrary to section one of the Criminal Attempts Act 1981. You do not have to say anything, but it may harm your defence if you fail to mention now something which you may later rely on in court. Anything you do say may be given in evidence.'

Owen Cottam made no comment and the custody officer noted that and indicated to Janet that they were done.

Cottam was led away.

I killed them. A normal bloke, she thought, an average family man. Nothing remarkable about him. A settled, uneventful life. Nothing that could ever have pointed to his having the capacity to slaughter his family. Not like the rest of the criminals they dealt with, their lives chaotic, their families fractured, haunted by abuse and neglect and poverty. Seeking solace in drink and drugs and confusing violence with love.

Janet didn't believe Owen Cottam had loved too much; rather that he'd mistaken possession, ownership, for love. Seeing his wife and children as chattels without free will and his own needs as paramount.

The cell door shut behind him with a clang that echoed along the corridor.

'Nice one, Janet,' said the custody sergeant.

Janet smiled and gave a nod. Glad it was done, glad it was all over.

23

'Gill thinks the grandmother will take the kids,' Janet said.

Rachel took another piece of garlic bread, dipped it in the oil and balsamic vinegar, savoured the tang. 'They'll not remember, will they? That age? Though she'll have to tell them eventually.'

'Doubt it. Though I can remember being in my high chair and my mum dancing. She reckons I was only two then.'

'I don't remember anything before school,' Rachel said, partly to stop Janet asking. 'Do you want that last bit?' She pointed at the bread.

'You have it,' Janet said, 'you need it more than I do. So – have you decided on your new kitchen?'

'What?' Then Rachel remembered in a rush. 'Oh, no, not bothering.'

Janet nodded, filled their glasses. 'I wanted to tell you,' she said, 'me flying off the handle, being under the weather . . .'

Rachel froze, expecting cancer or some wasting disease. Imagining Janet in a hospital bed shrinking away. This their Last Supper.

'. . . I'm fine.' Janet laughed. 'Least, I'm pretty sure I am. It's the menopause.'

'Oh, God,' said Rachel. 'So you're turning into an old bag?'

'It's the solidarity I love,' Janet said sarcastically. She took a drink. 'Just a new phase of life.'

'You think?' Rachel wasn't so sure. 'From what I hear, it's all dry skin and facial hair and bingo wings, isn't it?'

'And freedom from periods, the acquisition of a certain age and authority, perhaps,' Janet said. 'Your time will come.'

Rachel had another mouthful of wine. 'Godzilla's forgiven me,' she said, 'sort of.'

'Good. No more racing into burning buildings then, eh? I turn my back for five minutes . . .' Janet said, mock scolding.

'Sod off,' Rachel said. She sat back from the table while the waiter took their starter plates away.

'Funerals next week,' Janet said.

Rachel's heart stopped. She felt her skin chill. How the fuck had Janet found out?

'Gill'd like us to be there, Thursday, but if you can't face it . . .'

The Cottams! The Cottams' funerals! 'No, it's fine.' Rachel drank some wine quickly, felt her head swim.

'Course. Show respect,' she said. 'How are the kids, your kids, Elise and Taisie?' Rachel went on, thinking *change the bleeding subject*.

Janet looked at her, a smile in her eyes, but a question mark too. Of course it came out clumsy and Rachel wasn't in the habit of asking after them, but it always worked with Alison when Rachel wanted to escape scrutiny.

'They're great,' Janet said. 'Elise has righteousness down to a fine art and is practising her martyrdom skills and Taisie's up every other night with bad dreams and *in lurve* by day – a sight to behold.'

Their main meals arrived and they began to eat. Rachel's thoughts kept circling back to Cottam. 'He'll get life, right?' she said to Janet, not even needing to name him. 'But he won't do life, will he? He'll find a way to kill himself.'

'And there's me thinking this was a nice bit of socializing away from work,' Janet said.

Rachel let her complain, hung on for her answer.

'Yes – probably, eventually,' Janet said. 'We've done our bit. And we did good, *you* did good. Front pages, bet you.'

Rachel closed her eyes. She had already seen the copy the press office was sending out. Along with photos of her.

'What d'you reckon?' Janet said. 'Super-cop? That's always a popular one. Or, erm . . . Avenging Angel? Rachel to the Rescue?'

'Shut up,' Rachel said, a laugh undermining her very real irritation.

'If you can't stand the heat,' Janet said.

Rachel pointed her fork at her. 'You're the one having hot flushes.'

'Touché!' said Janet and picked up her glass, touching it to Rachel's. 'To us,' she said.

Rachel joined her, 'To us,' and downed her drink.

'What are you doing here?' Gill said. She had been called down to the front desk to find Sammy sitting there.

He swung his head, as though he was casting about for an explanation, then said, 'Dad said to tell you in person.'

Oh, God, no. Gill's mind Rolodexed through the possibilities: pregnancy, drugs, self-harm, expulsion.

Sammy had his hands stuffed into his pockets, his shoulders up to his ears, riddled with embarrassment. He looked about and she was aware that they could be overheard, that the reception area was perhaps not the best place for potentially devastating news.

'Come on, come with me.' She took him along to one of the small interview rooms, changed the sign on the door to occupied and followed him in. She sat down. Sammy loitered by the door. 'What is it?' she said, sounding much calmer than she felt. *HIV? Oh, God. Or hepatitis?* He didn't speak.

'Sammy?' Her stomach flipped over.

His face flooded with colour and she saw tears start in his eyes

Oh, bloody hell.

'I want to come home,' he said, sounding half his age. 'I don't want to stay at Dad's any more. I want to come home.'

Gill was stunned, waited in case there was more he had to say, in case there was a bombshell. 'That's it?'

'Yes,' he said, and sniffed.

'Is it because of the row you had?'

'No,' Sammy said.

'Because you'll do chores at mine same as you did before. More, probably.'

'I don't care about that. I just . . . I missed you,' he said awkwardly.

Now she was going to cry, which was ridiculous. 'Right.' She swallowed hard, looked at the ceiling tiles, the recessed lights. 'Fine, okay, and you've spoken to Dad?'

'Yes.'

'Right, and you've got your key?'

'Yes,' he said.

'Well, I won't be home until,' she glanced at the clock on the wall, 'well, another couple of hours.'

'I need to pack my stuff,' Sammy said.

'Okay,' Gill nodded. 'You go do that and I'll pick you up on my way back. Yes?'

'Okay.'

She stood up. 'Come here,' she said, opening her

arms, and he trudged forward, and she hugged him tight and he snuffled a bit. 'Good,' she said, ''cos I missed you too, you know. Apart from the sweaty feet. And the wet towels.'

'Mum!' His protest was half-hearted.

'Go on. I'll see you later.'

He loped off and Gill pinched the top of her nose and blinked and blew out breaths until she was fit to be seen in public again.

Cottam was pleading guilty and once he was up for sentencing everyone expected he'd be given a full-term life sentence. The story, with its power to fascinate, remained in the papers and they all knew there would be another flurry of articles once sentence was passed. And with them, fresh demands for Rachel to give interviews: radio, women's magazines, chat shows. She'd made it as plain as she could to Lisa that she would have to be dragged kicking and screaming and would rather Taser her tits than do any more PR. There was a difference between a news story in the midst of an investigation where the public were being encouraged to help the police and the sort of celebrity merry-go-round people wanted to stick her on.

Fortunately, Gill backed her up on that, especially when Rachel said she couldn't be sure she wouldn't end up speaking her mind.

Rachel was at home. She had spent the night before

bagging up her dad's stuff, ready to chuck. He'd an envelope containing half a dozen photographs, pictures of her and Alison and Dom as kids. None of her mum. The corners of the prints were curled and the images scratched with marks, spills or something on some. Alison could have them. Nothing else was worth keeping. Clothes not fit for anything but landfill, faded, full of tears and stains and round holes from cigarette burns. A plastic case with a comb and a toothbrush and an unopened bar of soap; small and cheap, like the packs they give out in the hostels. A tin of athlete's foot powder. Letters from the DWP about his benefits.

A life in three bin bags.

Rachel looked through the clutch of press cuttings: herself, three and four years ago. She tore them in half, then in half again, put them in an ashtray and took it outside. Set her lighter to it, watched the newsprint flare and shrivel and turn to flakes of ash. A gust of wind snatched at the remnants and blew them to dust. Swirling up and round.

Rachel fetched the bin bags out and stuffed them in the wheelie bin.

Then she rang Alison. The scabs on her hands had gone, leaving shiny, pink skin that still itched. She ran her nails over the heel of one thumb while she waited for a reply.

'Yes?' Alison sounding flustered, strained.

'I'm not coming,' Rachel said.

'What? Are you meeting us there?' Alison said.

'No. I'm not coming at all.' Rachel watched the boughs on the big tree by the road bend and sway. The leaves were dead now, crisp, red and brown. They rattled in the wind.

'What d'you mean?' Alison said. 'You can't not come. Dom's here, the car's on its way.'

'It's all paid for,' Rachel said, 'it's all sorted. It can happen whether I'm there or not. And I'm not.'

'Bloody hell, Rachel,' Alison said, 'this is the only chance you get to say goodbye. And when all's said and done, this is your father we're talking about. Your father.'

'Yeah, I know,' Rachel said, and hung up.

The phone went as she went back inside. *Janet calling*. 'Hi. Have you left yet?'

'Just about to. Why?' Rachel said.

'We've picked one up in Kirkholt. Twenty-two-year-old man, suspected domestic. Police called to the house twice in the last month. Boss wants you at the scene.'

'I'll go straight there,' Rachel said.

'I'll text you the postcode,' Janet said. 'See you later.'

'Yes.' Rachel felt the familiar rush, the leap of energy that came with a new case. The buzz that got her out of bed every day and kept her working for sixteen-hour stretches. The sweet, dark thrill of the chase.

Rachel was running.

Epilogue

Family Killer Cottam in Prison Suicide

The Ministry of Justice announced today that Owen Cottam (45) was found dead in his cell at Frankland High Security Prison in County Durham, in the early hours of yesterday morning. Cottam was serving a full-term life sentence for the murder of his wife Pamela, their daughter Penny, and his brother-in-law Michael Milne and two ten-year sentences for the attempted murder of Cottam's two young sons.

Landlord Cottam was the subject of a nationwide manhunt last year when he fled the Oldham pub where he and his family lived, taking the two boys with him. DC Rachel Bailey of Manchester Metropolitan Police is credited with finding and rescuing the children, who, doctors say, would soon have succumbed to death as a result of hypothermia and dehydration. The youngsters were reunited with their maternal grandmother and are now believed to be living in the Republic of Ireland.

The MoJ said: 'As with all deaths in custody, the independent Prisons and Probation Ombudsman will conduct an investigation.' The investigation will examine how Cottam, found hanging in his cell, was able to take his own life in spite of being classified as at risk and subject to suicide prevention procedures.

Financial difficulties and the end of Cottam's tenancy at the Journeys Inn were believed to be the factors which precipitated the murders. Criminal psychologist Professor Henry Threlfall said, 'The prospect of financial ruin and shame can be an intolerable burden for some men who believe it is their responsibility to provide for their family. When they are at risk of being exposed, a small minority will seek suicide rather than suffer the shame of their failure. In a few rare cases some individuals will also endeavour to take their family with them. A phenomenon which we are still trying to fully understand.'

Many thanks to Bill Scott-Kerr and Rachel Rayner and Transworld for inviting me to write a further two Scott & Bailey novels. Thanks to Sally Wainwright and Diane Taylor, whose wonderful characters continue to be a joy to work with, and to Suranne Jones, Lesley Sharp and Amelia Bullmore, who bring them to life in such memorable ways. Thanks also to Keith Dillon for generous help and advice about police work – any mistakes are mine. Some are deliberate!

The first book in the series . . .

DEAD TO ME

A SCOTT & BAILEY NOVEL

A daughter's death
A teenage girl is found brutally murdered in her squalid flat.

A mother's love
Her mother is devastated. She gave her child up to the care
system, only to lose her again, and is convinced that the
low-life boyfriend is to blame.

Two ordinary women, one extraordinary Job
DC Rachel Bailey has dragged herself up from a deprived
childhood and joined the Manchester Police. Rachel's boss
thinks her new recruit has bags of raw talent but straightlaced
DC Janet Scott, her reluctant partner, has her doubts.

**Together Scott and Bailey must hunt a killer,
but a life fighting crime can be no life at all . . .**

Buy it now in print and ebook!